PRAISE FOR MICHAEL CRICHTON AND
THE ANDROMEDA STRAIN

"*The Andromeda Strain* invented a new genre, the tech-nothriller. . . . [Crichton] could make most readers lose sleep all night and call in sick the next day."
—*San Francisco Chronicle*

"[Crichton is] one of the great storytellers of our age."
—*Newsday*

"Science fiction, which once frightened because it seemed so far-out, now frightens because it seems so near. *The Andromeda Strain* is as matter-of-fact as the skull-and-crossbones instructions on a bottle of poison—and just as chillingly effective."   —*Life*

"[An] intelligent page-turner."
—*The Washington Post Book World*

"[Crichton] is a master at blending edge-of-the-chair adventure with a scientific seminar, educating his readers as he entertains them."
—*St. Louis Post-Dispatch*

"Relentlessly suspenseful. . . . A hair-raising experience."   —*The Pittsburgh Press*

"Filled with gut-tightening tension."

—*San Antonio Express-News*

"*The Andromeda Strain*, a terrifying novel of biophysics, will leave you thinking Crichton was a visionary. Thirty years before researchers discovered the effects of microorganisms, Crichton predicted a virus just as deadly. . . . This one haunts you for years."

—*The Huffington Post*

MICHAEL CRICHTON

THE ANDROMEDA STRAIN

Michael Crichton was a writer, director, and producer, best known as the author of *Jurassic Park* and the creator of *ER*. One of the most recognizable names in literature and entertainment, Crichton sold more than 200 million copies of his books, which have been translated into forty languages and adapted into fifteen films.

www.michaelcrichton.com

BOOKS BY MICHAEL CRICHTON

FICTION

The Andromeda Strain
The Terminal Man
The Great Train Robbery
The 13th Warrior
(previously published as *Eaters of the Dead*)
Congo
Sphere
Jurassic Park
Rising Sun
Disclosure
The Lost World
Airframe
Timeline
Prey
State of Fear
Next
Pirate Latitudes
Micro (with Richard Preston)

NONFICTION

Five Patients
Jasper Johns
Electronic Life
Travels

THE
ANDROMEDA
STRAIN

MICHAEL CRICHTON

VINTAGE BOOKS

A Division of Penguin Random House LLC
New York

for
A.C.D., M.D.
who first proposed
the problem

FIRST VINTAGE BOOKS EDITION, JANUARY 2017

Copyright © 1969 by CrichtonSun, LLC

All rights reserved. Published in the United States by Vintage Books,
a division of Penguin Random House LLC, New York, and distributed
in Canada by Random House of Canada, a division of Penguin Random
House Canada Limited, Toronto. Originally published in hardcover
in the United States by Alfred A. Knopf, a division of Penguin Random
House LLC, New York, in 1969.

Vintage and colophon are registered trademarks
of Penguin Random House LLC.

The Cataloging-in-Publication Data is on file at The Library of Congress.

Vintage Books Trade Paperback ISBN: 978-1-101-97449-0
eBook ISBN: 978-0-307-81641-2

Author photograph © Jonathan Exley

www.vintagebooks.com

Printed in the United States of America
20 19 18 17 16 15 14 13 12

The survival value of human intelligence has
never been satisfactorily demonstrated.
                              JEREMY STONE

Increasing vision is increasingly expensive.
                              R. A. JANEK

ANDROMEDA STRAIN

THIS FILE IS CLASSIFIED TOP SECRET

Examination by unauthorized persons
is a criminal offense punishable
by fines and imprisonment up to
20 years and $20,000.

DO NOT ACCEPT FROM COURIER
IF SEAL IS BROKEN

The courier is required by law
to demand your card 7592. He
is not permitted to relinquish
this file without such proof of
identity.

MACHINE SCORE REVIEW BELOW

Acknowledgments

THIS BOOK RECOUNTS the five-day history of a major American scientific crisis.

As in most crises, the events surrounding the Andromeda Strain were a compound of foresight and foolishness, innocence and ignorance. Nearly everyone involved had moments of great brilliance, and moments of unaccountable stupidity. It is therefore impossible to write about the events without offending some of the participants.

However, I think it is important that the story be told. This country supports the largest scientific establishment in the history of mankind. New discoveries are constantly being made, and many of these discoveries have important political or social overtones. In the near future, we can expect more crises on the pattern of Andromeda. Thus I believe it is useful for the public to be made aware of the way in which scientific crises arise, and are dealt with.

In researching and recounting the history of the Andromeda Strain, I received the generous help of many people who felt as I did, and who encouraged me to tell the story accurately and in detail.

My particular thanks must go to Major General Willis A.

Haverford, United States Army; Lieutenant Everett J. Sloane, United States Navy (Ret.); Captain L. S. Waterhouse, United States Air Force (Vandenberg Special Projects Division); Colonel Henley Jackson and Colonel Stanley Friedrich, both of Wright Patterson; and Murray Charles of the Pentagon Press Division.

For their help in elucidating the background of the Wildfire Project, I must thank Roger White, National Aeronautics and Space Administration (Houston MSC); John Roble, NASA Kennedy Complex 13; Peter J. Mason, NASA Intelligence (Arlington Hall); Dr. Francis Martin, University of California (Berkeley) and the President's Science Advisory Council; Dr. Max Byrd, USIA; Kenneth Vorhees, White House Press Corps; and Professor Jonathan Percy of the University of Chicago (Genetics Department).

For their review of relevant chapters of the manuscript, and for their technical corrections and suggestions, I wish to thank Christian P. Lewis, Goddard Space Flight Center; Herbert Stanch, Avco, Inc.; James P. Baker, Jet Propulsion Laboratory; Carlos N. Sandos, California Institute of Technology; Dr. Brian Stack, University of Michigan; Edgar Blalock, Hudson Institute; Professor Linus Kjelling, the RAND Corporation; Dr. Eldredge Benson, National Institutes of Health.

Lastly, I wish to thank the participants in the Wildfire Project and the investigation of the so-called Andromeda Strain. All agreed to see me and, with many, my interviews lasted over a period of days. Furthermore, I was able to draw upon the transcripts of their debriefing, which are stored in Arlington Hall (Substation Seven) and which amounted to more than fifteen thousand pages of typewritten manuscript. This material, stored in twenty volumes, represents the full story of the events at Flatrock, Nevada, as told by each of the participants, and I was thus able to utilize their separate viewpoints in preparing a composite account.

This is a rather technical narrative, centering on complex issues of science. Wherever possible, I have explained the scientific questions, problems, and techniques. I have avoided the temptation to simplify both the issues and the answers, and if the reader must occasionally struggle through an arid passage of technical detail, I apologize.

I have also tried to retain the tension and excitement of events in these five days, for there is an inherent drama in the story of Andromeda, and if it is a chronicle of stupid, deadly blunders, it is also a chronicle of heroism and intelligence.

M. C.
Cambridge, Massachusetts
January 1969

day 1

CONTACT

1.

The Country of
Lost Borders

A MAN WITH BINOCULARS. That is how it began: with a man standing by the side of the road, on a crest overlooking a small Arizona town, on a winter night.

Lieutenant Roger Shawn must have found the binoculars difficult. The metal would be cold, and he would be clumsy in his fur parka and heavy gloves. His breath, hissing out into the moonlit air, would have fogged the lenses. He would be forced to pause to wipe them frequently, using a stubby gloved finger.

He could not have known the futility of this action. Binoculars were worthless to see into that town and uncover its secrets. He would have been astonished to learn that the men who finally succeeded used instruments a million times more powerful than binoculars.

There is something sad, foolish, and human in the image of Shawn leaning against a boulder, propping his arms on it, and holding the binoculars to his eyes. Though cumbersome, the binoculars would at least feel comfortable and familiar in his hands. It would be one of the last familiar sensations before his death.

We can imagine, and try to reconstruct, what happened from that point on.

Lieutenant Shawn swept over the town slowly and methodically. He could see it was not large, just a half-dozen wooden buildings, set out along a single main street. It was very quiet: no lights, no activity, no sound carried by the gentle wind.

He shifted his attention from the town to the surrounding hills. They were low, dusty, and blunted, with scrubby vegetation and an occasional withered yucca tree crusted in snow. Beyond the hills were more hills, and then the flat expanse of the Mojave Desert, trackless and vast. The Indians called it the Country of Lost Borders.

Lieutenant Shawn found himself shivering in the wind. It was February, the coldest month, and it was after ten. He walked back up the road toward the Ford Econovan, with the large rotating antenna on top. The motor was idling softly; it was the only sound he could hear. He opened the rear doors and climbed into the back, shutting the doors behind him.

He was enveloped in deep-red light: a night light, so that he would not be blinded when he stepped outside. In the red light the banks of instruments and electronic equipment glowed greenly.

Private Lewis Crane, the electronics technician, was there, also wearing a parka. He was hunched over a map, making calculations with occasional reference to the instruments before him.

Shawn asked Crane if he were certain they had arrived at the place, and Crane confirmed that they had. Both men were tired: they had driven all day from Vandenberg, in search of the latest Scoop satellite. Neither knew much about the Scoops, except that they were a series of secret capsules intended to analyze the upper atmosphere and then return. Shawn and Crane had the job of finding the capsules once they had landed.

In order to facilitate recovery, the satellites were fitted with electronic beepers that began to transmit signals when they came down to an altitude of five miles.

That was why the van had so much radio-directional equipment. In essence, it was performing its own triangulation. In Army parlance it was known as single-unit triangulation, and it was highly effective, though slow. The procedure was simple enough: the van stopped and fixed its position, recording the strength and direction of the radio beam from the satellite. Once this was done, it would be driven in the most likely direction of the satellite for a distance of twenty miles. Then it would stop and take new coordinates. In this way, a series of triangulation points could be mapped, and the van could proceed to the satellite by a zigzag path, stopping every twenty miles to correct any error. The method was slower than using two vans, but it was safer—the Army felt that two vans in an area might arouse suspicion.

For six hours, the van had been closing on the Scoop satellite. Now they were almost there.

Crane tapped the map with a pencil in a nervous way and announced the name of the town at the foot of the hill: Piedmont, Arizona. Population forty-eight; both men laughed over that, though they were both inwardly concerned. The Vandenberg ESA, or Estimated Site of Arrival, had been twelve miles north of Piedmont. Vandenberg computed this site on the basis of radar observations and 1410 computer trajectory projections. The estimates were not usually wrong by more than a few hundred yards.

Yet there was no denying the radio-directional equipment, which located the satellite beeper directly in the center of town. Shawn suggested that someone from the town might have seen it coming down—it would be glowing with the heat —and might have retrieved it, bringing it into Piedmont.

This was reasonable, except that a native of Piedmont who

happened upon an American satellite fresh from space would have told someone—reporters, police, NASA, the Army, *someone.*

But they had heard nothing.

Shawn climbed back down from the van, with Crane scrambling after him, shivering as the cold air struck him. Together, the two men looked out over the town.

It was peaceful, but completely dark. Shawn noticed that the gas station and the motel both had their lights doused. Yet they represented the only gas station and motel for miles.

And then Shawn noticed the birds.

In the light of the full moon he could see them, big birds, gliding in slow circles over the buildings, passing like black shadows across the face of the moon. He wondered why he hadn't noticed them before, and asked Crane what he made of them.

Crane said he didn't make anything of them. As a joke, he added, "Maybe they're buzzards."

"That's what they look like, all right," Shawn said.

Crane laughed nervously, his breath hissing out into the night. "But why should there be buzzards here? They only come when something is dead."

Shawn lit a cigarette, cupping his hands around the lighter, protecting the flame from the wind. He said nothing, but looked down at the buildings, the outline of the little town. Then he scanned the town once more with binoculars, but saw no signs of life or movement.

At length, he lowered the binoculars and dropped his cigarette onto the crisp snow, where it sputtered and died.

He turned to Crane and said, "We'd better go down and have a look."

2.

Vandenberg

THREE HUNDRED MILES AWAY, in the large, square, windowless room that served as Mission Control for Project Scoop, Lieutenant Edgar Comroe sat with his feet on his desk and a stack of scientific-journal articles before him. Comroe was serving as control officer for the night; it was a duty he filled once a month, directing the evening operations of the skeleton crew of twelve. Tonight, the crew was monitoring the progress and reports of the van coded Caper One, now making its way across the Arizona desert.

Comroe disliked this job. The room was gray and lighted with fluorescent lights; the tone was sparsely utilitarian and Comroe found it unpleasant. He never came to Mission Control except during a launch, when the atmosphere was different. Then the room was filled with busy technicians, each at work on a single complex task, each tense with the peculiar cold anticipation that precedes any spacecraft launch.

But nights were dull. Nothing ever happened at night. Comroe took advantage of the time and used it to catch up on reading. By profession he was a cardiovascular physiologist, with special interest in stresses induced at high-G accelerations.

Tonight, Comroe was reviewing a journal article titled "Stoichiometrics of Oxygen-Carrying Capacity and Diffusion Gradients with Increased Arterial Gas Tensions." He found it slow reading, and only moderately interesting. Thus he was willing to be interrupted when the overhead loudspeaker, which carried the voice transmissions from the van of Shawn and Crane, clicked on.

Shawn said, "This is Caper One to Vandal Deca. Caper One to Vandal Deca. Are you reading. Over."

Comroe, feeling amused, replied that he was indeed reading.

"We are about to enter the town of Piedmont and recover the satellite."

"Very good, Caper One. Leave your radio open."

"Roger."

This was a regulation of the recovery technique, as outlined in the Systems Rules Manual of Project Scoop. The SRM was a thick gray paperback that sat at one corner of Comroe's desk, where he could refer to it easily. Comroe knew that conversation between van and base was taped, and later became part of the permanent project file, but he had never understood any good reason for this. In fact, it had always seemed to him a straightforward proposition: the van went out, got the capsule, and came back.

He shrugged and returned to his paper on gas tensions, only half listening to Shawn's voice as it said, "We are now inside the town. We have just passed a gas station and a motel. All quiet here. There is no sign of life. The signals from the satellite are stronger. There is a church half a block ahead. There are no lights or activity of any kind."

Comroe put his journal down. The strained quality of Shawn's voice was unmistakable. Normally Comroe would have been amused at the thought of two grown men made jittery by entering a small, sleepy desert town. But he knew Shawn personally, and he knew that Shawn, whatever other virtues he might have, utterly lacked an imagination. Shawn could fall asleep in a horror movie. He was that kind of man.

Comroe began to listen.

Over the crackling static, he heard the rumbling of the van engine. And he heard the two men in the van talking quietly.

Shawn. "Pretty quiet around here."

Crane: "Yes sir."

There was a pause.

Crane: "Sir?"

Shawn: "Yes?"

Crane: "Did you see that?"

Shawn: "See what?"

Crane: "Back there, on the sidewalk. It looked like a body."

Shawn: "You're imagining things."

Another pause, and then Comroe heard the van come to a halt, brakes squealing.

Shawn: "Jesus."

Crane: "It's another one, sir."

Shawn: "Looks dead."

Crane: "Shall I—"

Shawn: "No. Stay in the van."

His voice became louder, more formal, as he ran through the call. "This is Caper One to Vandal Deca. Over."

Comroe picked up the microphone. "Reading you. What's happened?"

Shawn, his voice tight, said, "Sir, we see bodies. Lots of them. They appear to be dead."

"Are you certain, Caper One?"

"For Christ's sake," Shawn said. "Of course we're certain."

Comroe said mildly, "Proceed to the capsule, Caper One."

As he did so, he looked around the room. The twelve other men in the skeleton crew were staring at him, their eyes blank, unseeing. They were listening to the transmission.

The van rumbled to life again.

Comroe swung his feet off the desk and punched the red "Security" button on his console. That button automatically isolated the Mission Control room. No one would be allowed in or out without Comroe's permission.

Then he picked up the telephone and said, "Get me Major Manchek. M-A-N-C-H-E-K. This is a stat call. I'll hold."

Manchek was the chief duty officer for the month, the man directly responsible for all Scoop activities during February.

While he waited, he cradled the phone in his shoulder and lit a cigarette. Over the loudspeaker, Shawn could be heard to say, "Do they look dead to you, Crane?"

Crane: "Yes sir. Kind of peaceful, but dead."

Shawn: "Somehow they don't really look dead. There's something missing. Something funny . . . But they're all over. Must be dozens of them."

Crane: "Like they dropped in their tracks. Stumbled and fallen down dead."

Shawn: "All over the streets, on the sidewalks . . ."

Another silence, then Crane: "Sir!"

Shawn: "Jesus."

Crane: "You see him? The man in the white robe, walking across the street—"

Shawn: "I see him."

Crane: "He's just stepping over them like—"

Shawn: "He's coming toward us."

Crane: "Sir, look, I think we should get out of here, if you don't mind my—"

The next sound was a high-pitched scream, and a crunching noise. Transmission ended at this point, and Vandenberg Scoop Mission Control was not able to raise the two men again.

3.

Crisis

GLADSTONE, UPON HEARING OF the death of "Chinese" Gordon in Egypt, was reported to have muttered irritably that his general might have chosen a more propitious time to die: Gordon's death threw the Gladstone government into turmoil and crisis. An aide suggested that the circumstances were unique and unpredictable, to which Gladstone crossly answered: "All crises are the same."

He meant political crises, of course. There were no scientific crises in 1885, and indeed none for nearly forty years afterward. Since then there have been eight of major importance; two have received wide publicity. It is interesting that both the publicized crises—atomic energy and space capability—have concerned chemistry and physics, not biology.

This is to be expected. Physics was the first of the natural sciences to become fully modern and highly mathematical. Chemistry followed in the wake of physics, but biology, the retarded child, lagged far behind. Even in the time of Newton and Galileo, men knew more about the moon and other heavenly bodies than they did about their own.

It was not until the late 1940's that this situation changed. The postwar period ushered in a new era of biologic research, spurred by the discovery of antibiotics. Suddenly there was both enthusiasm and money for biology, and a torrent of discoveries poured forth: tranquilizers, steroid hormones, immunochemistry, the genetic code. By 1953 the first kidney was transplanted and by 1958 the first birth-control pills were tested. It was not long before biology was the fastest-growing field in all science; it was doubling its knowledge every ten years. Farsighted researchers talked seriously of changing genes, controlling evolution, regulating the mind—ideas that had been wild speculation ten years before.

And yet there had never been a biologic crisis. The Andromeda Strain provided the first.

According to Lewis Bornheim, a crisis is a situation in which a previously tolerable set of circumstances is suddenly, by the addition of another factor, rendered wholly intolerable. Whether the additional factor is political, economic, or scientific hardly matters: the death of a national hero, the instability of prices, or a technological discovery can all set events in motion. In this sense, Gladstone was right: all crises are the same.

The noted scholar Alfred Pockran, in his study of crises (*Culture, Crisis and Change*), has made several interesting points. First, he observes that every crisis has its beginnings long before the actual onset. Thus Einstein published his theories of relativity in 1905–15, forty years before his work culminated in the end of a war, the start of an age, and the beginnings of a crisis.

Similarly, in the early twentieth century, American, German, and Russian scientists were all interested in space travel, but only the Germans recognized the military potential of rockets. And after the war, when the German rocket installation at Peenemünde was cannibalized by the Soviets and Americans, it was only the Russians who made immediate, vigorous moves toward developing space capabilities. The Americans were content to tinker playfully with rockets—and ten years later, this resulted in an American scientific crisis involving Sputnik, American education, the ICBM, and the missile gap.

Pockran also observes that a crisis is compounded of individuals and personalities, which are unique:

> It is as difficult to imagine Alexander at the Rubicon, and Eisenhower at Waterloo, as it is difficult to imagine Darwin writing to Roosevelt about the potential for an atomic bomb. A crisis is made by men, who enter into the crisis with their own prejudices, propensities, and predispositions. A crisis is the sum of intuition and blind spots, a blend of facts noted and facts ignored.

> Yet underlying the uniqueness of each crisis is a disturbing sameness. A characteristic of all crises is their predictability, in retrospect. They seem to have a certain inevitability, they seem predestined. This is not true of all crises, but it is true of sufficiently many to make the most hardened historian cynical and misanthropic.

In the light of Pockran's arguments, it is interesting to consider the background and personalities involved in the Andromeda Strain. At the time of Andromeda, there had never been a crisis of biological science, and the first Americans faced with the facts were not disposed to think in terms of one. Shawn and Crane were capable but not thoughtful men, and Edgar Comroe, the night officer at Vandenberg, though a scientist, was not prepared to consider anything beyond the immediate irritation of a quiet evening ruined by an inexplicable problem.

According to protocol, Comroe called his superior officer, Major Arthur Manchek, and here the story takes a different turn. For Manchek was both prepared and disposed to consider a crisis of the most major proportions.

But he was not prepared to acknowledge it.

*   *   *

Major Manchek, his face still creased with sleep, sat on the edge of Comroe's desk and listened to the replay of the tape from the van.

When it was finished, he said, "Strangest damned thing I ever heard," and played it over again. While he did so, he carefully filled his pipe with tobacco, lit it, and tamped it down.

Arthur Manchek was an engineer, a quiet heavyset man plagued by labile hypertension, which threatened to end further promotions as an Army officer. He had been advised on many occasions to lose weight, but had been unable to do so. He was therefore considering abandoning the Army for a career as a scientist in private industry, where people did not care what your weight or blood pressure was.

Manchek had come to Vandenberg from Wright Patterson in Ohio, where he had been in charge of experiments in spacecraft landing methods. His job had been to develop a capsule shape that could touch down with equal safety on either land or sea. Manchek had succeeded in developing three new shapes that were promising; his success led to a promotion and transfer to Vandenberg.

Here he did administrative work, and hated it. People bored Manchek; the mechanics of manipulation and the vagaries of subordinate personality held no fascination for him. He often wished he were back at the wind tunnels of Wright Patterson.

Particularly on nights when he was called out of bed by some damnfool problem.

Tonight he felt irritable, and under stress. His reaction to this was characteristic: he became slow. He moved slowly, he thought slowly, he proceeded with a dull and plodding deliberation. It was the secret of his success. Whenever people around him became excited, Manchek seemed to grow more disinterested, until he appeared about to fall asleep. It was a trick he had for remaining totally objective and clear-headed.

Now he sighed and puffed on his pipe as the tape spun out for the second time.

"No communications breakdown, I take it?"

Comroe shook his head. "We checked all systems at this end. We are still monitoring the frequency." He turned on the radio, and hissing static filled the room. "You know about the audio screen?"

"Vaguely," Manchek said, suppressing a yawn. In fact, the audio screen was a system he had developed three years before. In simplest terms, it was a computerized way to find a needle in a haystack—a machine program that listened to apparently garbled, random sound and picked out certain irregularities. For example, the hubbub of conversation at an embassy cocktail party could be recorded and fed through the computer, which would pick out a single voice and separate it from the rest.

It had several intelligence applications.

"Well," Comroe said, "after the transmission ended, we got nothing but the static you hear now. We put it through the audio screen, to see if the computer could pick up a pattern. And we ran it through the oscilloscope in the corner."

Across the room, the green face of the scope displayed a jagged dancing white line—the summated sound of static.

"Then," Comroe said, "we cut in the computer. Like so."

He punched a button on his desk console. The oscilloscope line changed character abruptly. It suddenly became quieter, more regular, with a pattern of beating, thumping impulses.

"I see," Manchek said. He had, in fact, already identified the pattern and assessed its meaning. His mind was drifting elsewhere, considering other possibilities, wider ramifications.

"Here's the audio," Comroe said. He pressed another button and the audio version of the signal filled the room. It was a steady mechanical grinding with a repetitive metallic click.

Manchek nodded. "An engine. With a knock."

"Yes sir. We believe the van radio is still broadcasting, and that the engine is still running. That's what we're hearing now, with the static screened away."

"All right," Manchek said.

His pipe went out. He sucked on it for a moment, then lit it again, removed it from his mouth, and plucked a bit of tobacco from his tongue.

"We need evidence," he said, almost to himself. He was considering categories of evidence, and possible findings, contingencies . . .

"Evidence of what?" Comroe said.

Manchek ignored the question. "Have we got a Scavenger on the base?"

"I'm not sure, sir. If we don't, we can get one from Edwards."

"Then do it." Manchek stood up. He had made his decision, and now he felt tired again. An evening of telephone calls faced him, an evening of irritable operators and bad connections and puzzled voices at the other end.

"We'll want a flyby over that town," he said. "And a complete scan. All canisters to come directly. Alert the labs."

He also ordered Comroe to bring in the technicians, especially Jaggers. Manchek disliked Jaggers, who was effete and precious. But Manchek also knew that Jaggers was good, and tonight he needed a good man.

At 11:07 p.m., Samuel "Gunner" Wilson was moving at 645 miles per hour over the Mojave Desert. Up ahead in the moonlight, he saw the twin lead jets, their afterburners glowing angrily in the night sky. The planes had a heavy, pregnant look: phosphorus bombs were slung beneath the wings and belly.

Wilson's plane was different, sleek and long and black. It was a Scavenger, one of seven in the world.

The Scavenger was the operational version of the X-18. It was an intermediate-range reconnaissance jet aircraft fully equipped for day or night intelligence flights. It was fitted with two side-slung 16mm cameras, one for the visible spectrum, and one for low-frequency radiation. In addition it had a center-mount Homans infrared multispex camera as well as the usual electronic and radio-detection gear. All films and plates were, of course, processed automatically in the air, and were ready for viewing as soon as the aircraft returned to base.

All this technology made the Scavenger almost impossibly sensitive. It could map the outlines of a city in blackout, and could follow the movements of individual trucks and cars at eight thousand feet. It could detect a submarine to a depth of two hundred feet. It could locate harbor mines by wave-motion deformities and it could obtain a precise photograph of a factory from the residual heat of the building four hours after it had shut down.

So the Scavenger was the ideal instrument to fly over Piedmont, Arizona, in the dead of night.

Wilson carefully checked his equipment, his hands fluttering over the controls, touching each button and lever, watching the blinking green lights that indicated that all systems were in order.

His earphones crackled. The lead plane said lazily, "Coming up on the town, Gunner. You see it?"

He leaned forward in the cramped cockpit. He was low, only five hundred feet above ground, and for a moment he could see nothing but a blur of sand, snow, and yucca trees. Then, up ahead, buildings in the moonlight.

"Roger. I see it."

"Okay, Gunner. Give us room."

He dropped back, putting half a mile between himself and the other two planes. They were going into the P-square formation, for direct visualization of target by phosphorus flare. Direct visualization was not really necessary; Scavenger could function without it. But Vandenberg seemed insistent that they gather all possible information about the town.

The lead planes spread, moving wide until they were parallel to the main street of the town.

"Gunner? Ready to roll?"

Wilson placed his fingers delicately over the camera buttons. Four fingers: as if playing the piano.

"Ready."

"We're going in now."

The two planes swooped low, dipping gracefully toward the town. They were now very wide and seemingly inches above the ground as they began to release the bombs. As each struck the ground, a blazing white-hot sphere went up, bathing the town in an unearthly, glaring light and reflecting off the metal underbellies of the planes.

The jets climbed, their run finished, but Gunner did not see them. His entire attention, his mind and his body, was focused on the town.

"All yours, Gunner."

Wilson did not answer. He dropped his nose, cracked down his flaps, and felt a shudder as the plane sank sickeningly, like a stone, toward the ground. Below him, the area around the town was lighted for hundreds of yards in every direction. He pressed the camera buttons and felt, rather than heard, the vibrating whir of the cameras.

For a long moment he continued to fall, and then he shoved the stick forward, and the plane seemed to catch in the air, to grab, and lift and climb. He had a fleeting glimpse of the main street. He saw bodies, bodies everywhere, spreadeagled, lying in the streets, across cars . . .

"Jesus," he said.

And then he was up, still climbing, bringing the plane around in a slow arc, preparing for the descent into his second run and trying not to think of what he had seen. One of the first rules of air reconnaissance was "Ignore the scenery"; analysis and evaluation were not the job of the pilot. That was left to the experts, and pilots who forgot this, who became too interested in what they were photographing, got into trouble. Usually they crashed.

As the plane came down into a flat second run, he tried not to look at the ground. But he did, and again saw the bodies. The phosphorus flares were burning low, the lighting was darker, more sinister and subdued. But the bodies were still there: he had not been imagining it.

"Jesus," he said again. "Sweet Jesus."

The sign on the door said DATA PROSSEX EPSILON, and underneath, in red lettering, ADMISSION BY CLEARANCE CARD ONLY. Inside was a comfortable sort of briefing room: screen on one wall, a dozen steel-tubing and leather chairs facing it, and a projector in the back.

When Manchek and Comroe entered the room, Jaggers was already waiting for them, standing at the front of the room by the screen. Jaggers was a short man with a springy step and an eager, rather hopeful face. Though not well liked on the base, he was nonetheless the acknowledged master of reconnaissance interpretation. He had the sort of mind that delighted in small and puzzling details, and was well suited to his job.

Jaggers rubbed his hands as Manchek and Comroe sat down. "Well then," he said. "Might as well get right to it. I think we have something to interest you tonight." He nodded to the projectionist in the back. "First picture."

The room lights darkened. There was a mechanical click, and the screen lighted to show an aerial view of a small desert town.

"This is an unusual shot," Jaggers said. "From our files. Taken two months ago from Janos 12, our recon satellite. Orbiting at an altitude of one hundred and eighty-seven miles, as you know. The technical quality here is quite good. Can't read the license plates on the cars yet, but we're working on it. Perhaps by next year."

Manchek shifted in his chair, but said nothing.

"You can see the town here," Jaggers said. "Piedmont, Arizona. Population forty-eight, and not much to look at, even from one hundred and eighty-seven miles. Here's the general store; the gas station—notice how clearly you can read GULF—and the post office; the motel. Everything else you see is private residences. Church over here. Well: next picture."

Another click. This was dark, with a reddish tint, and was clearly an overview of the town in white and dark red. The outlines of the buildings were very dark.

"We begin here with the Scavenger IR plates. These are infrared films, as you know, which produce a picture on the basis of heat instead of light. Anything warm appears white on the picture; anything cold is black. Now then. You can see here that the buildings are dark—they are colder than the ground. As night comes on, the buildings give up their heat more rapidly."

"What are those white spots?" Comroe said. There were forty or fifty white areas on the film.

"Those," Jaggers said, "are bodies. Some inside houses, some in the street. By count, they number fifty. In the case of some of them, such as this one here, you can make out the four limbs and head clearly. This body is lying flat. In the street."

He lit a cigarette and pointed to a white rectangle. "As nearly as we can tell, this is an automobile. Notice it's got a bright white spot at one end. This means the motor is still running, still generating heat."

"The van," Comroe said. Manchek nodded.

"The question now arises," Jaggers said, "are all these people dead? We cannot be certain about that. The bodies appear to be of different temperatures. Forty-seven are rather cold, indicating death some time ago. Three are warmer. Two of those are in this car, here."

"Our men," Comroe said. "And the third?"

"The third is rather puzzling. You see him here, apparently

standing or lying curled in the street. Observe that he is quite white, and therefore quite warm. Our temperature scans indicate that he is about ninety-five degrees, which is a little on the cool side, but probably attributable to peripheral vasoconstriction in the night desert air. Drops his skin temperature. Next slide."

The third film flicked onto the screen.

Manchek frowned at the spot. "It's moved."

"Exactly. This film was made on the second passage. The spot has moved approximately twenty yards. Next picture."

A third film.

"Moved again!"

"Yes. An additional five or ten yards."

"So one person down there is alive?"

"That," Jaggers said, "is the presumptive conclusion."

Manchek cleared his throat. "Does that mean it's what you think?"

"Yes sir. It is what we think."

"There's a man down there, walking among the corpses?"

Jaggers shrugged and tapped the screen. "It is difficult to account for the data in any other manner, and—"

At that moment, a private entered the room with three circular metal canisters under his arm.

"Sir, we have films of the direct visualization by P-square."

"Run them," Manchek said.

The film was threaded into a projector. A moment later, Lieutenant Wilson was ushered into the room. Jaggers said, "I haven't reviewed these films yet. Perhaps the pilot should narrate."

Manchek nodded and looked at Wilson, who got up and walked to the front of the room, wiping his hands nervously on his pants. He stood alongside the screen and faced his audience, beginning in a flat monotone: "Sir, my flybys were made between 11:08 and 11:13 p.m. this evening. There were two, a start from the east and a return from the west, done at an average speed of two hundred and fourteen miles per hour, at a median altitude by corrected altimeter of eight hundred feet and an—"

"Just a minute, son," Manchek said, raising his hand. "This isn't a grilling. Just tell it naturally."

Wilson nodded and swallowed. The room lights went down and the projector whirred to life. The screen showed the town bathed in glaring white light as the plane came down over it.

"This is my first pass," Wilson said. "East to west, at 11:08. We're looking from the left-wing camera which is running at ninety-six frames per second. As you can see, my altitude is falling rapidly. Straight ahead is the main street of the target . . ."

He stopped. The bodies were clearly visible. And the van, stopped in the street, its rooftop antenna still turning slow revolutions. As the plane continued its run, approaching the van, they could see the driver collapsed over the steering wheel.

"Excellent definition," Jaggers said. "That fine-grain film really gives resolution when you need—"

"Wilson," Manchek said, "was telling us about his run."

"Yes sir," Wilson said, clearing his throat. He stared at the screen. "At this time I am right over target, where I observed the casualties you see here. My estimate at that time was seventy-five, sir."

His voice was quiet and tense. There was a break in the film, some numbers, and the image came on again.

"Now I am coming back for my second run," Wilson said. "The flares are already burning low but you can see—"

"Stop the film," Manchek said.

The projectionist froze the film at a single frame. It showed the long, straight main street of the town, and the bodies.

"Go back."

The film was run backward, the jet seeming to pull away from the street.

"There! Stop it now."

The frame was frozen. Manchek got up and walked close to the screen, peering off to one side.

"Look at this," he said, pointing to a figure. It was a man in knee-length white robes, standing and looking up at the plane. He was an old man, with a withered face. His eyes were wide.

"What do you make of this?" Manchek said to Jaggers.

Jaggers moved close. He frowned. "Run it forward a bit."

The film advanced. They could clearly see the man turn his head, roll his eyes, following the plane as it passed over him.

"Now backward," Jaggers said.

The film was run back. Jaggers smiled bleakly. "The man looks alive to me, sir."

"Yes," Manchek said crisply. "He certainly does."

And with that, he walked out of the room. As he left, he paused and announced that he was declaring a state of emergency; that everyone on the base was confined to quarters until further notice; that there would be no outside calls or communication; and that what they had seen in this room was confidential.

Outside in the hallway, he headed for Mission Control. Comroe followed him.

"I want you to call General Wheeler," Manchek said. "Tell him I have declared an SOE without proper authorization, and ask him to come down immediately." Technically no one but the commander had the right to declare a state of emergency.

Comroe said, "Wouldn't you rather tell him yourself?"

"I've got other things to do," Manchek said.

4.

Alert

WHEN ARTHUR MANCHEK stepped into the small soundproofed booth and sat down before the telephone, he knew exactly what he was going to do—but he was not very sure why he was doing it.

As one of the senior Scoop officers, he had received a briefing nearly a year before on Project Wildfire. It had been given, Manchek remembered, by a short little man with a dry, precise way of speaking. He was a university professor and he had outlined the project. Manchek had forgotten the details, except that there was a laboratory somewhere, and a team of five scientists who could be alerted to man the laboratory. The function of the team was investigation of possible extraterrestrial life forms introduced on American spacecraft returning to earth.

Manchek had not been told who the five men were; he knew only that a special Defense Department trunk line existed for calling them out. In order to hook into the line, one had only to dial the binary of some number. He reached into his pocket and withdrew his wallet, then fumbled for a moment until he found the card he had been given by the professor:

IN CASE OF FIRE
Notify Division 87
Emergencies Only

He stared at the card and wondered what exactly would happen if he dialed the binary of 87. He tried to imagine the sequence of events: Who would he talk to? Would someone call him back? Would there be an inquiry, a referral to higher authority?

He rubbed his eyes and stared at the card, and finally he shrugged. One way or the other, he would find out.

He tore a sheet of paper from the pad in front of him, next to the telephone, and wrote:

$$2^0 \quad 2^1 \quad 2^2 \quad 2^3 \quad 2^4 \quad 2^5 \quad 2^6 \quad 2^7$$

This was the basis of the binary system: base two raised to some power. Two to the zero power was one; two to the first was two; two squared was four; and so on. Manchek quickly wrote another line beneath:

2^0	2^1	2^2	2^3	2^4	2^5	2^6	2^7
1	2	4	8	16	32	64	128

Then he began to add up the numbers to get a total of 87. He circled these numbers:

2^0	2^1	2^2	2^3	2^4	2^5	2^6	2^7	
①	②	④	8	⑯	32	㉞	128	= 87

And then he drew in the binary code. Binary numbers were designed for computers which utilize an on-off, yes-no kind of language. A mathematician once joked that binary numbers were the way people who have only two fingers count. In essence, binary numbers translated normal numbers—which require nine digits, and decimal places—to a system that depended on only two digits, one and zero.

2^0	2^1	2^2	2^3	2^4	2^5	2^6	2^7
①1	②2	④4	8	⑯16	32	㊿64	128
1	1	1	0	1	0	1	0

Manchek looked at the number he had just written, and inserted the dashes: 1-110-1010. A perfectly reasonable telephone number.

Manchek picked up the telephone and dialed.

The time was exactly twelve midnight.

day 2

PIEDMONT

5.

The Early Hours

THE MACHINERY WAS THERE. The cables, the codes, the teleprinters had all been waiting dormant for two years. It only required Manchek's call to set the machinery in motion.

When he finished dialing, he heard a series of mechanical clicks, and then a low hum, which meant, he knew, that the call was being fed into one of the scrambled trunk lines. After a moment, the humming stopped and a voice said, "This is a recording. State your name and your message and hang up."

"Major Arthur Manchek, Vandenberg Air Force Base, Scoop Mission Control. I believe it is necessary to call up a Wildfire Alert. I have confirmatory visual data at this post, which has just been closed for security reasons."

As he spoke it occurred to him that it was all rather improbable. Even the tape recorder would disbelieve him. He continued to hold the telephone in his hand, somehow expecting an answer.

But there was none, only a click as the connection was automatically broken. The line was dead; he hung up and sighed. It was all very unsatisfying.

Manchek expected to be called back within a few minutes by Washington; he expected to receive many calls in the next few hours, and so remained at the phone. Yet he received no calls, for he did not know that the process he had initiated was automatic. Once mobilized, the Wildfire Alert would proceed ahead, and not be recalled for at least twelve hours.

Within ten minutes of Manchek's call, the following message clattered across the scrambled maximum-security cabler units of the nation:

■■■■■■■■ UNIT ■■■■■■■■

TOP SECRET

CODE FOLLOWS
AS
CBW 9/9/234/435/6778/90
PULG COORDINATES DELTA 8997

MESSAGE FOLLOWS
AS
WILDFIRE ALERT HAS BEEN CALLED.
REPEAT WILDFIRE ALERT HAS BEEN
CALLED. COORDINATES TO READ
NASA/AMC/NSC COMB DEC.
TIME OF COMMAND TO READ
LL-59-07 ON DATE.

FURTHER NOTATIONS
AS
PRESS BLACKFACE
POTENTIAL DIRECTIVE 7-L2
ALERT STATUS UNTIL FURTHER NOTICE

END MESSAGE

■■■■■■■■■■

DISENGAGE

This was an automatic cable. Everything about it, including the announcement of a press blackout and a possible directive 7-12, was automatic, and followed from Manchek's call.

Five minutes later, there was a second cable which named the men on the Wildfire team:

■■■■■■■■ UNIT ■■■■■■■■

TOP SECRET

CODE FOLLOWS
AS
CBW 9/9/234/435/6778/900

MESSAGE FOLLOWS
AS
THE FOLLOWING MALE AMERICAN
CITIZENS ARE BEING PLACED
ON ZED KAPPA STATUS. PREVIOUS
TOP SECRET CLEARANCE HAS BEEN
CONFIRMED. THE NAMES ARE +

STONE, JEREMY　　■■81
LEAVITT, PETER　　■■04
BARTON, CHARLES ■L51
CHRISTIANSENKRIKECANCEL THIS LINE CANCEL THIS LINE CAN
TO READ AS
KIRKE, CHRISTIAN ■142
HALL, MARK　　　 ■L77

ACCORD THESE MEN ZED KAPPA
STATUS UNTIL FURTHER NOTICE

END MESSAGE END MESSAGE

In theory, this cable was also quite routine; its purpose was to name the five members who were being given Zed Kappa status, the code for "OK" status. Unfortunately, however, the machine misprinted one of the names, and failed to reread the entire message. (Normally, when one of the printout units of a secret trunk line miswrote part of a message, the entire message was rewritten, or else it was reread by the computer to certify its corrected form.)

The message was thus open to doubt. In Washington and elsewhere, a computer expert was called in to confirm the accuracy of the message, by what is called "reverse tracing." The Washington expert expressed grave concern about the validity of the message since the machine was printing out other minor mistakes, such as "L" when it meant "I."

The upshot of all this was that the first two names on the list were accorded status, while the rest were not, pending confirmation.

Allison Stone was tired. At her home in the hills overlooking the Stanford campus, she and her husband, the chairman of the Stanford bacteriology department, had held a party for fifteen couples, and everyone had stayed late. Mrs. Stone was annoyed: she had been raised in official Washington, where one's second cup of coffee, offered pointedly without cognac, was accepted as a signal to go home. Unfortunately, she thought, academics did not follow the rules. She had served the second cup of coffee hours ago, and everybody was still there.

Shortly before one a.m., the doorbell rang. Answering it, she was surprised to see two military men standing side by side in the night. They seemed awkward and nervous to her, and she assumed they were lost; people often got lost driving through these residential areas at night.

"May I help you?"

"I'm sorry to disturb you, ma'am," one said politely. "But is this the residence of Dr. Jeremy Stone?"

"Yes," she said, frowning slightly. "It is."

She looked beyond the two men, to the driveway. A blue military sedan was parked there. Another man was standing by the car; he seemed to be holding something in his hand.

"Does that man have a gun?" she said.

"Ma'am," the man said, "we must see Dr. Stone at once, please."

It all seemed strange to her, and she found herself frightened. She looked across the lawn and saw a fourth man, moving up to the house and looking into the window. In the pale light streaming out onto the lawn, she could distinctly see the rifle in his hands.

"What's going on?"

"Ma'am, we don't want to disturb your party. Please call Dr. Stone to the door."

"I don't know if—"

"Otherwise, we will have to go get him," the man said.

She hesitated a moment, then said, "Wait here."

She stepped back and started to close the door, but one man had already slipped into the hall. He stood near the door, erect and very polite, with his hat in his hand. "I'll just wait here, ma'am," he said, and smiled at her.

She walked back to the party, trying to show nothing to the guests. Everyone was still talking and laughing; the room was noisy and dense with smoke. She found Jeremy in a corner, in the midst of some argument about riots. She touched his shoulder, and he disengaged himself from the group.

"I know this sounds funny," she said, "but there is some kind of Army man in the hall, and another outside, and two others with guns out on the lawn. They say they want to see you."

For a moment, Stone looked surprised, and then he nodded. "I'll take care of it," he said. His attitude annoyed her; he seemed almost to be expecting it.

"Well, if you knew about this, you might have told—"

"I didn't," he said. "I'll explain later."

He walked out to the hallway, where the officer was still waiting. She followed her husband.

Stone said, "I am Dr. Stone."

"Captain Morton," the man said. He did not offer to shake hands. "There's a fire, sir."

"All right," Stone said. He looked down at his dinner jacket. "Do I have time to change?"

"I'm afraid not, sir."

To her astonishment, Allison saw her husband nod quietly. "All right."

He turned to her and said, "I've got to leave." His face was blank and expressionless, and it seemed to her like a nightmare, his face like that, while he spoke. She was confused, and afraid.

"When will you be back?"

"I'm not sure. A week or two. Maybe longer."

She tried to keep her voice low, but she couldn't help it, she was upset. "What is it?" she said. "Are you under arrest?"

"No," he said, with a slight smile. "It's nothing like that. Make my apologies to everyone, will you?"

"But the guns—"

"Mrs. Stone," the military man said, "it's our job to protect your husband. From now on, nothing must be allowed to happen to him."

"That's right," Stone said. "You see, I'm suddenly an important person." He smiled again, an odd, crooked smile, and gave her a kiss.

And then, almost before she knew what was happening, he was walking out the door, with Captain Morton on one side of him and the other man on the other. The man with the rifle wordlessly fell into place behind them; the man by the car saluted and opened the door.

Then the car lights came on, and the doors slammed shut, and the car backed down the drive and drove off into the night. She was still standing by the door when one of her guests came up behind her and said, "Allison, are you all right?"

And she turned, and found she was able to smile and say, "Yes, it's nothing. Jeremy had to leave. The lab called him: another one of his late-night experiments going wrong."

The guest nodded and said, "Shame. It's a delightful party."

In the car, Stone sat back and stared at the men. He recalled that their faces were blank and expressionless. He said, "What have you got for me?"

"Got, sir?"

"Yes, dammit. What did they give you for me? They must have given you something."

"Oh. Yes sir."

He was handed a slim file. Stenciled on the brown cardboard cover was PROJECT SUMMARY: SCOOP.

"Nothing else?" Stone said.

"No sir."

Stone sighed. He had never heard of Project Scoop before; the file would have to be read carefully. But it was too dark in the car to read; there would be time for that later, on the airplane. He found himself thinking back over the last five years, back to the rather odd symposium on Long Island, and the rather odd little speaker from England who had, in his own way, begun it all.

In the summer of 1962, J. J. Merrick, the English biophysicist, presented a paper to the Tenth Biological Symposium at Cold Spring Harbor, Long Island. The paper was entitled "Frequencies of Biologic Contact According to Speciation Probabilities." Merrick was a rebellious, unorthodox scientist whose reputation for clear thinking was not enhanced by his recent divorce or the presence of the handsome blond secretary he had brought with him to the symposium. Following the presentation of his paper, there was little serious discussion of Merrick's ideas, which were summarized at the end of the paper.

I must conclude that the first contact with extraterrestrial life will be determined by the known probabilities of speciation. It is an undeniable fact that complex organisms are rare on earth, while simple organisms flourish in abundance. There are millions of species of bacteria, and thousands of species of insects. There are only a few species of primates, and only four of great apes. There is but one species of man.

With this frequency of speciation goes a corresponding frequency in numbers. Simple creatures are much more common than complex organisms. There are three billion men on the earth, and that seems a great many until we consider that ten or even one hundred times that number of bacteria can be contained within a large flask.

All available evidence on the origin of life points to an evolutionary progression from simple to complex life forms. This is true on earth. It is probably true throughout the universe. Shapley, Merrow, and others have calculated the number of viable planetary systems in the near universe. My own calculations, indicated earlier in the paper, consider the relative abundance of different organisms throughout the universe.

My aim has been to determine the probability of contact between man and another life form. That probability is as follows:

FORM	PROBABILITY
Unicellular organisms or less (naked genetic information)	.7840
Multicellular organisms, simple	.1940
Multicellular organisms, complex but lacking coordinated central nervous system	.0140
Multicellular organisms with integrated organ systems including nervous system	.0078
Multicellular organisms with complex nervous system capable of handling 7+ data (human capability)	.0002
	1.0000

These considerations lead me to believe that the first human interaction with extraterrestrial life will consist of contact with organisms similar to, if not identical to, earth bacteria or viruses. The consequences of such contact are disturbing when one recalls that 3 per cent of all earth bacteria are capable of exerting some deleterious effect upon man.

Later, Merrick himself considered the possibility that the first contact would consist of a plague brought back from the moon by the first men to go there. This idea was received with amusement by the assembled scientists.

One of the few who took it seriously was Jeremy Stone. At the age of thirty-six, Stone was perhaps the most famous person attending the symposium that year. He was professor of bacteriology at Stanford, a post he had held since he was thirty, and he had just won the Nobel Prize.

The list of Stone's achievements—disregarding the particular series of experiments that led to the Nobel Prize—is astonishing. In 1955, he was the first to use the technique of multiplicative counts for bacterial colonies. In 1957, he developed a method for liquid-pure suspension. In 1960, Stone presented a radical new theory of operon activity in E. coli and S. tabuli, and developed evidence for the physical nature of the inducer and repressor substances. His 1958 paper on linear viral transformations opened broad new lines of scientific inquiry, particularly among the Pasteur Institute group in Paris, which subsequently won the Nobel Prize in 1966.

In 1961, Stone himself won the Nobel Prize. The award was given for work on bacterial mutant reversion that he had done in his spare time as a law student at Michigan, when he was twenty-six.

Perhaps the most significant thing about Stone was that he had done Nobel-caliber work as a law student, for it demonstrated the depth and range of his interests. A friend once said of him: "Jeremy knows everything, and is fascinated by the rest." Already he was being compared to Einstein and to

Bohr as a scientist with a conscience, an overview, an appreciation of the significance of events.

Physically, Stone was a thin, balding man with a prodigious memory that catalogued scientific facts and blue jokes with equal facility. But his most outstanding characteristic was a sense of impatience, the feeling he conveyed to everyone around him that they were wasting his time. He had a bad habit of interrupting speakers and finishing conversations, a habit he tried to control with only limited success. His imperious manner, when added to the fact that he had won the Nobel Prize at an early age, as well as the scandals of his private life —he was four times married, twice to the wives of colleagues —did nothing to increase his popularity.

Yet it was Stone who, in the early 1960's, moved forward in government circles as one of the spokesmen for the new scientific establishment. He himself regarded this role with tolerant amusement—"a vacuum eager to be filled with hot gas," he once said—but in fact his influence was considerable.

By the early 1960's America had reluctantly come to realize that it possessed, as a nation, the most potent scientific complex in the history of the world. Eighty per cent of all scientific discoveries in the preceding three decades had been made by Americans. The United States had 75 per cent of the world's computers, and 90 per cent of the world's lasers. The United States had three and a half times as many scientists as the Soviet Union and spent three and a half times as much money on research; the U.S. had four times as many scientists as the European Economic Community and spent seven times as much on research. Most of this money came, directly or indirectly, from Congress, and Congress felt a great need for men to advise them on how to spend it.

During the 1950's, all the great advisers had been physicists: Teller and Oppenheimer and Bruckman and Weidner. But ten years later, with more money for biology and more concern for it, a new group emerged, led by DeBakey in Houston,

Farmer in Boston, Heggerman in New York, and Stone in California.

Stone's prominence was attributable to many factors: the prestige of the Nobel Prize; his political contacts; his most recent wife, the daughter of Senator Thomas Wayne of Indiana; his legal training. All this combined to assure Stone's repeated appearance before confused Senate subcommittees—and gave him the power of any trusted adviser.

It was this same power that he used so successfully to implement the research and construction leading to Wildfire.

Stone was intrigued by Merrick's ideas, which paralleled certain concepts of his own. He explained these in a short paper entitled "Sterilization of Spacecraft," printed in *Science* and later reprinted in the British journal *Nature*. The argument stated that bacterial contamination was a two-edged sword, and that man must protect against both edges.

Previous to Stone's paper, most discussion of contamination dealt with the hazards to other planets of satellites and probes inadvertently carrying earth organisms. This problem was considered early in the American space effort; by 1959, NASA had set strict regulations for sterilization of earth-origin probes.

The object of these regulations was to prevent contamination of other worlds. Clearly, if a probe were being sent to Mars or Venus to search for new life forms, it would defeat the purpose of the experiment for the probe to carry earth bacteria with it.

Stone considered the reverse situation. He stated that it was equally possible for extraterrestrial organisms to contaminate the earth via space probes. He noted that spacecraft that burned up in reentry presented no problem, but "live" returns —manned flights, and probes such as the Scoop satellites— were another matter entirely. Here, he said, the question of contamination was very great.

His paper created a brief flurry of interest but, as he later said, "nothing very spectacular." Therefore, in 1963 he began an informal seminar group that met twice monthly in Room 410, on the top floor of the Stanford Medical School biochemistry wing, for lunch and discussion of the contamination problem. It was this group of five men—Stone and John Black of Stanford, Samuel Holden and Terence Lisset of Cal Med, and Andrew Weiss of Berkeley biophysics—that eventually formed the early nucleus of the Wildfire Project. They presented a petition to the President in 1965, in a letter consciously patterned after the Einstein letter to Roosevelt, in 1940, concerning the atomic bomb.

Response to the letter was gratifyingly prompt. Twenty-four hours later, Stone received a call from one of the President's advisers, and the following day he flew to Washington to confer with the President and members of the National Security Council. Two weeks after that, he flew to Houston to discuss further plans with NASA officials.

Although Stone recalls one or two cracks about "the goddam penitentiary for bugs," most scientists he talked with regarded the project favorably. Within a month, Stone's informal team was hardened into an official committee to study problems of contamination and draw up recommendations.

This committee was put on the Defense Department's Advance Research Projects List and funded through the Defense Department. At that time, the ARPL was heavily invested in chemistry and physics—ion sprays, reversal duplication, pimeson substrates—but there was growing interest in biologic problems. Thus one ARPL group was concerned with electronic pacing of brain function (a euphemism for mind control); a second had prepared a study of biosynergics, the future possible combinations of man and machines implanted inside the body; still another was evaluating Project Ozma, the search for extraterrestrial life conducted in 1961–4. A fourth group was engaged in preliminary design of a machine that would carry out all human functions and would be self-duplicating.

All these projects were highly theoretical, and all were staffed by prestigious scientists. Admission to the ARPL was a mark of considerable status, and it ensured future funds for implementation and development.

Therefore, when Stone's committee submitted an early draft of the Life Analysis Protocol, which detailed the way any living thing could be studied, the Defense Department responded with an outright appropriation of $22,000,000 for the construction of a special isolated laboratory. (This rather large sum was felt to be justified since the project had application to other studies already under way. In 1965, the whole field of sterility and contamination was one of major importance. For example, NASA was building a Lunar Receiving Laboratory, a high-security facility for Apollo astronauts returning from the moon and possibly carrying bacteria or viruses harmful to man. Every astronaut returning from the moon would be quarantined in the LRL for three weeks, until decontamination was complete. Further, the problems of "clean rooms" of industry, where dust and bacteria were kept at a minimum, and the "sterile chambers" under study at Bethesda, were also major. Aseptic environments, "life islands," and sterile support systems seemed to have great future significance, and Stone's appropriation was considered a good investment in all these fields.)

Once money was funded, construction proceeded rapidly. The eventual result, the Wildfire Laboratory, was built in 1966 in Flatrock, Nevada. Design was awarded to the naval architects of the Electric Boat Division of General Dynamics, since GD had considerable experience designing living quarters on atomic submarines, where men had to live and work for prolonged periods.

The plan consisted of a conical underground structure with five floors. Each floor was circular, with a central service core of wiring, plumbing, and elevators. Each floor was more sterile than the one above; the first floor was nonsterile, the second moderately sterile, the third stringently sterile, and so on. Passage from one floor to another was not free; personnel had to undergo decontamination and quarantine procedures in passing either up or down.

Once the laboratory was finished, it only remained to select the Wildfire Alert team, the group of scientists who would study any new organism. After a number of studies of team composition, five men were selected, including Jeremy Stone himself. These five were prepared to mobilize immediately in the event of a biologic emergency.

Barely two years after his letter to the President, Stone was satisfied that "this country has the capability to deal with an unknown biologic agent." He professed himself pleased with the response of Washington and the speed with which his ideas had been implemented. But privately, he admitted to friends that it had been almost too easy, that Washington had agreed to his plans almost too readily.

Stone could not have known the reasons behind Washington's eagerness, or the very real concern many government officials had for the problem. For Stone knew nothing, until the night he left the party and drove off in the blue military sedan, of Project Scoop.

"It was the fastest thing we could arrange, sir," the Army man said.

Stone stepped onto the airplane with a sense of absurdity. It was a Boeing 727, completely empty, the seats stretching back in long unbroken rows.

"Sit first class, if you like," the Army man said, with a slight smile. "It doesn't matter." A moment later he was gone. He was not replaced by a stewardess but by a stern MP with a pistol on his hip who stood by the door as the engines started, whining softly in the night.

Stone sat back with the Scoop file in front of him and began to read. It made fascinating reading; he went through it quickly, so quickly that the MP thought his passenger must be merely glancing at the file. But Stone was reading every word.

Scoop was the brainchild of Major General Thomas Sparks, head of the Army Medical Corps, Chemical and Biological Warfare Division. Sparks was responsible for the research of the CBW installations at Fort Detrick, Maryland, Harley, Indiana, and Dugway, Utah. Stone had met him once or twice, and remembered him as being mild-mannered and bespectacled. Not the sort of man to be expected in the job he held.

Reading on, Stone learned that Project Scoop was contracted to the Jet Propulsion Laboratory of the California Institute of Technology in Pasadena in 1963. Its avowed aim was the collection of any organisms that might exist in "near space," the upper atmosphere of the earth. Technically speaking, it was an Army project, but it was funded through the National Aeronautics and Space Administration, a supposedly civilian organization. In fact, NASA was a government agency with a heavy military commitment; 43 per cent of its contractual work was classified in 1963.

In theory, JPL was designing a satellite to enter the fringes of space and collect organisms and dust for study. This was considered a project of pure science—almost curiosity—and was thus accepted by all the scientists working on the study.

In fact, the true aims were quite different.

The true aims of Scoop were to find new life forms that might benefit the Fort Detrick program. In essence, it was a study to discover new biological weapons of war.

Detrick was a rambling structure in Maryland dedicated to

the discovery of chemical-and-biological-warfare weapons. Covering 1,300 acres, with a physical plant valued at $100,-000,000, it ranked as one of the largest research facilities of any kind in the United States. Only 15 per cent of its findings were published in open scientific journals; the rest were classified, as were the reports from Harley and Dugway. Harley was a maximum-security installation that dealt largely with viruses. In the previous ten years, a number of new viruses had been developed there, ranging from the variety coded Carrie Nation (which produces diarrhea) to the variety coded Arnold (which causes clonic seizures and death). The Dugway Proving Ground in Utah was larger than the state of Rhode Island and was used principally to test poison gases such as Tabun, Sklar, and Kuff-11.

Few Americans, Stone knew, were aware of the magnitude of U.S. research into chemical and biological warfare. The total government expenditure in CBW exceeded half a billion dollars a year. Much of this was distributed to academic centers such as Johns Hopkins, Pennsylvania, and the University of Chicago, where studies of weapons systems were contracted under vague terms. Sometimes, of course, the terms were not so vague. The Johns Hopkins program was devised to evaluate "studies of actual or potential injuries and illnesses, studies on diseases of potential biological-warfare significance, and evaluation of certain chemical and immunological responses to certain toxoids and vaccines."

In the past eight years, none of the results from Johns Hopkins had been published openly. Those from other universities, such as Chicago and UCLA, had occasionally been published, but these were considered within the military establishment to be "trial balloons"—examples of ongoing research intended to intimidate foreign observers. A classic was the paper by Tendron and five others entitled "Researches into a Toxin Which Rapidly Uncouples Oxidative Phosphorylation Through Cutaneous Absorption."

The paper described, but did not identify, a poison that would kill a person in less than a minute and was absorbed through the skin. It was recognized that this was a relatively minor achievement compared to other toxins that had been devised in recent years.

With so much money and effort going into CBW, one might think that new and more virulent weapons would be continuously perfected. However, this was not the case from 1961 to 1965; the conclusion of the Senate Preparedness Subcommittee in 1961 was that "conventional research has been less than satisfactory" and that "new avenues and approaches of inquiry" should be opened within the field.

That was precisely what Major General Thomas Sparks intended to do, with Project Scoop.

In final form, Scoop was a program to orbit seventeen satellites around the earth, collecting organisms and bringing them back to the surface. Stone read the summaries of each previous flight.

Scoop I was a gold-plated satellite, cone-shaped, weighing thirty-seven pounds fully equipped. It was launched from Vandenberg Air Force Base in Purisima, California, on March 12, 1966. Vandenberg is used for west-to-east orbits, as opposed to Cape Kennedy, which launches east-to-west; Vandenberg had the additional advantage of maintaining better secrecy than Kennedy.

Scoop I orbited for six days before being brought down. It landed successfully in a swamp near Athens, Georgia. Unfortunately, it was found to contain only standard earth organisms.

Scoop II burned up in reentry, as a result of instrumentation failure. Scoop III also burned up, though it had a new type of plastic-and-tungsten-laminate heat shield.

Scoops IV and V were recovered intact from the Indian Ocean and the Appalachian foothills, but neither contained radically new organisms; those collected were harmless variants of S. *albus*, a common contaminant of normal human skin. These failures led to a further increase in sterilization procedures prior to launch.

Scoop VI was launched on New Year's Day, 1967. It incorporated all the latest refinements from earlier attempts. High hopes rode with the revised satellite, which returned eleven days later, landing near Bombay, India. Unknown to anyone, the 34th Airborne, then stationed in Evreux, France, just outside Paris, was dispatched to recover the capsule. The 34th was on alert whenever a spaceflight went up, according to the procedures of Operation Scrub, a plan first devised to protect Mercury and Gemini capsules should one be forced to land in Soviet Russia or Eastern Bloc countries. Scrub was the primary reason for keeping a single paratroop division in Western Europe in the first half of the 1960's.

Scoop VI was recovered uneventfully. It was found to contain a previously unknown form of unicellular organism, coccobacillary in shape, gram-negative, coagulase, and triokinase-positive. However, it proved generally benevolent to all living things with the exception of domestic female chickens, which it made moderately ill for a four-day period.

Among the Detrick staff, hope dimmed for the successful recovery of a pathogen from the Scoop program. Nonetheless, Scoop VII was launched soon after Scoop VI. The exact date is classified but it is believed to be February 5, 1967. Scoop VII immediately went into stable orbit with an apogee of 317 miles and a perigee of 224 miles. It remained in orbit for two and a half days. At that time, the satellite abruptly left stable orbit for unknown reasons, and it was decided to bring it down by radio command.

The anticipated landing site was a desolate area in northeastern Arizona.

Midway through the flight, his reading was interrupted by an officer who brought him a telephone and then stepped a respectful distance away while Stone talked.

"Yes?" Stone said, feeling odd. He was not accustomed to talking on the telephone in the middle of an airplane trip.

"General Marcus here," a tired voice said. Stone did not know General Marcus. "I just wanted to inform you that all members of the team have been called in, with the exception of Professor Kirke."

"What happened?"

"Professor Kirke is in the hospital," General Marcus said. "You'll get further details when you touch down."

The conversation ended; Stone gave the telephone back to the officer. He thought for a minute about the other men on the team, and wondered at their reactions as they were called out of bed.

There was Leavitt, of course. He would respond quickly. Leavitt was a clinical microbiologist, a man experienced in the treatment of infectious disease. Leavitt had seen enough plagues and epidemics in his day to know the importance of quick action. Besides, there was his ingrained pessimism, which never deserted him. (Leavitt had once said, "At my wedding, all I could think of was how much alimony she'd cost me.") He was an irritable, grumbling, heavyset man with a morose face and sad eyes, which seemed to peer ahead into a bleak and miserable future; but he was also thoughtful, imaginative, and not afraid to think daringly.

Then there was the pathologist, Burton, in Houston. Stone had never liked Burton very well, though he acknowledged his scientific talent. Burton and Stone were different: where Stone was organized, Burton was sloppy; where Stone was controlled, Burton was impulsive; where Stone was confident, Burton was nervous, jumpy, petulant. Colleagues referred to Burton as "the Stumbler," partly because of his tendency to trip over his untied shoelaces and baggy trouser cuffs and partly because of his talent for tumbling by error into one important discovery after another.

And then Kirke, the anthropologist from Yale, who apparently was not going to be able to come. If the report was true, Stone knew he was going to miss him. Kirke was an ill-informed and rather foppish man who possessed, as if by accident, a superbly logical brain. He was capable of grasping the essentials of a problem and manipulating them to get the necessary result; though he could not balance his own checkbook, mathematicians often came to him for help in resolving highly abstract problems.

Stone was going to miss that kind of brain. Certainly the fifth man would be no help. Stone frowned as he thought about Mark Hall. Hall had been a compromise candidate for the team; Stone would have preferred a physician with experience in metabolic disease, and the choice of a surgeon instead had been made with the greatest reluctance. There had been great pressure from Defense and the AEC to accept Hall, since those groups believed in the Odd Man Hypothesis; in the end, Stone and the others had given in.

Stone did not know Hall well; he wondered what he would say when he was informed of the alert. Stone could not have known of the great delay in notifying members of the team. He did not know, for instance, that Burton, the pathologist, was not called until five a.m., or that Peter Leavitt, the microbiologist, was not called until six thirty, the time he arrived at the hospital.

And Hall was not called until five minutes past seven.

It was, Mark Hall said later, "a horrifying experience. In an instant, I was taken from the most familiar of worlds and plunged into the most unfamiliar." At six forty-five, Hall was in the washroom adjacent to OR 7, scrubbing for his first case of the day. He was in the midst of a routine he had carried out daily for several years; he was relaxed and joking with the resident, scrubbing with him.

When he finished, he went into the operating room, holding

his arms before him, and the instrument nurse handed him a towel, to wipe his hands dry. Also in the room was another resident, who was prepping the body for surgery—applying iodine and alcohol solutions—and a circulating nurse. They all exchanged greetings.

At the hospital, Hall was known as a swift, quick-tempered, and unpredictable surgeon. He operated with speed, working nearly twice as fast as other surgeons. When things went smoothly, he laughed and joked as he worked, kidding his assistants, the nurses, the anesthetist. But if things did not go well, if they became slow and difficult, Hall could turn blackly irritable.

Like most surgeons, he was insistent upon routine. Everything had to be done in a certain order, in a certain way. If not, he became upset.

Because the others in the operating room knew this, they looked up toward the overhead viewing gallery with apprehension when Leavitt appeared. Leavitt clicked on the intercom that connected the upstairs room to the operating room below and said, "Hello, Mark."

Hall had been draping the patient, placing green sterile cloths over every part of the body except for the abdomen. He looked up with surprise. "Hello, Peter," he said.

"Sorry to disturb you," Leavitt said. "But this is an emergency."

"Have to wait," Hall said. "I'm starting a procedure."

He finished draping and called for the skin knife. He palpated the abdomen, feeling for the landmarks to begin his incision.

"It can't wait," Leavitt said.

Hall paused. He set down the scalpel and looked up. There was a long silence.

"What the hell do you mean, it can't wait?"

Leavitt remained calm. "You'll have to break scrub. This is an emergency."

"Look, Peter, I've got a patient here. Anesthetized. Ready to go. I can't just walk—"

"Kelly will take over for you."

Kelly was one of the staff surgeons.

"Kelly?"

"He's scrubbing now," Leavitt said. "It's all arranged. I'll expect to meet you in the surgeon's change room. In about thirty seconds."

And then he was gone.

Hall glared at everyone in the room. No one moved, or spoke. After a moment, he stripped off his gloves and stomped out of the room, swearing once, very loudly.

Hall viewed his own association with Wildfire as tenuous at best. In 1966 he had been approached by Leavitt, the chief of bacteriology of the hospital, who had explained in a sketchy way the purpose of the project. Hall found it all rather amusing and had agreed to join the team, if his services ever became necessary; privately, he was confident that nothing would ever come of Wildfire.

Leavitt had offered to give Hall the files on Wildfire and to keep him up to date on the project. At first, Hall politely took the files, but it soon became clear that he was not bothering to read them, and so Leavitt stopped giving them to him. If anything, this pleased Hall, who preferred not to have his desk cluttered.

A year before, Leavitt had asked him whether he wasn't curious about something that he had agreed to join and that might at some future time prove dangerous.

Hall had said, "No."

Now, in the doctors' room, Hall regretted those words. The doctors' room was a small place, lined on all four walls with lockers; there were no windows. A large coffeemaker sat in the center of the room, with a stack of paper cups alongside.

Leavitt was pouring himself a cup, his solemn, basset-hound face looking mournful.

"This is going to be awful coffee," he said. "You can't get a decent cup anywhere in a hospital. Hurry and change."

Hall said, "Do you mind telling me first why—"

"I mind, I mind," Leavitt said. "Change: there's a car waiting outside and we're already late. Perhaps too late."

He had a gruffly melodramatic way of speaking that had always annoyed Hall.

There was a loud slurp as Leavitt sipped the coffee. "Just as I suspected," he said. "How can you tolerate it? Hurry, please."

Hall unlocked his locker and kicked it open. He leaned against the door and stripped away the black plastic shoe covers that were worn in the operating room to prevent buildup of static charges. "Next, I suppose you're going to tell me this has to do with that damned project."

"Exactly," Leavitt said. "Now try to hurry. The car is waiting to take us to the airport, and the morning traffic is bad."

Hall changed quickly, not thinking, his mind momentarily stunned. Somehow he had never thought it possible. He dressed and walked out with Leavitt toward the hospital entrance. Outside, in the sunshine, he could see the olive U.S. Army sedan pulled up to the curb, its light flashing. And he had a sudden, horrible realization that Leavitt was not kidding, that nobody was kidding, and that some kind of awful nightmare was coming true.

For his own part, Peter Leavitt was irritated with Hall. In general, Leavitt had little patience with practicing physicians. Though he had an M.D. degree, Leavitt had never practiced, preferring to devote his time to research. His field was clinical microbiology and epidemiology, and his specialty was parasitology. He had done parasitic research all over the world; his work had led to the discovery of the Brazilian tapeworm,

Taenia renzi, which he had characterized in a paper in 1953.

As he grew older, however, Leavitt had stopped traveling. Public health, he was fond of saying, was a young man's game; when you got your fifth case of intestinal amebiasis, it was time to quit. Leavitt got his fifth case in Rhodesia in 1955. He was dreadfully sick for three months and lost forty pounds. Afterward, he resigned his job in the public health service. He was offered the post of chief of microbiology at the hospital, and he had taken it, with the understanding that he would be able to devote a good portion of his time to research.

Within the hospital he was known as a superb clinical bacteriologist, but his real interest remained parasites. In the period from 1955 to 1964 he published a series of elegant metabolic studies on *Ascaris* and *Necator* that were highly regarded by other workers in the field.

Leavitt's reputation had made him a natural choice for Wildfire, and it was through Leavitt that Hall had been asked to join. Leavitt knew the reasons behind Hall's selection, though Hall did not.

When Leavitt had asked him to join, Hall had demanded to know why. "I'm just a surgeon," he had said.

"Yes," Leavitt said. "But you know electrolytes."

"So?"

"That may be important. Blood chemistries, pH, acidity and alkalinity, the whole thing. That may be vital, when the time comes."

"But there are a lot of electrolyte people," Hall had pointed out. "Many of them better than me."

"Yes," Leavitt had said. "But they're all married."

"So what?"

"We need a single man."

"Why?"

"It's necessary that one member of the team be unmarried."

"That's crazy," Hall had said.

"Maybe," Leavitt had said. "Maybe not."

* * *

They left the hospital and walked up to the Army sedan. A young officer was waiting stiffly, and saluted as they came up.

"Dr. Hall?"

"Yes."

"May I see your card, please?"

Hall gave him the little plastic card with his picture on it. He had been carrying the card in his wallet for more than a year; it was a rather strange card—with just a name, a picture, and a thumbprint, nothing more. Nothing to indicate that it was an official card.

The officer glanced at it, then at Hall, and back to the card. He handed it back.

"Very good, sir."

He opened the rear door of the sedan. Hall got in and Leavitt followed, shielding his eyes from the flashing red light on the car top. Hall noticed it.

"Something wrong?"

"No. Just never liked flashing lights. Reminds me of my days as an ambulance driver, during the war." Leavitt settled back and the car started off. "Now then," he said. "When we reach the airfield, you will be given a file to read during the trip."

"What trip?"

"You'll be taking an F-104," Leavitt said.

"Where?"

"Nevada. Try to read the file on the way. Once we arrive, things will be very busy."

"And the others in the team?"

Leavitt glanced at his watch. "Kirke has appendicitis and is in the hospital. The others have already begun work. Right now, they are in a helicopter, over Piedmont, Arizona."

"Never heard of it," Hall said.

"Nobody has," Leavitt said, "until now."

6.

Piedmont

At 9:59 a.m. on the same morn-
ing, a K-4 jet helicopter lifted off the concrete of Vandenberg's
maximum-security hangar MSH-9 and headed east, toward
Arizona.

The decision to lift off from an MSH was made by Major
Manchek, who was concerned about the attention the suits
might draw. Because inside the helicopter were three men, a
pilot and two scientists, and all three wore clear plastic inflata-
ble suits, making them look like obese men from Mars, or, as
one of the hangar maintenance men put it, "like balloons
from the Macy's parade."

As the helicopter climbed into the clear morning sky, the
two passengers in the belly looked at each other. One was
Jeremy Stone, the other Charles Burton. Both men had arrived
at Vandenberg just a few hours before—Stone from Stanford
and Burton from Baylor University in Houston.

Burton was fifty-four, a pathologist. He held a professorship
at Baylor Medical School and served as a consultant to the
NASA Manned Spaceflight Center in Houston. Earlier he
had done research at the National Institutes in Bethesda. His
field had been the effects of bacteria on human tissues.

It is one of the peculiarities of scientific development that such a vital field was virtually untouched when Burton came to it. Though men had known germs caused disease since Henle's hypothesis of 1840, by the middle of the twentieth century there was still nothing known about why or how bacteria did their damage. The specific mechanisms were unknown.

Burton began, like so many others in his day, with *Diplococcus pneumoniae,* the agent causing pneumonia. There was great interest in pneumococcus before the advent of penicillin in the forties; after that, both interest and research money evaporated. Burton shifted to *Staphylococcus aureus,* a common skin pathogen responsible for "pimples" and "boils." At the time he began his work, his fellow researchers laughed at him; staphylococcus, like pneumococcus, was highly sensitive to penicillin. They doubted Burton would ever get enough money to carry on his work.

For five years, they were right. The money was scarce, and Burton often had to go begging to foundations and philanthropists. Yet he persisted, patiently elucidating the coats of the cell wall that caused a reaction in host tissue and helping to discover the half-dozen toxins secreted by the bacteria to break down tissue, spread infection, and destroy red cells.

Suddenly, in the 1950's, the first penicillin-resistant strains of staph appeared. The new strains were virulent, and produced bizarre deaths, often by brain abscess. Almost overnight Burton found his work had assumed major importance; dozens of labs around the country were changing over to study staph; it was a "hot field." In a single year, Burton watched his grant appropriations jump from $6,000 a year to $300,000. Soon afterward, he was made a professor of pathology.

Looking back, Burton felt no great pride in his accomplishment; it was, he knew, a matter of luck, of being in the right place and doing the right work when the time came.

He wondered what would come of being here, in this helicopter, now.

Sitting across from him, Jeremy Stone tried to conceal his distaste for Burton's appearance. Beneath the plastic suit Burton wore a dirty plaid sport shirt with a stain on the left breast pocket; his trousers were creased and frayed and even his hair, Stone felt, was unruly and untidy.

He stared out the window, forcing himself to think of other matters. "Fifty people," he said, shaking his head. "Dead within eight hours of the landing of Scoop VII. The question is one of spread."

"Presumably airborne," Burton said.

"Yes. Presumably."

"Everyone seems to have died in the immediate vicinity of the town," Burton said. "Are there reports of deaths farther out?"

Stone shook his head. "I'm having the Army people look into it. They're working with the highway patrol. So far, no deaths have turned up outside."

"Wind?"

"A stroke of luck," Stone said. "Last night the wind was fairly brisk, nine miles an hour to the south and steady. But around midnight, it died. Pretty unusual for this time of year, they tell me."

"But fortunate for us."

"Yes." Stone nodded. "We're fortunate in another way as well. There is no important area of habitation for a radius of nearly one hundred and twelve miles. Outside that, of course, there is Las Vegas to the north, San Bernardino to the west, and Phoenix to the east. Not nice, if the bug gets to any of them."

"But as long as the wind stays down, we have time."

"Presumably," Stone said.

For the next half hour, the two men discussed the vector problem with frequent reference to a sheaf of output maps drawn up during the night by Vandenberg's computer division. The output maps were highly complex analyses of geographic problems; in this case, the maps were visualizations of the southwestern United States, weighted for wind direction and population.

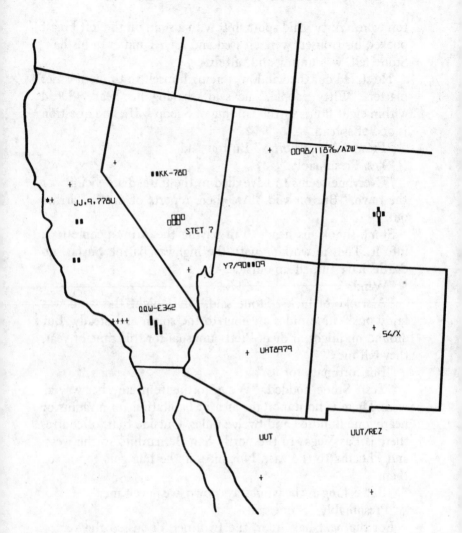

A NOTE ON THE OUTPUT MAPS: these three maps are intended as examples of the staging of computerbase output mapping. The first map is relatively standard, with the addition of computer coordinates around population centers and other important areas.

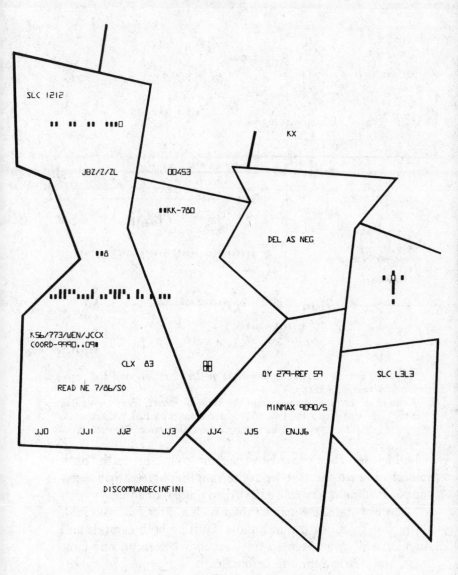

The second map has been weighted to account for wind and population factors, and is consequently distorted.

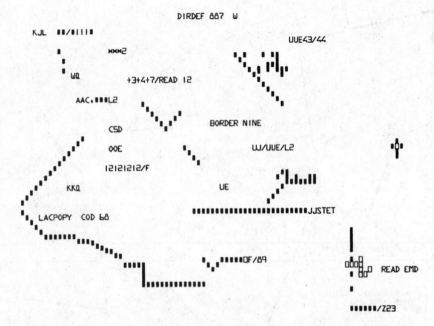

The third map is a computer projection of the effects of wind and population in a specific "scenario."

None of these output maps is from the Wildfire Project. They are similar, but they represent output from a CBW scenario, not the actual Wildfire work.

(*courtesy General Autonomics Corporation*)

Discussion then turned to the time course of death. Both men had heard the tape from the van; they agreed that everyone at Piedmont seemed to have died quite suddenly.

"Even if you slit a man's throat with a razor," Burton said, "you won't get death that rapidly. Cutting both carotids and jugulars still allows ten to forty seconds before unconsciousness, and nearly a minute before death."

"At Piedmont, it seems to have occurred in a second or two."

Burton shrugged. "Trauma," he suggested. "A blow to the head."

"Yes. Or a nerve gas."

"Certainly possible."

"It's that, or something very much like it," Stone said. "If it was an enzymatic block of some kind—like arsenic or strychnine—we'd expect fifteen or thirty seconds, perhaps longer. But a block of nervous transmission, or a block of the neuromuscular junction, or cortical poisoning—that could be very swift. It could be instantaneous."

"If it is a fast-acting gas," Burton said, "it must have high diffusibility across the lungs—"

"Or the skin," Stone said. "Mucous membranes, anything. Any porous surface."

Burton touched the plastic of his suit. "If this gas is so highly diffusible . . . "

Stone gave a slight smile. "We'll find out, soon enough."

Over the intercom, the helicopter pilot said, "Piedmont approaching, gentlemen. Please advise."

Stone said, "Circle once and give us a look at it."

The helicopter banked steeply. The two men looked out and saw the town below them. The buzzards had landed during the night, and were thickly clustered around the bodies.

"I was afraid of that," Stone said.

"They may represent a vector for infectious spread," Burton said. "Eat the meat of infected people, and carry the organisms away with them."

Stone nodded, staring out the window.

"What do we do?"

"Gas them," Stone said. He flicked on the intercom to the pilot. "Have you got the canisters?"

"Yes sir."

"Circle again, and blanket the town."

"Yes sir."

The helicopter tilted, and swung back. Soon the two men could not see the ground for the clouds of pale-blue gas.

"What is it?"

"Chlorazine," Stone said. "Highly effective, in low concentrations, on aviary metabolism. Birds have a high metabolic rate. They are creatures that consist of little more than feathers and muscle; their heartbeats are usually about one-twenty, and many species eat more than their own weight every day."

"The gas is an uncoupler?"

"Yes. It'll hit them hard."

The helicopter banked away, then hovered. The gas slowly cleared in the gentle wind, moving off to the south. Soon they could see the ground again. Hundreds of birds lay there; a few flapped their wings spastically, but most were already dead.

Stone frowned as he watched. Somewhere, in the back of his mind, he knew he had forgotten something, or ignored something. Some fact, some vital clue, that the birds provided and he must not overlook.

Over the intercom, the pilot said, "Your orders, sir?"

"Go to the center of the main street," Stone said, "and drop the rope ladder. You are to remain twenty feet above ground. Do not put down. Is that clear?"

"Yes sir."

"When we have climbed down, you are to lift off to an altitude of five hundred feet."

"Yes sir."

"Return when we signal you."

"Yes sir."

"And should anything happen to us—"

"I proceed directly to Wildfire," the pilot said, his voice dry.

"Correct."

The pilot knew what that meant. He was being paid according to the highest Air Force pay scales: he was drawing regular pay plus hazardous-duty pay, plus non-wartime special-services pay, plus mission-over-hostile-territory pay, plus bonus airtime pay. He would receive more than a thousand dollars for this day's work, and his family would receive an additional ten thousand dollars from the short-term life insurance should he not return.

There was a reason for the money: if anything happened to Burton and Stone on the ground, the pilot was ordered to fly directly to the Wildfire installation and hover thirty feet above ground until such time as the Wildfire group had determined the correct way to incinerate him, and his airplane, in midair.

He was being paid to take a risk. He had volunteered for the job. And he knew that high above, circling at twenty thousand feet, was an Air Force jet with air-to-air missiles. It was the job of the jet to shoot down the helicopter should the pilot suffer a last-minute loss of nerve and fail to go directly to Wildfire.

"Don't slip up," the pilot said. "Sir."

The helicopter maneuvered over the main street of the town and hung in midair. There was a rattling sound: the rope ladder being released. Stone stood and pulled on his helmet. He snapped shut the sealer and inflated his clear suit, puffing it up around him. A small bottle of oxygen on his back would provide enough air for two hours of exploration.

He waited until Burton had sealed his suit, and then Stone opened the hatch and stared down at the ground. The helicopter was raising a heavy cloud of dust.

Stone clicked on his radio. "All set?"

"All set."

Stone began to climb down the ladder. Burton waited a moment, then followed. He could see nothing in the swirling dust, but finally felt his shoes touch the ground. He released the ladder and looked over. He could barely make out Stone's suit, a dim outline in a gloomy, dusky world.

The ladder pulled away as the helicopter lifted into the sky. The dust cleared. They could see.

"Let's go," Stone said.

Moving clumsily in their suits, they walked down the main street of Piedmont.

7.

"An Unusual Process"

SCARCELY TWELVE HOURS after the first known human contact with the Andromeda Strain was made at Piedmont, Burton and Stone arrived in the town. Weeks later, in their debriefing sessions, both men recalled the scene vividly, and described it in detail.

The morning sun was still low in the sky; it was cold and cheerless, casting long shadows over the thinly snow-crusted ground. From where they stood, they could look up and down the street at the gray, weathered wooden buildings; but what they noticed first was the silence. Except for a gentle wind that whined softly through the empty houses, it was deathly silent. Bodies lay everywhere, heaped and flung across the ground in attitudes of frozen surprise.

But there was no sound—no reassuring rumble of an automobile engine, no barking dog, no shouting children.

Silence.

The two men looked at each other. They were painfully aware of how much there was to learn, to do. Some catastrophe had struck this town, and they must discover all they could about it. But they had practically no clues, no points of departure.

They knew, in fact, only two things. First, that the trouble apparently began with the landing of Scoop VII. And second, that death had overtaken the people of the town with astonishing rapidity. If it was a disease from the satellite, then it was like no other in the history of medicine.

For a long time the men said nothing, but stood in the street, looking about them, feeling the wind tug at their oversized suits. Finally, Stone said, "Why are they all outside, in the street? If this was a disease that arrived at night, most of the people would be indoors."

"Not only that," Burton said, "they're mostly wearing pajamas. It was a cold night last night. You'd think they would have stopped to put on a jacket, or a raincoat. Something to keep warm."

"Maybe they were in a hurry."

"To do what?" Burton said.

"To see something," Stone said, with a helpless shrug.

Burton bent over the first body they came to. "Odd," he said. "Look at the way this fellow is clutching his chest. Quite a few of them are doing that."

Looking at the bodies, Stone saw that the hands of many were pressed to their chests, some flat, some clawing.

"They didn't seem to be in pain," Stone said. "Their faces are quite peaceful."

"Almost astonished, in fact," Burton nodded. "These people look cut down, caught in midstride. But clutching their chests."

"Coronary?" Stone said.

"Doubt it. They should grimace—it's painful. The same with a pulmonary embolus."

"If it was fast enough, they wouldn't have time."

"Perhaps. But somehow I think these people died a painless death. Which means they are clutching their chests because—"

"They couldn't breathe," Stone said.

Burton nodded. "It's possible we're seeing asphyxiation.

Rapid, painless, almost instantaneous asphyxiation. But I doubt it. If a person can't breathe, the first thing he does is loosen his clothing, particularly around the neck and chest. Look at that man there—he's wearing a tie, and he hasn't touched it. And that woman with the tightly buttoned collar."

Burton was beginning to regain his composure now, after the initial shock of the town. He was beginning to think clearly. They walked up to the van, standing in the middle of the street, its lights still shining weakly. Stone reached in to turn off the lights. He pushed the stiff body of the driver back from the wheel and read the name on the breast pocket of the parka.

"Shawn."

The man sitting rigidly in the back of the van was a private named Crane. Both men were locked in rigor mortis. Stone nodded to the equipment in the back.

"Will that still work?"

"I think so," Burton said.

"Then let's find the satellite. That's our first job. We can worry later about—"

He stopped. He was looking at the face of Shawn, who had obviously pitched forward hard onto the steering wheel at the moment of death. There was a large, arc-shaped cut across his face, shattering the bridge of his nose and tearing the skin.

"I don't get it," Stone said.

"Get what?" Burton said.

"This injury. Look at it."

"Very clean," Burton said. "Remarkably clean, in fact. Practically no bleeding . . . "

Then Burton realized. He started to scratch his head in astonishment, but his hand was stopped by the plastic helmet.

"A cut like that," he said, "on the face. Broken capillaries, shattered bone, torn scalp veins—it should bleed like hell."

"Yes," Stone said. "It should. And look at the other bodies. Even where the vultures have chewed at the flesh: no bleeding."

Burton stared with increasing astonishment. None of the bodies had lost even a drop of blood. He wondered why they had not noticed it before.

"Maybe the mechanism of action of this disease—"

"Yes," Stone said. "I think you may be right." He grunted and dragged Shawn out of the van, working to pull the stiff body from behind the wheel. "Let's get that damned satellite," he said. "This is really beginning to worry me."

Burton went to the back and pulled Crane out through the rear doors, then climbed in as Stone turned the ignition. The starter turned over sluggishly, and the engine did not catch.

Stone tried to start the van for several seconds, then said, "I don't understand. The battery is low, but it should still be enough—"

"How's your gas?" Burton said.

There was a pause, and Stone swore loudly. Burton smiled, and crawled out of the back. Together they walked up the street to the gas station, found a bucket, and filled it with gas from the pump after spending several moments trying to decide how it worked. When they had the gas, they returned to the van, filled the tank, and Stone tried again.

The engine caught and held. Stone grinned. "Let's go."

Burton scrambled into the back, turned on the electronic equipment, and started the antenna rotating. He heard the faint beeping of the satellite.

"The signal's weak, but still there. Sounds over to the left somewhere."

Stone put the van in gear. They rumbled off, swerving around the bodies in the street. The beeping grew louder. They continued down the main street, past the gas station and the general store. The beeping suddenly grew faint.

"We've gone too far. Turn around."

It took a while for Stone to find reverse on the gearshift, and then they doubled back, tracing the intensity of the sound. It was another fifteen minutes before they were able to locate the origin of the beeps to the north, on the outskirts of the town.

Finally, they pulled up before a plain single-story wood-frame house. A sign creaked in the wind: Dr. Alan Benedict.

"Might have known," Stone said. "They'd take it to the doctor."

The two men climbed out of the van and went up to the house. The front door was open, banging in the breeze. They entered the living room and found it empty. Turning right, they came to the doctor's office.

Benedict was there, a pudgy, white-haired man. He was seated before his desk, with several textbooks laid open. Along one wall were bottles, syringes, pictures of his family and several others showing men in combat uniforms. One showed a group of grinning soldiers; the scrawled words: "For Benny, from the boys of 87, Anzio."

Benedict himself was staring blankly toward a corner of the room, his eyes wide, his face peaceful.

"Well," Burton said, "Benedict certainly didn't make it out-side—"

And then they saw the satellite.

It was upright, a sleek polished cone three feet high, and its edges had been cracked and seared from the heat of reentry. It had been opened crudely, apparently with the help of a pair of pliers and chisel that lay on the floor next to the capsule.

"The bastard opened it," Stone said. "Stupid son of a bitch."

"How was he to know?"

"He might have asked somebody," Stone said. He sighed. "Anyway, he knows now. And so do forty-nine other people." He bent over the satellite and closed the gaping, triangular hatch. "You have the container?"

Burton produced the folded plastic bag and opened it out. Together they slipped it over the satellite, then sealed it shut.

"I hope to hell there's something left," Burton said.

"In a way," Stone said softly, "I hope there isn't."

They turned their attention to Benedict. Stone went over to him and shook him. The man fell rigidly from his chair onto the floor.

Burton noticed the elbows, and suddenly became excited. He leaned over the body. "Come on," he said to Stone. "Help me."

"Do what?"

"Strip him down."

"Why?"

"I want to check the lividity."

"But why?"

"Just wait," Burton said. He began unbuttoning Benedict's shirt and loosening his trousers. The two men worked silently for some moments, until the doctor's body was naked on the floor.

"There," Burton said, standing back.

"I'll be damned," Stone said.

There was no dependent lividity. Normally, after a person died, blood seeped to the lowest points, drawn down by gravity. A person who died in bed had a purple back from accumulated blood. But Benedict, who had died sitting up, had no blood in the tissue of his buttocks or thighs.

Or in his elbows, which had rested on the arms of the chair.

"Quite a peculiar finding," Burton said. He glanced around the room and found a small autoclave for sterilizing instruments. Opening it, he removed a scalpel. He fitted it with a blade—carefully, so as not to puncture his airtight suit—and then turned back to the body.

"We'll take the most superficial major artery and vein," he said.

"Which is?"

"The radial. At the wrist."

Holding the scalpel carefully, Burton drew the blade along the skin of the inner wrist, just behind the thumb. The skin pulled back from the wound, which was completely bloodless.

He exposed fat and subcutaneous tissue. There was no bleeding.

"Amazing."

He cut deeper. There was still no bleeding from the incision. Suddenly, abruptly, he struck a vessel. Crumbling red-black material fell out onto the floor.

"I'll be damned," Stone said again.

"Clotted solid," Burton said.

"No wonder the people didn't bleed."

Burton said, "Help me turn him over." Together, they got the corpse onto its back, and Burton made a deep incision into the medial thigh, cutting down to the femoral artery and vein. Again there was no bleeding, and when they reached the artery, as thick as a man's finger, it was clotted into a firm, reddish mass.

"Incredible."

He began another incision, this time into the chest. He exposed the ribs, then searched Dr. Benedict's office for a very sharp knife. He wanted an osteotome, but could find none. He settled for the chisel that had been used to open the capsule. Using this he broke away several ribs to expose the lungs and the heart. Again there was no bleeding.

Burton took a deep breath, then cut open the heart, slicing into the left ventricle.

The interior was filled with red, spongy material. There was no liquid blood at all.

"Clotted solid," he said. "No question."

"Any idea what can clot people this way?"

"The whole vascular system? Five quarts of blood? No." Burton sat heavily in the doctor's chair and stared at the body he had just cut open. "I've never heard of anything like it. There's a thing called disseminated intravascular coagulation, but it's rare and requires all sorts of special circumstances to initiate it."

"Could a single toxin initiate it?"

"In theory, I suppose. But in fact, there isn't a toxin in the world—"

He stopped.

"Yes," Stone said. "I suppose that's right."

He picked up the satellite designated Scoop VII and carried it outside to the van. When he came back, he said, "We'd better search the houses."

"Beginning here?"

"Might as well," Stone said.

It was Burton who found Mrs. Benedict. She was a pleasant-looking middle-aged lady sitting in a chair with a book on her lap; she seemed about to turn the page. Burton examined her briefly, then heard Stone call to him.

He walked to the other end of the house. Stone was in a small bedroom, bent over the body of a young teen-age boy on the bed. It was obviously his room: psychedelic posters on the walls, model airplanes on a shelf to one side.

The boy lay on his back in bed, eyes open, staring at the ceiling. His mouth was open. In one hand, an empty tube of model-airplane cement was tightly clenched; all over the bed were empty bottles of airplane dope, paint thinner, turps.

Stone stepped back. "Have a look."

Burton looked in the mouth, reached a finger in, touched the now-hardened mass. "Good God," he said.

Stone was frowning. "This took time," he said. "Regardless of what made him do it, it took time. We've obviously been oversimplifying events here. Everyone did not die instantaneously. Some people died in their homes; some got out into the street. And this kid here . . ."

He shook his head. "Let's check the other houses."

On the way out, Burton returned to the doctor's office, stepping around the body of the physician. It gave him a strange feeling to see the wrist and leg sliced open, the chest exposed—but no bleeding. There was something wild and inhuman about that. As if bleeding were a sign of humanity. Well, he thought, perhaps it is. Perhaps the fact that we bleed to death makes us human.

For Stone, Piedmont was a puzzle challenging him to crack its secret. He was convinced that the town could tell him everything about the nature of the disease, its course and effects. It was only a matter of putting together the data in the proper way.

But he had to admit, as they continued their search, that the data were confusing:

A house that contained a man, his wife, and their young daughter, all sitting around the dinner table. They had apparently been relaxed and happy, and none of them had had time to push back their chairs from the table. They remained frozen in attitudes of congeniality, smiling at each other across the plates of now-rotting food, and flies. Stone noticed the flies, which buzzed softly in the room. He would, he thought, have to remember the flies.

An old woman, her hair white, her face creased. She was smiling gently as she swung from a noose tied to a ceiling rafter. The rope creaked as it rubbed against the wood of the rafter.

At her feet was an envelope. In a careful, neat, unhurried hand: "To whom it may concern."

Stone opened the letter and read it. "The day of judgment is at hand. The earth and the waters shall open up and mankind shall be consumed. May God have mercy on my soul and upon those who have shown mercy to me. To hell with the others. Amen."

Burton listened as the letter was read. "Crazy old lady," he said. "Senile dementia. She saw everyone around her dying, and she went nuts."

"And killed herself?"

"Yes, I think so."

"Pretty bizarre way to kill herself, don't you think?"

"That kid also chose a bizarre way," Burton said.

Stone nodded.

Roy O. Thompson, who lived alone. From his greasy coveralls they assumed he ran the town gas station. Roy had apparently filled his bathtub with water, then knelt down, stuck his head in, and held it there until he died. When they found him his body was rigid, holding himself under the surface of the water; there was no one else around, and no sign of struggle.

"Impossible," Stone said. "No one can commit suicide that way."

Lydia Everett, a seamstress in the town who had quietly gone out to the back yard, sat in a chair, poured gasoline over herself, and struck a match. Next to the remains of her body they found the scorched gasoline can.

William Arnold, a man of sixty sitting stiffly in a chair in the living room, wearing his World War I uniform. He had been a captain in that war, and he had become a captain again, briefly, before he shot himself through the right temple with a Colt .45. There was no blood in the room when they found him; he appeared almost ludicrous, sitting there with a clean, dry hole in his head.

A tape recorder stood alongside him, his left hand resting on the case. Burton looked at Stone questioningly, then turned it on.

A quavering, irritable voice spoke to them.

"You took your sweet time coming, didn't you? Still I am glad you have arrived at last. We are in need of reinforcements. I tell you, it's been one hell of a battle against the Hun. Lost

40 per cent last night, going over the top, and two of our officers are out with the rot. Not going well, not at all. If only Gary Cooper was here. We need men like that, the men who made America strong. I can't tell you how much it means to me, with those giants out there in the flying saucers. Now they're burning us down, and the gas is coming. You can see them die and we don't have gas masks. None at all. But I won't wait for it. I am going to do the proper thing now. I regret that I have but one life to kill for my country."

The tape ran on, but it was silent.

Burton turned it off. "Crazy," he said. "Stark raving mad."

Stone nodded.

"Some of them died instantly, and the others . . . went quietly nuts."

"But we seem to come back to the same basic question. Why? What was the difference?"

"Perhaps there's a graded immunity to this bug," Burton said. "Some people are more susceptible than others. Some people are protected, at least for a time."

"You know," Stone said, "there was that report from the flybys, and those films of a man alive down here. One man in white robes."

"You think he's still alive?"

"Well, I wonder," Stone said. "Because if some people survived longer than others—long enough to dictate a taped speech, or to arrange a hanging—then you have to ask yourself if someone maybe didn't survive for a very long time. You have to ask yourself if there isn't someone in this town who is *still* alive."

It was then that they heard the sound of crying.

At first it seemed like the sound of the wind, it was so high and thin and reedy, but they listened, feeling puzzled at first, and then astonished. The crying persisted, interrupted by little hacking coughs.

They ran outside.

It was faint, and difficult to localize. They ran up the street, and it seemed to grow louder; this spurred them on.

And then, abruptly, the sound stopped.

The two men came to a halt, gasping for breath, chests heaving. They stood in the middle of the hot, deserted street and looked at each other.

"Have we lost our minds?" Burton said.

"No," Stone said. "We heard it, all right."

They waited. It was absolutely quiet for several minutes. Burton looked down the street, at the houses, and the jeep van parked at the other end, in front of Dr. Benedict's house.

The crying began again, very loud now, a frustrated howl.

The two men ran.

It was not far, two houses up on the right side. A man and a woman lay outside, on the sidewalk, fallen and clutching their chests. They ran past them and into the house. The crying was still louder; it filled the empty rooms.

They hurried upstairs, clambering up, and came to the bedroom. A large double bed, unmade. A dresser, a mirror, a closet.

And a small crib.

They leaned over, pulling back the blankets from a small, very red-faced, very unhappy infant. The baby immediately stopped crying long enough to survey their faces, enclosed in the plastic suits.

Then it began to howl again.

"Scared hell out of it," Burton said. "Poor thing."

He picked it up gingerly and rocked it. The baby continued to scream. Its toothless mouth was wide open, its cheeks purple, and the veins stood out on its forehead.

"Probably hungry," Burton said.

Stone was frowning. "It's not very old. Can't be more than a couple of months. Is it a he or a she?"

Burton unwrapped the blankets and checked the diapers. "He. And he needs to be changed. And fed." He looked around the room. "There's probably a formula in the kitchen . . ."

"No," Stone said. "We don't feed it."

"Why not?"

"We don't do anything to that child until we get it out of this town. Maybe feeding is part of the disease process; maybe the people who weren't hit so hard or so fast were the ones who hadn't eaten recently. Maybe there's something protective about this baby's diet. Maybe . . ." He stopped. "But whatever it is, we can't take a chance. We've got to wait and get him into a controlled situation."

Burton sighed. He knew that Stone was right, but he also knew that the baby hadn't been fed for at least twelve hours. No wonder the kid was crying.

Stone said, "This is a very important development. It's a major break for us, and we've got to protect it. I think we should go back immediately."

"We haven't finished our head count."

Stone shook his head. "Doesn't matter. We have something much more valuable than anything we could hope to find. We have a survivor."

The baby stopped crying for a moment, stuck its finger in its mouth, and looked questioningly up at Burton. Then, when he was certain no food was forthcoming, he began to howl again.

"Too bad," Burton said, "he can't tell us what happened."

"I'm hoping he can," Stone said.

They parked the van in the center of the main street, beneath the hovering helicopter, and signaled for it to descend with the ladder. Burton held the infant, and Stone held the Scoop satellite—strange trophies, Stone thought, from a very strange town. The baby was quiet now; he had finally tired of crying and was sleeping fitfully, awakening at intervals to whimper, then sleep again.

The helicopter descended, spinning up swirls of dust. Burton wrapped the blankets about the baby's face to protect him. The ladder came down and he climbed up, with difficulty.

Stone waited on the ground, standing with the capsule in the wind and dust and thumpy noise from the helicopter.

And, suddenly, he realized that he was not alone on the street. He turned, and saw a man behind him.

He was an old man, with thin gray hair and a wrinkled, worn face. He wore a long nightgown that was smudged with dirt and yellowed with dust, and his feet were bare. He stumbled and tottered toward Stone. His chest was heaving with exertion beneath the nightgown.

"Who are you?" Stone said. But he knew: the man in the pictures. The one who had been photographed by the airplane.

"You . . ." the man said.

"Who are you?"

"You . . . did it . . ."

"What is your name?"

"Don't hurt me . . . I'm not like the others . . ."

He was shaking with fear as he stared at Stone in his plastic suit. Stone thought, We must look strange to him. Like men from Mars, men from another world.

"Don't hurt me . . ."

"We won't hurt you," Stone said. "What is your name?"

"Jackson. Peter Jackson. Sir. Please don't hurt me." He waved to the bodies in the street. "I'm not like the others . . ."

"We won't hurt you," Stone said again.

"You hurt the others . . ."

"No. We didn't."

"They're dead."

"We had nothing—"

"You're lying," he shouted, his eyes wide. "You're lying to me. You're not human. You're only pretending. You know

I'm a sick man. You know you can pretend with me. I'm a sick man. I'm bleeding, I know. I've had this . . . this . . . this . . ."

He faltered, and then doubled over, clutching his stomach and wincing in pain.

"Are you all right?"

The man fell to the ground. He was breathing heavily, his skin pale. There was sweat on his face.

"My stomach," he gasped. "It's my stomach."

And then he vomited. It came up heavy, deep-red, rich with blood.

"Mr. Jackson—"

But the man was not awake. His eyes were closed and he was lying on his back. For a moment, Stone thought he was dead, but then he saw the chest moving, slowly, very slowly, but moving.

Burton came back down.

"Who is he?"

"Our wandering man. Help me get him up."

"Is he alive?"

"So far."

"I'll be damned," Burton said.

They used the power winch to hoist up the unconscious body of Peter Jackson, and then lowered it again to raise the capsule. Then, slowly, Burton and Stone climbed the ladder into the belly of the helicopter.

They did not remove their suits, but instead clipped on a second bottle of oxygen to give them another two hours of breathing time. That would be sufficient to carry them to the Wildfire installation.

The pilot established a radio connection to Vandenberg so that Stone could talk with Major Manchek.

"What have you found?" Manchek said.

"The town is dead. We have good evidence for an unusual process at work."

"Be careful," Manchek said. "This is an open circuit."

"I am aware of that. Will you order up a 7–12?"

"I'll try. You want it now?"

"Yes, now."

"Piedmont?"

"Yes."

"You have the satellite?"

"Yes, we have it."

"All right," Manchek said. "I'll put through the order."

8.

Directive 7-12

DIRECTIVE 7–12 WAS A PART of the final Wildfire Protocol for action in the event of a biologic emergency. It called for the placement of a limited thermonuclear weapon at the site of exposure of terrestrial life to exogenous organisms. The code for the directive was Cautery, since the function of the bomb was to cauterize the infection —to burn it out, and thus prevent its spread.

As a single step in the Wildfire Protocol, Cautery had been agreed upon by the authorities involved—Executive, State, Defense, and AEC—after much debate. The AEC, already unhappy about the assignment of a nuclear device to the Wildfire laboratory, did not wish Cautery to be accepted as a program; State and Defense argued that any aboveground thermonuclear detonation, for whatever purpose, would have serious repercussions internationally.

The President finally agreed to Directive 7–12, but insisted that he retain control over the decision to use a bomb for Cautery. Stone was displeased with this arrangement, but he was forced to accept it; the President had been under considerable pressure to reject the whole idea and had compromised only after much argument. Then, too, there was the Hudson Institute study.

The Hudson Institute had been contracted to study possible consequences of Cautery. Their report indicated that the President would face four circumstances (scenarios) in which he might have to issue the Cautery order. According to degree of seriousness, the scenarios were:

1. *A satellite or manned capsule lands in an unpopulated area of the United States.* The President may cauterize the area with little domestic uproar and small loss of life. The Russians may be privately informed of the reasons for breaking the Moscow Treaty of 1963 forbidding aboveground nuclear testing.

2. *A satellite or manned capsule lands in a major American city.* (The example was Chicago.) The Cautery will require destruction of a large land area and a large population, with great domestic consequences and secondary international consequences.

3. *A satellite or manned capsule lands in a major neutralist urban center.* (New Delhi was the example.) The Cautery will entail American intervention with nuclear weapons to prevent further spread of disease. According to the scenarios, there were seventeen possible consequences of American-Soviet interaction following the destruction of New Delhi. Twelve led directly to thermonuclear war.

4. *A satellite or manned capsule lands in a major Soviet urban center.* (The example was Stalingrad.) Cautery will require the United States to inform the Soviet Union of what has happened and to advise that the Russians themselves destroy the city. According to the Hudson Institute scenario, there were six possible consequences of American-Russian interaction following this event, and all six led directly to war. It was therefore advised that if a satellite fell within Soviet or Eastern Bloc territory the United States not inform the Russians of what had happened. The basis of this decision was the prediction that a Russian plague would kill between two and five million people, while combined Soviet-American losses

from a thermonuclear exchange involving both first- and second-strike capabilities would come to more than two hundred and fifty million persons.

As a result of the Hudson Institute report, the President and his advisers felt that control of Cautery, and responsibility for it, should remain within political, not scientific, hands. The ultimate consequences of the President's decision could not, of course, have been predicted at the time it was made.

Washington came to a decision within an hour of Manchek's report. The reasoning behind the President's decision has never been clear, but the final result was plain enough:

The President elected to postpone calling Directive 7–12 for twenty-four to forty-eight hours. Instead, he called out the National Guard and cordoned off the area around Piedmont for a radius of one hundred miles. And he waited.

9.

Flatrock

MARK WILLIAM HALL, M.D., sat in
the tight rear seat of the F-104 fighter and stared over the
top of the rubber oxygen mask at the file on his knees. Leavitt
had given it to him just before takeoff—a heavy, thick wad of
paper bound in gray cardboard. Hall was supposed to read
it during the flight, but the F-104 was not made for reading;
there was barely enough room in front of him to hold his
hands clenched together, let alone open a file and read.

Yet Hall was reading it.

On the cover of the file was stenciled WILDFIRE, and underneath, an ominous note:

> THIS FILE IS CLASSIFIED TOP SECRET.
> Examination by unauthorized persons
> is a criminal offense punishable
> by fines and imprisonment up to
> 20 years and $20,000.

When Leavitt gave him the file, Hall had read the note and
whistled.

"Don't you believe it," Leavitt said.

"Just a scare?"

"Scare, hell," Leavitt said. "If the wrong man reads this
file, he just disappears."

"Nice."

"Read it," Leavitt said, "and you'll see why."

The plane flight had taken an hour and forty minutes, cruising in eerie, perfect silence at 1.8 times the speed of sound. Hall had skimmed through most of the file; reading it, he had found, was impossible. Much of its bulk of 274 pages consisted of cross-references and interservice notations, none of which he could understand. The first page was as bad as any of them:

THIS IS PAGE ___1___ OF __274__ PAGES

PROJECT: WILDFIRE
AUTHORITY: NASA/AMC
CLASSIFICATION: TOP SECRET (NTK BASIS)
PRIORITY: NATIONAL (DX)
SUBJECT: Initiation of high-security facility to prevent dispersion of toxic extraterrestrial agents.
CROSSFILE: Project CLEAN, Project ZERO CONTAMINANTS, Project CAUTERY

SUMMARY OF FILE CONTENTS:

By executive order, construction of a facility initiated January 1965. Planning stage March 1965. Consultants Fort Detrick and General Dynamics (EBD) July 1965. Recommendation for multistory facility in isolated location for investigation of possible or probable contaminatory agents. Specifications reviewed August 1965. Approval with revision same date. Final drafts drawn and filed AMC under WILDFIRE (copies Detrick, Hawkins). Choice of site northeast Montana, reviewed August 1965. Choice of site southwest Arizona, reviewed August 1965. Choice of site northwest Nevada, reviewed September 1965. Nevada site approved October 1965.

Construction completed July 1966. Funding NASA, AMC, DEFENSE (unaccountable reserves). Congressional appropriation for maintenance and personnel under same.

Major alterations: millipore filters, see page 74. Self-destruct capacity (nuclear), page 88. Ultraviolet irradiators removed, see page 81. Single Man Hypothesis (Odd Man Hypothesis), page 255.

PERSONNEL SUMMARIES HAVE BEEN ELIMINATED FROM THIS FILE. PERSONNEL MAY BE FOUND IN AMC (WILDFIRE) FILES ONLY.

The second page listed the basic parameters of the system, as laid down by the original Wildfire planning group. This specified the most important concept of the installation, namely that it would consist of roughly similar, descending levels, all underground. Each would be more sterile than the one above.

THIS IS PAGE ___2___ OF __274__ PAGES

PROJECT: WILDFIRE

PRIMARY PARAMETERS

1. THERE ARE TO BE FIVE STAGES:

Stage I: Non-decontaminated, but clean. Approximates sterility of hospital operating room or NASA clean room. No time delay of entrance.

Stage II: Minimal sterilization procedures: hexachlorophene and methitol bath, not requiring total immersion. One-hour delay with clothing change.

Stage III: Moderate sterilization procedures: total-immersion bath, UV irradiation, followed by two-hour delay for preliminary testing. Afebrile infections of UR and GU tracts permitted to pass. Viral symptomatology permitted to pass.

Stage IV: Maximal sterilization procedures: total immersion in four baths of biocaine, monochlorophin, xantholysin, and prophyne with intermediate thirty-minute UV and IR irradiation. All infection halted at this stage on basis of symptomatology or clinical signs. Routine screening of all personnel. Six-hour delay.

Stage V: Redundant sterilization procedures: no further immersions or testing, but destruct clothing x2 per day. Prophylactic antibiotics for forty-eight hours. Daily screen for superinfection, first eight days.

2. EACH STAGE INCLUDES:

1. Resting quarters, individual
2. Recreation quarters, including movie and game room
3. Cafeteria, automatic
4. Library, with main journals transmitted by Xerox or TV from main library Level I.
5. Shelter, a high-security antimicrobial complex with safety in event of level contamination.
6. Laboratories:
    a) biochemistry, with all necessary equipment for automatic amino-acid analysis, sequence determination, O/R potentials, lipid and carbohydrate determinations on human, animal, other subjects.
    b) pathology, with EM, phase and LM, microtomes and curing rooms. Five full-time technicians each level. One autopsy room. One room for experimental animals.
    c) microbiology, with all facilities for growth, nutrient, analytic, immunologic studies. Subsections bacterial, viral, parasitic, other.
    d) pharmacology, with material for dose-relation and receptor site specificity studies of known compounds. Pharmacy to include drugs as noted in appendix.
    e) main room, experimental animals. 75 genetically pure strains of mice; 27 of rat; 17 of cat; 12 of dog; 8 of primate.
    f) nonspecific room for previously unplanned experiments.
8. Surgery: for care and treatment of staff, including operating-room facilities for acute emergencies.
9. Communications: for contact with other levels by audiovisual and other means.

COUNT YOUR PAGES
REPORT ANY MISSING
PAGES AT ONCE
COUNT YOUR PAGES

As Hall continued to read, he found that only on Level I, the topmost floor, would there be a large computer complex for data analysis, but that this computer would serve all other levels on a time-sharing basis. This was considered feasible since, for biologic problems, real time was unimportant in relation to computer time, and multiple problems could be fed and handled at once.

He was leafing through the rest of the file, looking for the part that interested him—the Odd Man Hypothesis—when he came upon a page that was rather unusual.

THIS IS PAGE __255__ OF __274__ PAGES

BY THE AUTHORITY OF THE DEPARTMENT OF DEFENSE
THIS PAGE FROM A HIGH-SECURITY FILE HAS BEEN DELETED

THE PAGE IS NUMBER: two hundred fifty-five / 255

THE FILE IS CODED: Wildfire

THE SUBJECT MATTER
DELETED IS: Odd Man Hypothesis

PLEASE NOTE THAT THIS CONSTITUTES A LEGAL DELETION
FROM THE FILE WHICH NEED NOT BE REPORTED BY THE
READER.

MACHINE SCORE REVIEW BELOW

255 WILDFIRE 255

Hall was frowning at the page, wondering what it meant, when the pilot said, "Dr. Hall?"

"Yes."

"We have just passed the last checkpoint, sir. We will touch down in four minutes."

"All right." Hall paused. "Do you know where, exactly, we are landing?"

"I believe," said the pilot, "that it is Flatrock, Nevada."

"I see," Hall said.

A few minutes later, the flaps went down, and he heard a whine as the airplane slowed.

Nevada was the ideal site for Wildfire. The Silver State ranks seventh in size, but forty-ninth in population; it is the least-dense state in the Union after Alaska. Particularly when one considers that 85 per cent of the state's 440,000 people live in Las Vegas, Reno, or Carson City, the population density of 1.2 persons per square mile seems well suited for projects such as Wildfire, and indeed many have been located there.

Along with the famous atomic site at Vinton Flats, there is the Ultra-Energy Test Station at Martindale, and the Air Force Medivator Unit near Los Gados. Most of these facilities are in the southern triangle of the state, having been located there in the days before Las Vegas swelled to receive twenty million visitors a year. More recently, government test stations have been located in the northwest corner of Nevada, which is still relatively isolated. Pentagon classified lists include five new installations in that area; the nature of each is unknown.

10.

Stage I

HALL LANDED SHORTLY AFTER NOON, the hottest part of the day. The sun beat down from a pale, cloudless sky and the airfield asphalt was soft under his feet as he walked from the airplane to the small quonset hut at the edge of the runway. Feeling his feet sink into the surface, Hall thought that the airfield must have been designed primarily for night use; at night it would be cold, the asphalt solid.

The quonset hut was cooled by two massive, grumbling air conditioners. It was furnished sparsely: a card table in one corner, at which two pilots sat, playing poker and drinking coffee. A guard in the corner was making a telephone call; he had a machine gun slung over his shoulder. He did not look up as Hall entered.

There was a coffee machine near the telephone. Hall went over with his pilot and they each poured a cup. Hall took a sip and said, "Where's the town, anyway? I didn't see it as we were coming in."

"Don't know, sir."

"Have you been here before?"

"No sir. It's not on the standard runs."

"Well, what exactly does this airfield serve?"

At that moment, Leavitt strode in and beckoned to Hall. The bacteriologist led him through the back of the quonset and then out into the heat again, to a light-blue Falcon sedan parked in the rear. There were no identifying marks of any kind on the car; there was no driver. Leavitt slipped behind the wheel and motioned for Hall to get in.

As Leavitt put the car in gear, Hall said, "I guess we don't rate any more."

"Oh yes. We rate. But drivers aren't used out here. In fact, we don't use any more personnel than we have to. The number of wagging tongues is kept to a minimum."

They set off across desolate, hilly countryside. In the distance were blue mountains, shimmering in the liquid heat of the desert. The road was pock-marked and dusty; it looked as if it hadn't been used for years.

Hall mentioned this.

"Deceptive," Leavitt said. "We took great pains about it. We spent nearly five thousand dollars on this road."

"Why?"

Leavitt shrugged. "Had to get rid of the tractor treadmarks. A hell of a lot of heavy equipment has moved over these roads, at one time or another. Wouldn't want anyone to wonder why."

"Speaking of caution," Hall said after a pause, "I was reading in the file. Something about an atomic self-destruct device—"

"What about it?"

"It exists?"

"It exists."

Installation of the device had been a major stumbling block in the early plans for Wildfire. Stone and the others had insisted that they retain control over the detonate/no detonate decision; the AEC and the Executive branch had been reluctant. No atomic device had been put in private hands before.

Stone argued that in the event of a leak in the Wildfire lab, there might not be time to consult with Washington and get a Presidential detonate order. It was a long time before the President agreed that this might be true.

"I was reading," Hall said, "that this device is somehow connected with the Odd Man Hypothesis."

"It is."

"How? The page on Odd Man was taken from my file."

"I know," Leavitt said. "We'll talk about it later."

The Falcon turned off the potted road onto a dirt track. The sedan raised a heavy cloud of dust, and despite the heat, they were forced to roll up the windows. Hall lit a cigarette.

"That'll be your last," Leavitt said.

"I know. Let me enjoy it."

On their right, they passed a sign that said GOVERNMENT PROPERTY KEEP OFF, but there was no fence, no guard, no dogs —just a battered, weatherbeaten sign.

"Great security measures," Hall said.

"We try not to arouse suspicion. The security is better than it looks."

They proceeded another mile, bouncing along the dirt rut, and then came over a hill. Suddenly Hall saw a large, fenced circle perhaps a hundred yards in diameter. The fence, he noticed, was ten feet high and sturdy; at intervals it was laced with barbed wire. Inside was a utilitarian wooden building, and a field of corn.

"Corn?" Hall said.

"Rather clever, I think."

They came to the entrance gate. A man in dungarees and a T-shirt came out and opened it for them; he held a sandwich in one hand and was chewing vigorously as he unlocked the gate. He winked and smiled and waved them through, still chewing. The sign by the gate said:

GOVERNMENT PROPERTY
U.S. DEPARTMENT OF AGRICULTURE
DESERT RECLAMATION TEST STATION

Leavitt drove through the gates and parked by the wooden building. He left the keys on the dashboard and got out. Hall followed him.

"Now what?"

"Inside," Leavitt said. They entered the building, coming directly into a small room. A man in a Stetson hat, checked sport shirt, and string tie sat at a rickety desk. He was reading a newspaper and, like the man at the gate, eating his lunch. He looked up and smiled pleasantly.

"Howdy," he said.

"Hello," Leavitt said.

"Help you folks?"

"Just passing through," Leavitt said. "On the way to Rome."

The man nodded. "Have you got the time?"

"My watch stopped yesterday," Leavitt said.

"Durn shame," the man said.

"It's because of the heat."

The ritual completed, the man nodded again. And they walked past him, out of the anteroom and down a corridor. The doors had hand-printed labels: "Seedling Incubation"; "Moisture Control"; "Soil Analysis." A half-dozen people were at work in the building, all of them dressed casually, but all of them apparently busy.

"This is a real agricultural station," Leavitt said. "If necessary, that man at the desk could give you a guided tour, explaining the purpose of the station and the experiments that are going on. Mostly they are attempting to develop a strain of corn that can grow in low-moisture, high-alkalinity soil."

"And the Wildfire installation?"

"Here," Leavitt said. He opened a door marked "Storage" and they found themselves staring at a narrow cubicle lined with rakes and hoes and watering hoses.

"Step in," Leavitt said.

Hall did. Leavitt followed and closed the door behind him. Hall felt the floor sink and they began to descend, rakes and hoses and all.

In a moment, he found himself in a modern, bare room, lighted by banks of cold overhead fluorescent lights. The walls were painted red. The only object in the room was a rectangular, waist-high box that reminded Hall of a podium. It had a glowing green glass top.

"Step up to the analyzer," Leavitt said. "Place your hands flat on the glass, palms down."

Hall did. He felt a faint tingling in his fingers, and then the machine gave a buzz.

"All right. Step back." Leavitt placed his hands on the box, waited for the buzz, and then said, "Now we go over here. You mentioned the security arrangements; I'll show them to you before we enter Wildfire."

He nodded to a door across the room.

"What was that thing?"

"Finger- and palm-print analyzer," Leavitt said. "It is fully automatic. Reads a composite of ten thousand dermatographic lines so it can't make a mistake; in its storage banks it has a record of the prints of everyone cleared to enter Wildfire."

Leavitt pushed through the door.

They were faced with another door, marked SECURITY, which slid back noiselessly. They entered a darkened room in which a single man sat before banks of green dials.

"Hello, John," Leavitt said to the man. "How are you?"

"Good, Dr. Leavitt. Saw you come in."

Leavitt introduced Hall to the security man, who then demonstrated the equipment to Hall. There were, the man explained, two radar scanners located in the hills overlooking the installation; they were well concealed but quite effective. Then closer in, impedence sensors were buried in the ground; they signaled the approach of any animal life weighing more than one hundred pounds. The sensors ringed the base.

"We've never missed anything yet," the man said. "And if we do . . . " He shrugged. To Leavitt: "Going to show him the dogs?"

"Yes," Leavitt said.

They walked through into an adjoining room. There were nine large cages there, and the room smelled strongly of animals. Hall found himself looking at nine of the largest German shepherds he had ever seen.

They barked at him as he entered, but there was no sound in the room. He watched in astonishment as they opened their mouths and threw their heads forward in a barking motion.

No sound.

"These are Army-trained sentry dogs," the security man said. "Bred for viciousness. You wear leather clothes and heavy gloves when you walk them. They've undergone laryngectomies, which is why you can't hear them. Silent and vicious."

Hall said, "Have you ever, uh, used them?"

"No," the security man said. "Fortunately not."

They were in a small room with lockers. Hall found one with his name on it.

"We change in here," Leavitt said. He nodded to a stack of pink uniforms in one corner. "Put those on, after you have removed everything you are wearing."

Hall changed quickly. The uniforms were loose-fitting one-piece suits that zipped up the side. When they had changed they proceeded down a passageway.

Suddenly an alarm sounded and a gate in front of them slid closed abruptly. Overhead, a white light began to flash. Hall was confused, and it was only much later that he remembered Leavitt looked away from the flashing light.

"Something's wrong," Leavitt said. "Did you remove everything?"

"Yes," Hall said.

"Rings, watch, everything?"

Hall looked at his hands. He still had his watch on.

"Go back," Leavitt said. "Put it in your locker."

Hall did. When he came back, they started down the corridor a second time. The gate remained open, and there was no alarm.

"Automatic as well?" Hall said.

"Yes," Leavitt said. "It picks up any foreign object. When we installed it, we were worried because we knew it would pick up glass eyes, cardiac pacemakers, false teeth—anything at all. But fortunately nobody on the project has these things."

"Fillings?"

"It is programmed to ignore fillings."

"How does it work?"

"Some kind of capacitance phenomenon. I don't really understand it," Leavitt said.

They passed a sign that said:

YOU ARE NOW ENTERING LEVEL I
PROCEED DIRECTLY TO IMMUNIZATION CONTROL

Hall noticed that all the walls were red. He mentioned this to Leavitt.

"Yes," Leavitt said. "All levels are painted a different color. Level I is red; II, yellow; III, white; IV, green; and V, blue."

"Any particular reason for the choice?"

"It seems," Leavitt said, "that the Navy sponsored some studies a few years back on the psychological effects of colored environments. Those studies have been applied here."

They came to Immunization. A door slid back revealing three glass booths. Leavitt said, "Just sit down in one of them."

"I suppose this is automatic, too?"

"Of course."

Hall entered a booth and closed the door behind him. There was a couch, and a mass of complex equipment. In front of the couch was a television screen, which showed several lighted points.

"Sit down," said a flat mechanical voice. "Sit down. Sit down."

He sat on the couch.

"Observe the screen before you. Place your body on the couch so that all points are obliterated."

He looked at the screen. He now saw that the points were arranged in the shape of a man:

```
                    *


            *               *


         *                     *


     *       *         *         *


         *               *



         *               *
```

He shifted his body, and one by one the spots disappeared.

"Very good," said the voice. "We may now proceed. State your name for the record. Last name first, first name last."

"Mark Hall," he said.

"State your name for the record. Last name first, first name last."

Simultaneously, on the screen appeared the words:

SUBJECT HAS GIVEN UNCODABLE RESPONSE

"Hall, Mark."

"Thank you for your cooperation," said the voice. "Please recite, 'Mary had a little lamb.'"

"You're kidding," Hall said.

There was a pause, and the faint sound of relays and circuits clicking. The screen again showed:

SUBJECT HAS GIVEN UNCODABLE RESPONSE

"Please recite."

Feeling rather foolish, Hall said, "Mary had a little lamb, her fleece was white as snow, and everywhere that Mary went, the lamb was sure to go."

Another pause. Then the voice: "Thank you for your cooperation." And the screen said:

ANALYZER CONFIRMS IDENTITY
HALL, MARK

"Please listen closely," said the mechanical voice. "You will answer the following questions with a yes or no reply. Make no other response. Have you received a smallpox vaccination within the last twelve months?"

"Yes."

"Diphtheria?"

"Yes."

"Typhoid and paratyphoid A and B?"

"Yes."

"Tetanus toxoid?"

"Yes."

"Yellow fever?"

"Yes, yes, yes. I had them all."

"Just answer the question please. Uncooperative subjects waste valuable computer time."

"Yes," Hall said, subdued. When he had joined the Wildfire team, he had undergone immunizations for everything imaginable, even plague and cholera, which had to be renewed every six months, and gamma-globulin shots for viral infection.

"Have you ever contracted tuberculosis or other mycobacterial disease, or had a positive skin test for tuberculosis?"

"No."

"Have you ever contracted syphilis or other spirochetal disease, or had a positive serological test for syphilis?"

"No."

"Have you contracted within the past year any gram-positive bacterial infection, such as streptococcus, staphylococcus, or pneumococcus?"

"No."

"Any gram-negative infection, such as gonococcus, meningeococcus, proteus, pseudomonas, salmonella, or shigella?"

"No."

"Have you contracted any recent or past fungal infection, including blastomycosis, histoplasmosis, or coccidiomycosis, or had a positive skin test for any fungal disease?"

"No."

"Have you had any recent viral infection, including poliomyelitis, hepatitis, mononucleosis, mumps, measles, varicella, or herpes?"

"No."

"Any warts?"

"No."

"Have you any known allergies?"

"Yes, to ragweed pollen."

On the screen appeared the words:

ROGEEN PALEN

And then after a moment:

UNCODABLE RESPONSE

"Please repeat your response slowly for our memory cells."

Very distinctly, he said, "Ragweed pollen."

On the screen:

RAGWEED POLLEN   CODED

"Are you allergic to albumin?" continued the voice.

"No."

"This ends the formal questions. Please undress and return to the couch, obliterating the points as before."

He did so. A moment later, an ultraviolet lamp swung out on a long arm and moved close to his body. Next to the lamp was some kind of scanning eye. Watching the screen he could see the computer print of the scan, beginning with his feet.

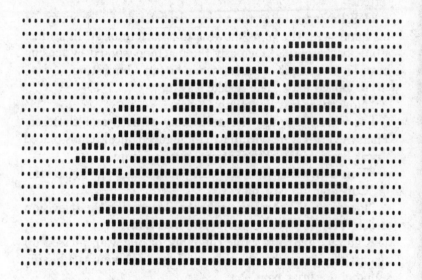

"This is a scan for fungus," the voice announced. After several minutes, Hall was ordered to lie on his stomach, and the process was repeated. He was then told to lie on his back once more and align himself with the dots.

"Physical parameters will now be measured," the voice said. "You are requested to lie quietly while the examination is conducted."

A variety of leads snaked out at him and were attached by mechanical hands to his body. Some he could understand— the half-dozen leads over his chest for an electrocardiogram, and twenty-one on his head for an electroencephalogram. But others were fixed on his stomach, his arms, and his legs.

"Please raise your left hand," said the voice.

Hall did. From above, a mechanical hand came down, with an electric eye fixed on either side of it. The mechanical hand examined Hall's.

"Place your hand on the board to the left. Do not move. You will feel a slight prick as the intravenous needle is inserted."

Hall looked over at the screen. It flashed a color image of his hand, with the veins showing in a pattern of green against a blue background. Obviously the machine worked by sensing heat. He was about to protest when he felt a brief sting.

He looked back. The needle was in.

"Now then, just lie quietly. Relax."

For fifteen seconds, the machinery whirred and clattered. Then the leads were withdrawn. The mechanical hands placed a neat Band-Aid over the intravenous puncture.

"This completes your physical parameters," the voice said.

"Can I get dressed now?"

"Please sit up with your right shoulder facing the television screen. You will receive pneumatic injections."

A gun with a thick cable came out of one wall, pressed up against the skin of his shoulder, and fired. There was a hissing sound and a brief pain.

"Now you may dress," said the voice. "Be advised that you may feel dizzy for a few hours. You have received booster immunizations and gamma G. If you feel dizzy, sit down. If you suffer systemic effects such as nausea, vomiting, or fever, report at once to Level Control. Is that clear?"

"Yes."

"The exit is to your right. Thank you for your cooperation. This recording is now ended."

*   *   *

Hall walked with Leavitt down a long red corridor. His arm ached from the injection.

"That machine," Hall said. "You'd better not let the AMA find out about it."

"We haven't," Leavitt said.

In fact, the electronic body analyzer had been developed by Sandeman Industries in 1965, under a general government contract to produce body monitors for astronauts in space. It was understood by the government at that time that such a device, though expensive at a cost of $87,000 each, would eventually replace the human physician as a diagnostic instrument. The difficulties, for both doctor and patient, of adjusting to this new machine were recognized by everyone. The government did not plan to release the EBA until 1971, and then only to certain large hospital facilities.

Walking along the corridor, Hall noticed that the walls were slightly curved.

"Where exactly are we?"

"On the perimeter of Level I. To our left are all the laboratories. To the right is nothing but solid rock."

Several people were walking in the corridor. Everyone wore pink jumpsuits. They all seemed serious and busy.

"Where are the others on the team?" Hall said.

"Right here," Leavitt said. He opened a door marked CONFERENCE 7, and they entered a room with a large hardwood table. Stone was there, standing stiffly erect and alert, as if he had just taken a cold shower. Alongside him, Burton, the pathologist, somehow appeared sloppy and confused, and there was a kind of tired fright in his eyes.

They all exchanged greetings and sat down. Stone reached into his pocket and removed two keys. One was silver, the other red. The red one had a chain attached to it. He gave it to Hall.

"Put it around your neck," he said.

Hall looked at it. "What's this?"

Leavitt said, "I'm afraid Mark is still unclear about the Odd Man."

"I thought that he would read it on the plane—"

"His file was edited."

"I see." Stone turned to Hall. "You know nothing about the Odd Man?"

"Nothing," Hall said, frowning at the key.

"Nobody told you that a major factor in your selection to the team was your single status?"

"What does that have to do—"

"The fact of the matter is," Stone said, "that you are the Odd Man. You are the key to all this. Quite literally."

He took his own key and walked to a corner of the room. He pushed a hidden button and the wood paneling slid away to reveal a burnished metal console. He inserted his key into a lock and twisted it. A green light on the console flashed on; he stepped back. The paneling slid into place.

"At the lowest level of this laboratory is an automatic atomic self-destruct device," Stone said. "It is controlled from within the laboratory. I have just inserted my key and armed the mechanism. The device is ready for detonation. The key on this level cannot be removed; it is now locked in place. Your key, on the other hand, can be inserted and removed again. There is a three-minute delay between the time detonation locks in and the time the bomb goes off. That period is to provide you time to think, and perhaps call it all off."

Hall was still frowning. "But why me?"

"Because you are single. We had to have one unmarried man."

Stone opened a briefcase and withdrew a file. He gave it to Hall. "Read that."

It was a Wildfire file.

"Page 255," Stone said.

Hall turned to it.

Project: Wildfire

ALTERATIONS

1. Millipore Filters, insertion into ventilatory system. Initial spec filters unilayer styrilene, with maximal efficiency of 97.4% trapping. Replaced in 1966 when Upjohn developed filters capable of trapping organisms of size up to one micron. Trapping at 90% efficiency per leaf, causing triple-layered membrance to give results of 99.9%. Infective ratio of .1% remainder too low to be harmful. Cost factor of four- or five-layered membrance removing all but .001% considered prohibitive for added gain. Tolerance parameter of 1/1,000 considered sufficient. Installation completed 8/12/66.

2. Atomic Self-Destruct Device, change in detonator close-gap timers. See AEC/Def file 77-12-0918.

3. Atomic Self-Destruct Device, revision of core maintenance schedules for K technicians, see AEC/Warburg file 77-14-0004.

4. Atomic Self-Destruct Device, final command decision change. See AEC/Def file 77-14-0023. SUMMARY APPENDED.

SUMMARY OF ODD MAN HYPOTHESIS: First tested as null hypothesis by Wildfire advisory committee. Grew out of tests conducted by USAF (NORAD) to determine reliability of commanders in making life/death decisions. Tests involved decisions in ten scenario contexts, with prestructured alternatives drawn up by Walter Reed Psychiatric Division, after n-order test analysis by biostatistics unit, NIH, Bethesda.

Test given to SAC pilots and groundcrews, NORAD workers, and others involved in decision-making or positive-action capacity. Ten scenarios drawn up by Hudson Institute; subjects required to make YES/NO decision in each case. Decisions always involved thermo-nuclear or chem-biol destruction of enemy targets.

Data on 7420 subjects tested by $H_1 H_2$ program for multifactorial analysis of variance; later test by ANOVAR program; final discrimination by CLASSIF program. NIH biostat summarizes this program as follows:

It is the object of this program to determine the effectiveness of assigning individuals to distinct groups on the basis of scores which can be quantified. The program produces group contours and probability of classification for individuals as a control of data.

Program prints: mean scores for groups, contour confidence limits, and scores of individual test subjects.

K G Borgrand

K.G. Borgrand, Ph.D. NIH

RESULTS OF ODD MAN STUDY: The study concluded that married individuals performed differently from single individuals on several parameters of the test. Hudson Institute provided mean answers, i.e. theoretical "right" decisions, made by computer on basis of data given in scenario. Conformance of study groups to these right answers produced an index of effectiveness, a measure of the extent to which correct decisions were made.

Group	Index of Effectiveness
Married males	.343
Married females	.399
Single females	.402
Single males	.824

The data indicate that married men choose the correct decision only once in three times, while single men choose correctly four out of five times. The group of single males was then broken down further, in search of highly accurate subgroups within that classification.

Group	Index of Effectiveness
Single males, total	.824
Military:	
commissioned officer	.655
noncommissioned officer	.624

Technical:
   engineers   .877
   ground crews   .901
Service:
   maintenance and utility   .758
Professional:
   scientists   .946

These results concerning the relative skill of decision-making individuals should not be interpreted hastily. Although it would appear
that janitors are better decision-makers than generals, the situation is
in reality more complex. PRINTED SCORES ARE SUMMATIONS OF
TEST AND INDIVIDUAL VARIATIONS. DATA MUST BE
INTERPRETED WITH THIS IN MIND. Failure to do so may lead to
totally erroneous and dangerous assumptions.

     Application of study to Wildfire command personnel conducted at
request of AEC at time of implantation of self-destruct nuclear
capacity. Test given to all Wildfire personnel; results filed under
CLASSIF WILDFIRE: GENERAL PERSONNEL (see ref. 77-14-0023).
Special testing for command group.

Name	Index of Effectiveness
Burton	.543
Reynolds	.601
Kirke	.614
Stone	.687
Hall	.899

     Results of special testing confirm the Odd Man Hypothesis, that
an unmarried male should carry out command decisions involving
thermonuclear or chem-biol destruct contexts.

    When Hall had finished reading, he said, "It's crazy."
    "Nonetheless," Stone said, "it was the only way we could
get the government to put control of the weapon in our
hands."

"You really expect me to put in my key, and fire that thing?"

"I'm afraid you don't understand," Stone said. "The detonation mechanism is automatic. Should breakthrough of the organism occur, with contamination of all Level V, detonation will take place within three minutes *unless* you lock in your key, and call it off."

"Oh," Hall said, in a quiet voice.

11.

Decontamination

A BELL RANG SOMEWHERE on the
level; Stone glanced up at the wall clock. It was late. He began
the formal briefing, talking rapidly, pacing up and down the
room, hands moving constantly.

"As you know," he said, "we are on the top level of a five-
story underground structure. According to protocol it will take
us nearly twenty-four hours to descend through the sterilization and decontamination procedures to the lowest level.
Therefore we must begin immediately. The capsule is already
on its way."

He pressed a button on a console at the head of the table,
and a television screen glowed to life, showing the cone-shaped
satellite in a plastic bag, making its descent. It was being
cradled by mechanical hands.

"The central core of this circular building," Stone said,
"contains elevators and service units—plumbing, wiring, that
sort of thing. That is where you see the capsule now. It will be
deposited shortly in a maximum-sterilization assembly on the
lowest level."

He went on to explain that he had brought back two other
surprises from Piedmont. The screen shifted to show Peter

Jackson, lying on a litter, with intravenous lines running into both arms.

"This man apparently survived the night. He was the one walking around when the planes flew over, and he was still alive this morning."

"What's his status now?"

"Uncertain," Stone said. "He is unconscious, and he was vomiting blood earlier today. We've started intravenous dextrose to keep him fed and hydrated until we can get down to the bottom."

Stone flicked a button and the screen showed the baby. It was howling, strapped down to a tiny bed. An intravenous bottle was running into a vein in the scalp.

"This little fellow also survived last night," Stone said. "So we brought him along. We couldn't really leave him, since a Directive 7–12 was being called. The town is now destroyed by a nuclear blast. Besides, he and Jackson are living clues which may help us unravel this mess."

Then, for the benefit of Hall and Leavitt, the two men disclosed what they had seen and learned at Piedmont. They reviewed the findings of rapid death, the bizarre suicides, the clotted arteries and the lack of bleeding.

Hall listened in astonishment. Leavitt sat shaking his head. When they were through, Stone said, "Questions?"

"None that won't keep," Leavitt said.

"Then let's get started," Stone said.

They began at a door, which said in plain white letters: TO LEVEL II. It was an innocuous, straightforward, almost mundane sign. Hall had expected something more—perhaps a stern guard with a machine gun, or a sentry to check passes. But there was nothing, and he noticed that no one had badges, or clearance cards of any kind.

He mentioned this to Stone. "Yes," Stone said. "We decided

against badges early on. They are easily contaminated and difficult to sterilize; usually they are plastic and high-heat sterilization melts them."

The four men passed through the door, which clanged shut heavily and sealed with a hissing sound. It was airtight. Hall faced a tiled room, empty except for a hamper marked "clothing." He unzipped his jumpsuit and dropped it into the hamper; there was a brief flash of light as it was incinerated.

Then, looking back, he saw that on the door through which he had come was a sign: "Return to Level I is NOT Possible Through this Access."

He shrugged. The other men were already moving through the second door, marked simply EXIT. He followed them and stepped into clouds of steam. The odor was peculiar, a faint woodsy smell that he guessed was scented disinfectant. He sat down on a bench and relaxed, allowing the steam to envelop him. It was easy enough to understand the purpose of the steam room: the heat opened the pores, and the steam would be inhaled into the lungs.

The four men waited, saying little, until their bodies were coated with a sheen of moisture, and then walked into the next room.

Leavitt said to Hall, "What do you think of this?"

"It's like a goddam Roman bath," Hall said.

The next room contained a shallow tub ("Immerse Feet ONLY") and a shower. ("Do not swallow shower solution. Avoid undue exposure to eyes and mucous membranes.") It was all very intimidating. He tried to guess what the solutions were by smell, but failed; the shower was slippery, though, which meant it was alkaline. He asked Leavitt about this, and Leavitt said the solution was alpha chlorophin at pH 7.7. Leavitt said that whenever possible, acidic and alkaline solutions were alternated.

"When you think about it," Leavitt said, "we've faced up to quite a planning problem here. How to disinfect the human body—one of the dirtiest things in the known universe—without killing the person at the same time. Interesting."

He wandered off. Dripping wet from the shower, Hall looked around for a towel but found none. He entered the next room and blowers turned on from the ceiling in a rush of hot air. From the sides of the room, UV lights clicked on, bathing the room in an intense purple light. He stood there until a buzzer sounded, and the dryers turned off. His skin tingled slightly as he entered the last room, which contained clothing. They were not jumpsuits, but rather like surgical uniforms—light-yellow, a loose-fitting top with a V-neck and short sleeves; elastic banded pants; low rubber-soled shoes, quite comfortable, like ballet slippers.

The cloth was soft, some kind of synthetic. He dressed and stepped with the others through a door marked EXIT TO LEVEL II. He entered the elevator and waited as it descended.

Hall emerged to find himself in a corridor. The walls here were painted yellow, not red as they had been on Level I. The people wore yellow uniforms. A nurse by the elevator said, "The time is 2:47 p.m., gentlemen. You may continue your descent in one hour."

They went to a small room marked INTERIM CONFINEMENT. It contained a half-dozen couches with plastic disposable covers over them.

Stone said, "Better relax. Sleep if you can. We'll need all the rest we can get before Level V." He walked over to Hall. "How did you find the decontamination procedure?"

"Interesting," Hall said. "You could sell it to the Swedes and make a fortune. But somehow I expected something more rigorous."

"Just wait," Stone said. "It gets tougher as you go. Physicals on Levels III and IV. Afterward there will be a brief conference."

Then Stone lay down on one of the couches and fell instantly asleep. It was a trick he had learned years before, when he had been conducting experiments around the clock. He learned to squeeze in an hour here, two hours there. He found it useful.

The second decontamination procedure was similar to the first. Hall's yellow clothing, though he had worn it just an hour, was incinerated.

"Isn't that rather wasteful?" he asked Burton.

Burton shrugged. "It's paper."

"Paper? That cloth?"

Burton shook his head. "Not cloth. Paper. New process."

They stepped into the first total-immersion pool. Instructions on the wall told Hall to keep his eyes open under water. Total immersion, he soon discovered, was guaranteed by the simple device of making the connection between the first room and the second an underwater passage. Swimming through, he felt a slight burning of his eyes, but nothing bad.

The second room contained a row of six boxes, glass-walled, looking rather like telephone booths. Hall approached one and saw a sign that said, "Enter and close both eyes. Hold arms slightly away from body and stand with feet one foot apart. Do not open eyes until buzzer sounds. BLINDNESS MAY RESULT FROM EXPOSURE TO LONG-WAVE RADIATION."

He followed the directions and felt a kind of cold heat on his body. It lasted perhaps five minutes, and then he heard the buzzer and opened his eyes. His body was dry. He followed the others to a corridor, consisting of four showers. Walking down the corridor, he passed beneath each shower in turn. At the end, he found blowers, which dried him, and then clothing. This time the clothing was white.

They dressed, and took the elevator down to Level III.

There were four nurses waiting for them; one took Hall to an examining room. It turned out to be a two-hour physical examination, given not by a machine but by a blank-faced, thorough young man. Hall was annoyed, and thought to himself that he preferred the machine.

The doctor did everything, including a complete history: birth, education, travel, family history, past hospitalizations and illnesses. And an equally complete physical. Hall became angry; it was all so damned unnecessary. But the doctor shrugged and kept saying, "It's routine."

After two hours, he rejoined the others, and proceeded to Level IV.

Four total-immersion baths, three sequences of ultraviolet and infrared light, two of ultrasonic vibrations, and then something quite astonishing at the end. A steel-walled cubicle, with a helmet on a peg. The sign said, "This is an ultraflash apparatus. To protect head and facial hair, place metal helmet securely on head, then press button below."

Hall had never heard of ultraflash, and he followed directions, not knowing what to expect. He placed the helmet over his head, then pressed the button.

There was a single, brief, dazzling burst of white light, followed by a wave of heat that filled the cubicle. He felt a moment of pain, so swift he hardly recognized it until it was over. Cautiously, he removed the helmet and looked at his body. His skin was covered with a fine, white ash—and then he realized that the ash was his skin, or had been: the machine had burned away the outer epithelial layers. He proceeded to a shower and washed the ash off. When he finally reached the dressing room, he found green uniforms.

Another physical. This time they wanted samples of everything: sputum, oral epithelium, blood, urine, stool. He submitted passively to the tests, examinations, questions. He was tired, and was beginning to feel disoriented. The repetitions, the new experiences, the colors on the walls, the same bland artificial light . . .

Finally, he was brought back to Stone and the others. Stone said, "We have six hours on this level—that's protocol, waiting while they do the lab tests on us—so we might as well sleep. Down the corridor are rooms, marked with your names. Further down is the cafeteria. We'll meet there in five hours for a conference. Right?"

Hall found his room, marked with a plastic door tag. He entered, surprised to find it quite large. He had been expecting something the size of a Pullman cubicle, but this was bigger and better-furnished. There was a bed, a chair, a small desk, and a computer console with built-in TV set. He was curious about the computer, but also very tired. He lay down on the bed and fell asleep quickly.

Burton could not sleep. He lay in his bed on Level IV and stared at the ceiling, thinking. He could not get the image of that town out of his mind, or those bodies, lying in the street without bleeding . . .

Burton was not a hematologist, but his work had involved some blood studies. He knew that a variety of bacteria had effects on blood. His own research with staphylococcus, for example, had shown that this organism produced two enzymes that altered blood.

One was the so-called exotoxin, which destroyed skin and dissolved red cells. Another was a coagulase, which coated the bacteria with protein to inhibit destruction by white cells.

So it was possible that bacteria could alter blood. And it could do it many different ways: strep produced an enzyme, streptokinase, that dissolved coagulated plasma. Clostridia and pneumococci produced a variety of hemolysins that destroyed red cells. Malaria and amebae also destroyed red cells, by digesting them as food. Other parasites did the same thing.

So it was possible.

But it didn't help them in finding out how the Scoop organism worked.

Burton tried to recall the sequence for blood clotting. He remembered that it operated like a kind of waterfall: one enzyme was set off, and activated, which acted on a second enzyme, which acted on a third; the third on a fourth; and so on, down through twelve or thirteen steps, until finally blood clotted.

And vaguely he remembered the rest, the details: all the intermediate steps, the necessary enzymes, the metals, ions, local factors. It was horribly complex.

He shook his head and tried to sleep.

Leavitt, the clinical microbiologist, was thinking through the steps in isolation and identification of the causative organism. He had been over it before; he was one of the original founders of the group, one of the men who developed the Life Analysis Protocol. But now, on the verge of putting that plan into effect, he had doubts.

Two years before, sitting around after lunch, talking speculatively, it had all seemed wonderful. It had been an amusing intellectual game then, a kind of abstract test of wits. But now, faced with a real agent that caused real and bizarre death, he wondered whether all their plans would prove to be so effective and so complete as they once thought.

The first steps were simple enough. They would examine the capsule minutely and culture everything onto growth media. They would be hoping like hell to come up with an organism that they could work with, experiment on, and identify.

And after that, attempt to find out how it attacked. There

was already the suggestion that it killed by clotting the blood; if that turned out to be the case, they had a good start, but if not, they might waste valuable time following it up.

The example of cholera came to mind. For centuries, men had known that cholera was a fatal disease, and that it caused severe diarrhea, sometimes producing as much as thirty quarts of fluid a day. Men knew this, but they somehow assumed that the lethal effects of the disease were unrelated to the diarrhea; they searched for something else: an antidote, a drug, a way to kill the organism. It was not until modern times that cholera was recognized as a disease that killed through dehydration primarily; if you could replace a victim's water losses rapidly, he would survive the infection without other drugs or treatment.

Cure the symptoms, cure the disease.

But Leavitt wondered about the Scoop organism. Could they cure the disease by treating the blood clotting? Or was the clotting secondary to some more serious disorder?

There was also another concern, a nagging fear that had bothered him since the earliest planning stages of Wildfire. In those early meetings, Leavitt had argued that the Wildfire team might be committing extraterrestrial murder.

Leavitt had pointed out that all men, no matter how scientifically objective, had several built-in biases when discussing life. One was the assumption that complex life was larger than simple life. It was certainly true on the earth. As organisms became more intelligent, they grew larger, passing from the single-celled stage to multicellular creatures, and then to larger animals with differentiated cells working in groups called organs. On earth, the trend had been toward larger and more complex animals.

But this might not be true elsewhere in the universe. In other places, life might progress in the opposite direction— toward smaller and smaller forms. Just as modern human technology had learned to make things smaller, perhaps highly advanced evolutionary pressures led to smaller life forms. There were distinct advantages to smaller forms: less consumption of raw materials, cheaper spaceflight, fewer feeding problems . . .

Perhaps the most intelligent life form on a distant planet was no larger than a flea. Perhaps no larger than a bacterium. In that case, the Wildfire Project might be committed to destroying a highly developed life form, without ever realizing what it was doing.

This concept was not unique to Leavitt. It had been proposed by Merton at Harvard, and by Chalmers at Oxford. Chalmers, a man with a keen sense of humor, had used the example of a man looking down on a microscope slide and seeing the bacteria formed into the words "Take us to your leader." Everyone thought Chalmers's idea highly amusing.

Yet Leavitt could not get it out of his mind. Because it just might turn out to be true.

Before he fell asleep, Stone thought about the conference coming up. And the business of the meteorite. He wondered what Nagy would say, or Karp, if they knew about the meteorite.

Probably, he thought, it would drive them insane. Probably it will drive us all insane.

And then he slept.

Delta sector was the designation of three rooms on Level I that contained all communications facilities for the Wildfire installation. All intercom and visual circuits between levels were routed through there, as were cables for telephone and teletype from the outside. The trunk lines to the library and the central storage unit were also regulated by delta sector.

In essence it functioned as a giant switchboard, fully computerized. The three rooms of delta sector were quiet; all that could be heard was the soft hum of spinning tape drums and the muted clicking of relays. Only one person worked here, a single man sitting at a console, surrounded by the blinking lights of the computer.

There was no real reason for the man to be there; he performed no necessary function. The computers were self-regulating, constructed to run check patterns through their circuits every twelve minutes; the computers shut down automatically if there was an abnormal reading.

According to protocol, the man was required to monitor MCN communications, which were signaled by the ringing of a bell on the teleprinter. When the bell rang, he notified the five level command centers that the transmission was received. He was also required to report any computer dysfunction to Level I command, should that unlikely event occur.

day 3

WILDFIRE

12.

The Conference

"TIME TO WAKE UP, SIR."

Mark Hall opened his eyes. The room was lit with a steady, pale fluorescent light. He blinked and rolled over on his stomach.

"Time to wake up, sir."

It was a beautiful female voice, soft and seductive. He sat up in bed and looked around the room: he was alone.

"Hello?"

"Time to wake up, sir."

"Who are you?"

"Time to wake up, sir."

He reached over and pushed a button on the nightstand by his bed. A light went off. He waited for the voice again, but it did not speak.

It was, he thought, a hell of an effective way to wake a man up. As he slipped into his clothes, he wondered how it worked. It was not a simple tape, because it worked as a response of some sort. The message was repeated only when Hall spoke.

To test his theory, he pushed the nightstand button again. The voice said softly, "Do you wish something, sir?"

"I'd like to know your name, please."

"Will that be all, sir?"

"Yes, I believe so."

"Will that be all, sir?"

He waited. The light clicked off. He slipped into his shoes and was about to leave when a male voice said, "This is the answering-service supervisor, Dr. Hall. I wish you would treat the project more seriously."

Hall laughed. So the voice responded to comments, and taped his replies. It was a clever system.

"Sorry," he said, "I wasn't sure how the thing worked. The voice is quite luscious."

"The voice," said the supervisor heavily, "belongs to Miss Gladys Stevens, who is sixty-three years old. She lives in Omaha and makes her living taping messages for SAC crews and other voice-reminder systems."

"Oh," Hall said.

He left the room and walked down the corridor to the cafeteria. As he walked, he began to understand why submarine designers had been called in to plan Wildfire. Without his wristwatch, he had no idea of the time, or even whether it was night or day. He found himself wondering whether the cafeteria would be crowded, wondering whether it was dinner time or breakfast time.

As it turned out, the cafeteria was almost deserted. Leavitt was there; he said the others were in the conference room. He pushed a glass of dark-brown liquid over to Hall and suggested he have breakfast.

"What's this?" Hall said.

"Forty-two-five nutrient. It has everything needed to sustain the average seventy-kilogram man for eighteen hours."

Hall drank the liquid, which was syrupy and artificially flavored to taste like orange juice. It was a strange sensation, drinking brown orange juice, but not bad after the initial shock. Leavitt explained that it had been developed for the astronauts, and that it contained everything except air-soluble vitamins.

"For that, you need this pill," he said.

Hall swallowed the pill, then got himself a cup of coffee from a dispenser in the corner. "Any sugar?"

Leavitt shook his head. "No sugar anywhere here. Nothing that might provide a bacterial growth medium. From now on, we're all on high-protein diets. We'll make all the sugar we need from the protein breakdown. But we won't be getting any sugar into the gut. Quite the opposite."

He reached into his pocket.

"Oh, no."

"Yes," Leavitt said. He gave him a small capsule, sealed in aluminum foil.

"No," Hall said.

"Everyone else has them. Broad-spectrum. Stop by your room and insert it before you go into the final decontamination procedures."

"I don't mind dunking myself in all those foul baths," Hall said. "I don't mind being irradiated. But I'll be goddammed—"

"The idea," Leavitt said, "is that you be as nearly sterile as possible on Level V. We have sterilized your skin and mucous membranes of the respiratory tract as best we can. But we haven't done a thing about the GI tract yet."

"Yes," Hall said, "but suppositories?"

"You'll get used to it. We're all taking them for the first four days. Not, of course, that they'll do any good," he said, with the familiar wry, pessimistic look on his face. He stood. "Let's go to the conference room. Stone wants to talk about Karp."

"Who?"

"Rudolph Karp."

Rudolph Karp was a Hungarian-born biochemist who came to the United States from England in 1951. He obtained a position at the University of Michigan and worked steadily and quietly for five years. Then, at the suggestion of colleagues at

the Ann Arbor observatory, Karp began to investigate meteorites with the intent of determining whether they harbored life,
or showed evidence of having done so in the past. He took the
proposal quite seriously and worked with diligence, writing no
papers on the subject until the early 1960's, when Calvin and
Vaughn and Nagy and others were writing explosive papers on
similar subjects.

The arguments and counter-arguments were complex, but
boiled down to a simple substrate: whenever a worker would
announce that he had found a fossil, or a proteinaceous hydro-
carbon, or other indication of life within a meteorite, the critics
would claim sloppy lab technique and contamination with
earth-origin matter and organisms.

Karp, with his careful, slow techniques, was determined to
end the arguments once and for all. He announced that he
had taken great pains to avoid contamination: each meterorite
he examined had been washed in twelve solutions, including
peroxide, iodine, hypertonic saline and dilute acids. It was
then exposed to intense ultraviolet light for a period of two
days. Finally, it was submerged in a germicidal solution and
placed in a germ-free, sterile isolation chamber; further work
was done within the chamber.

Karp, upon breaking open his meteorites, was able to isolate
bacteria. He found that they were ring-shaped organisms,
rather like a tiny undulating inner tube, and he found they
could grow and multiply. He claimed that, while they were
essentially similar to earthly bacteria in structure, being based
upon proteins, carbohydrates, and lipids, they had no cell
nucleus and therefore their manner of propagation was a
mystery.

Karp presented his information in his usual quiet, unsensa-
tional manner, and hoped for a good reception. He did not receive one; instead, he was laughed down by the Seventh
Conference of Astrophysics and Geophysics, meeting in Lon-
don in 1961. He became discouraged and set his work with

meteorites aside; the organisms were later destroyed in an accidental laboratory explosion on the night of June 27, 1963.

Karp's experience was almost identical to that of Nagy and the others. Scientists in the 1960's were not willing to entertain notions of life existing in meteorites; all evidence presented was discounted, dismissed, and ignored.

A handful of people in a dozen countries remained intrigued, however. One of them was Jeremy Stone; another was Peter Leavitt. It was Leavitt who, some years before, had formulated the Rule of 48. The Rule of 48 was intended as a humorous reminder to scientists, and referred to the massive literature collected in the late 1940's and the 1950's concerning the human chromosome number.

For years it was stated that men had forty-eight chromosomes in their cells; there were pictures to prove it, and any number of careful studies. In 1953, a group of American researchers announced to the world that the human chromosome number was forty-six. Once more, there were pictures to prove it, and studies to confirm it. But these researchers also went back to reexamine the old pictures, and the old studies—and found only forty-six chromosomes, not forty-eight.

Leavitt's Rule of 48 said simply, "All Scientists Are Blind." And Leavitt had invoked his rule when he saw the reception Karp and others received. Leavitt went over the reports and the papers and found no reason to reject the meteorite studies out of hand; many of the experiments were careful, well reasoned, and compelling.

He remembered this when he and the other Wildfire planners drew up the study known as the Vector Three. Along with the Toxic Five, it formed one of the firm theoretical bases for Wildfire.

The Vector Three was a report that considered a crucial question: If a bacterium invaded the earth, causing a new disease, where would that bacterium come from?

After consultation with astronomers and evolutionary theories, the Wildfire group concluded that bacteria could come from three sources.

The first was the most obvious—an organism, from another planet or galaxy, which had the protection to survive the extremes of temperature and vacuum that existed in space. There was no doubt that organisms could survive—there was, for instance, a class of bacteria known as thermophilic that thrived on extreme heat, multiplying enthusiastically in temperatures as high as 70° C. Further, it was known that bacteria had been recovered from Egyptian tombs, where they had been sealed for thousands of years. These bacteria were still viable.

The secret lay in the bacteria's ability to form spores, molding a hard calcific shell around themselves. This shell enabled the organism to survive freezing or boiling, and, if necessary, thousands of years without food. It combined all the advantages of a space suit with those of suspended animation.

There was no doubt that a spore could travel through space. But was another planet or galaxy the most *likely* source of contamination for the earth?

Here, the answer was no. The most likely source was the closest source—the earth itself.

The report suggested that bacteria could have left the surface of the earth eons ago, when life was just beginning to emerge from the oceans and the hot, baked continents. Such bacteria would depart before the fishes, before the primitive mammals, long before the first ape-man. The bacteria would head up into the air, and slowly ascend until they were literally in space. Once there, they might evolve into unusual forms, perhaps even learning to derive energy for life directly from the sun, instead of requiring food as an energy source. These organisms might also be capable of direct conversion of energy to matter.

Leavitt himself suggested the analogy of the upper atmosphere and the depths of the sea as equally inhospitable environments, but equally viable. In the deepest, blackest regions of the oceans, where oxygenation was poor, and where light never reached, life forms were known to exist in abundance. Why not also in the far reaches of the atmosphere? True, oxygen was scarce. True, food hardly existed. But if creatures could live miles beneath the surface, why could they not also live five miles above it?

And if there were organisms out there, and if they had departed from the baking crust of the earth long before the first men appeared, then they would be foreign to man. No immunity, no adaptation, no antibodies would have been developed. They would be primitive aliens to modern man, in the same way that the shark, a primitive fish unchanged for a hundred million years, was alien and dangerous to modern man, invading the oceans for the first time.

The third source of contamination, the third of the vectors, was at the same time the most likely and the most troublesome. This was contemporary earth organisms, taken into space by inadequately sterilized spacecraft. Once in space, the organisms would be exposed to harsh radiation, weightlessness, and other environmental forces that might exert a mutagenic effect, altering the organisms.

So that when they came down, they would be different.

Take up a harmless bacteria—such as the organism that causes pimples, or sore throats—and bring it back in a new form, virulent and unexpected. It might do anything. It might show a preference for the aqueous humor of the inner eye, and invade the eyeball. It might thrive on the acid secretions of the stomach. It might multiply on the small currents of electricity afforded by the human brain itself, drive men mad.

This whole idea of mutated bacteria seemed farfetched and unlikely to the Wildfire people. It is ironic that this should be the case, particularly in view of what happened to the Andromeda Strain. But the Wildfire team staunchly ignored both the evidence of their own experience—that bacteria mutate rapidly and radically—and the evidence of the Biosatellite tests, in which a series of earth forms were sent into space and later recovered.

Biosatellite II contained, among other things, several species of bacteria. It was later reported that the bacteria had reproduced at a rate twenty to thirty times normal. The reasons were still unclear, but the results unequivocal: space could affect reproduction and growth.

And yet no one in Wildfire paid attention to this fact, until it was too late.

Stone reviewed the information quickly, then handed each of them a cardboard file. "These files," he said, "contain a transcript of autoclock records of the entire flight of Scoop VII. Our purpose in reviewing the transcript is to determine, if possible, what happened to the satellite while it was in orbit."

Hall said, "Something happened to it?"

Leavitt explained. "The satellite was scheduled for a six-day orbit, since the probability of collecting organisms is proportional to time in orbit. After launch, it was in stable orbit. Then, on the second day, it went out of orbit."

Hall nodded.

"Start," Stone said, "with the first page."

Hall opened his file.

AUTOCLOCK TRANSCRIPT
PROJECT: SCOOP VII
LAUNCHDATE:
ABRIDGED VERSION. FULL TRANSCRIPT
STORED VAULTS 179-99, VDBG COMPLEX
EPSILON.

HOURS MIN SEC PROCEDURE

T MINUS TIME

0002   01   05   Vandenberg Launchpad Block 9, Scoop Mission
                    Control, reports systems check on schedule.

| 0001 | 39 | 52 | Scoop MC holds for fuel check reported from Ground Control. |

STOP CLOCK — STOP CLOCK. REALTIME LOSS 12 MINUTES.

| 0001 | 39 | 52 | Count resumed. Clock corrected. |

| 0000 | 41 | 12 | Scoop MC holds 20 seconds for Launchpad Block 9 check. Clock not stopped for built-in hold. |

| 0000 | 30 | 00 | Gantry removed. |

| 0000 | 24 | 00 | Final craft systems check. |

| 0000 | 19 | 00 | Final capsule systems check. |

| 0000 | 13 | 00 | Final systems checks read as negative. |

| 0000 | 07 | 12 | Cable decoupling. |

| 0000 | 01 | 07 | Stat-link decoupling. |

| 0000 | 00 | 05 | Ignition. |

| 0000 | 00 | 04 | Launchpad Block 9 clears all systems. |

| 0000 | 00 | 00 | Core clamps released. Launch. |

T PLUS TIME

| 0000 | 00 | 06 | Stable. Speed 6 fps. Smooth EV approach. |

| 0000 | 00 | 09 | Tracking reported. |

| 0000 | 00 | 11 | Tracking confirmed. |

| 0000 | 00 | 27 | Capsule monitors at g 1.9. Equipment check clear. |

| 0000 | 01 | 00 | Launchpad Block 9 clears rocket and capsule systems for orbit. |

"No point in dwelling on this," Stone said. "It is the record of a perfect launch. There is nothing here, in fact, nothing for the next ninety-six hours of flight, to indicate any difficulty on board the spacecraft. Now turn to page 10."

They all turned.

TRACK TRANSCRIPT CONT'D
SCOOP VII
LAUNCHDATE: —
ABRIDGED VERSION

HOURS	MIN	SEC	PROCEDURE
0096	10	12	Orbital check stable as reported by Grand Bahama Station.
0096	34	19	Orbital check stable as reported by Sydney.
0096	47	34	Orbital check stable as reported by Vdbg.
0097	04	12	Orbital check stable but system malfunction reported by Kennedy Station.
0097	05	18	Malfunction confirmed.
0097	07	22	Malfunction confirmed by Grand Bahama. Computer reports orbital instability.
0097	34	54	Sydney reports orbital instability.
0097	39	02	Vandenberg computations indicate orbital decay.
0098	27	14	Vandenberg Scoop Mission Control orders radio reentry.
0099	12	56	Reentry code transmitted.
0099	13	13	Houston reports initiation of reentry. Stabilized flightpath.

"What about voice communication during the critical period?"

"There were linkups between Sydney, Kennedy, and Grand Bahama, all routed through Houston. Houston had the big computer as well. But in this instance, Houston was just helping out; all decisions came from Scoop Mission Control in Vandenberg. We have the voice communication at the back of the file. It's quite revealing."

TRANSCRIPT OF VOICE COMMUNICATIONS
SCOOP MISSION CONTROL
VANDENBERG AFB
HOURS 0096:59 TO 0097:39
THIS IS A CLASSIFIED TRANSCRIPT.
IT HAS NOT BEEN ABRIDGED OR EDITED.

HOURS	MIN	SEC	COMMUNICATION
0096	59	00	HELLO KENNEDY THIS IS SCOOP MISSION CONTROL. AT THE END OF 96 HOURS OF FLIGHT TIME WE HAVE STABLE ORBITS FROM ALL STATIONS. DO YOU CONFIRM.
0097	00	00	I think we do, Scoop. Our check is going through now. Hold this line open for a few minutes, fellows.
0097	03	31	Hello, Scoop MC. This is Kennedy. We have a stable orbit confirmation for you on the last passby. Sorry about the delay but there is an instrument snag somewhere here.
0097	03	34	KENNEDY PLEASE CLARIFY. IS YOUR SNAG ON THE GROUND OR ALOFT.
0097	03	39	I am sorry we have no tracer yet. We think it is on the ground.
0097	04	12	Hello, Scoop MC. This is Kennedy. We have a preliminary report of system malfunction aboard

HOURS	MIN	SEC	COMMUNICATION
			your spacecraft. Repeat we have a preliminary report of malfunction in the air. Awaiting confirmation.
0097	04	15	KENNEDY PLEASE CLARIFY SYSTEM INVOLVED.
0097	04	18	I'm sorry they haven't given me that. I assume they are waiting for final confirmation of the malfunction.
0097	04	21	DOES YOUR ORBITAL CHECK AS STABLE STILL HOLD.
0097	04	22	Vandenberg, we have confirmed your orbital check as stable. Repeat the orbit is stable.
0097	05	18	Ah, Vandenberg, I am afraid we also confirm readings consistent with system malfunction on board your spacecraft. These include the stationary rotor elements and spanner units going to mark twelve. I repeat mark twelve.
0097	05	30	HAVE YOU RUN CONSISTENCY CHECK ON YOUR COMPUTERS.
0097	05	35	Sorry fellows but our computers check out. We read it as a real malfunction.
0097	05	45	HELLO, HOUSTON. OPEN THE LINE TO SYDNEY, WILL YOU. WE WANT CONFIRMATION OF DATA.
0097	05	51	Scoop Mission Control, This is Sydney Station. We confirm our last reading. There was nothing wrong with the spacecraft on its last passby here.
0097	06	12	OUR COMPUTER CHECK INDICATES NO SYSTEMS MALFUNCTION AND GOOD ORBITAL STABILITY ON SUMMATED

HOURS　MIN　SEC　COMMUNICATION

			DATA. WE QUESTION KENNEDY GROUND INSTRUMENT FAILURE.
0097	06	18	This is Kennedy, Scoop MC. We have run repeat checkouts at this end. Our reading of system malfunction remains. Have you got something from Bahama.
0097	06	23	NEGATIVE, KENNEDY. STANDING BY.
0097	06	36	HOUSTON, THIS IS SCOOP MC. CAN YOUR PROJECTION GROUP GIVE US ANYTHING.
0097	06	46	Scoop, at this time we cannot. Our computers have insufficient data. They still read stable orbit with all systems going.
0097	07	22	Scoop MC, this is Grand Bahama Station. We report passby of your craft Scoop Seven according to schedule. Preliminary radar fixes were normal with question of increased transit time. Please hold for systems telemetry.
0097	07	25	HOLDING, GRAND BAHAMA.
0097	07	29	Scoop MC, we are sorry to say we confirm Kennedy observations. Repeat, we confirm Kennedy observations of systems malfunction. Our data are on the trunk to Houston. Can they be routed to you as well.
0097	07	34	NO, WE WILL WAIT FOR HOUSTON'S PRINTOUT. THEY HAVE LARGER PREDICTIVE BANKING UNITS.
0097	07	36	Scoop MC, Houston has the Bahama Data. It is going through the Dispar Program. Give us ten seconds.
0097	07	47	Scoop MC, this is Houston. The Dispar Program confirms systems malfunction. Your vehicle is

HOURS	MIN	SEC	COMMUNICATION
			now in unstable orbit with increased transit time of zero point three seconds per unit of arc. We are analyzing orbital parameters at this time. Is there anything further you wish as interpreted data.
0097	07	59	NO, HOUSTON. SOUNDS LIKE YOU'RE DOING BEAUTIFULLY.
0097	08	10	Sorry, Scoop. Bad break.
0097	08	18	GET US THE DECAY RATIOS AS SOON AS POSSIBLE. COMMAND WISHES TO MAKE A DECISION ON INSTRUMENTATION TAKEDOWN WITHIN THE NEXT TWO ORBITS.
0097	08	32	Understand, Scoop. Our condolences here.
0097	11	35	Scoop, Houston Projection Group has confirmed orbital instability and decay ratios are now being passed by the data trunk to your station.
0097	11	44	HOW DO THEY LOOK, HOUSTON.
0097	11	51	Bad.
0097	11	59	NOT UNDERSTOOD. PLEASE REPEAT.
0097	12	07	Bad: B as in broken, A as in awful, D as in dropping.
0097	12	15	HOUSTON, DO YOU HAVE A CAUSATION. THAT SATELLITE HAS BEEN IN EXCELLENT ORBIT FOR NEARLY ONE HUNDRED HOURS. WHAT HAPPENED TO IT.
0097	12	29	Beats us. We wonder about collision. There is a good wobble component to the new orbit.
0097	12	44	HOUSTON, OUR COMPUTERS ARE WORKING THROUGH THE TRANSMITTED DATA. WE

HOURS	MIN	SEC	COMMUNICATION
			AGREE A COLLISION. HAVE YOU GUYS GOT SOMETHING IN THE NEIGHBORHOOD.
0097	13	01	Air Force Skywatch confirms our report that we we have nothing around your baby, Scoop.
0097	13	50	HOUSTON, OUR COMPUTERS ARE READING THIS AS A RANDOM EVENT. PROBABILITIES GREATER THAN ZERO POINT SEVEN NINE.
0097	15	00	We can add nothing. Looks reasonable. Are you going to bring it down.
0097	15	15	WE ARE HOLDING ON THAT DECISION, HOUSTON. WE WILL NOTIFY AS SOON AS IT IS MADE.
0097	17	54	HOUSTON, OUR COMMAND GROUP HAS RAISED THE QUESTION OF WHETHER ******** ***********************
0097	17	59	[reply from Houston deleted]
0097	18	43	[Scoop query to Houston deleted]
0097	19	03	[reply from Houston deleted]
0097	19	11	AGREE, HOUSTON. WE WILL MAKE OUR DECISION AS SOON AS WE HAVE FINAL CONFIRMATION OF ORBITAL SHUTDOWN FROM SYDNEY. IS THIS ACCEPTABLE.
0097	19	50	Perfectly, Scoop. We are standing by.
0097	24	32	HOUSTON, WE ARE REWORKING OUR DATA AND NO LONGER CONSIDER THAT *********** IS LIKELY.
0097	24	39	Roger, Scoop.
0097	29	13	HOUSTON, WE ARE STANDING BY FOR SYDNEY.

HOURS	MIN	SEC	COMMUNICATION
0097	34	54	Scoop Mission Control, this is Sydney Station. We have just followed the passby of your vehicle. Our initial readings confirm a prolonged transit time. It is quite striking at this time.
0097	35	12	THANK YOU, SYDNEY.
0097	35	22	Bit of nasty luck, Scoop. Sorry.
0097	39	02	THIS IS SCOOP MISSION CONTROL TO ALL STATIONS. OUR COMPUTERS HAVE JUST CALCULATED THE ORBITAL DECAY FOR THE VEHICLE AND WE FIND IT TO BE COMING DOWN AS A PLUS FOUR. STANDBY FOR THE FINAL DECISION AS TO WHEN WE WILL BRING IT DOWN.

Hall said, "What about the deleted passages?"

"Major Manchek at Vandenberg told me," Stone said, "that they had to do with the Russian craft in the area. The two stations eventually concluded that the Russians had not, either accidentally or purposely, brought down the Scoop satellite. No one has since suggested differently."

They nodded.

"It's tempting," Stone said. "The Air Force maintains a watchdog facility in Kentucky that tracks all satellites in earth orbit. It has a dual function, both to follow old satellites known to be in orbit and to track new ones. There are twelve satellites in orbit at this time that cannot be accounted for; in other words, they are not ours, and are not the result of announced Soviet launches. It is thought that some of these represent navigation satellites for Soviet submarines. Others are presumed to be spy satellites. But the important thing is that Russian or not, there are a hell of a lot of satellites up there. As of last Friday, the Air Force reported five hundred and eighty-seven orbiting bodies around the earth. This includes some old, nonfunctioning satellites from the American Explorer series and the Russian Sputnik series. It also includes boosters and final stages—anything in stable orbit large enough to reflect back a radar beam."

"That's a lot of satellites."

"Yes, and there are probably many more. The Air Force thinks there is a lot of junk out there—nuts, bolts, scraps of metal—all in more or less stable orbit. No orbit, as you know, is completely stable. Without frequent corrections, any satellite will eventually decay out and spiral down to earth, burning up in the atmosphere. But that may be years, even decades, after the launch. In any event, the Air Force estimates that the total number of individual orbiting objects could be anything up to seventy-five thousand."

"So a collision with a piece of junk is possible."

"Yes. Possible."

"How about a meteor?"

"That is the other possibility, and the one Vandenberg favors. A random event, most likely a meteor."

"Any showers these days?"

"None, apparently. But that does not rule out a meteor collision."

Leavitt cleared his throat. "There is still another possibility."

Stone frowned. He knew that Leavitt was imaginative, and that this trait was both a strength and a defect. At times, Leavitt could be startling and exciting; at others, merely irritating. "It's rather farfetched," Stone said, "to postulate debris from some extragalactic source other than—"

"I agree," Leavitt said. "Hopelessly farfetched. No evidence for it whatever. But I don't think we can afford to ignore the possibility."

A gong sounded softly. A lush female voice, which Hall now recognized as that of Gladys Stevens of Omaha, said softly, "You may proceed to the next level, gentlemen."

13.

Level V

LEVEL V WAS PAINTED a quiet shade of blue, and they all wore blue uniforms. Burton showed Hall around.

"This floor," he said, "is like all the others. It's circular. Arranged in a series of concentric circles, actually. We're on the outer perimeter now; this is where we live and work. Cafeteria, sleeping rooms, everything is out here. Just inside is a ring of laboratories. And inside that, sealed off from us, is the central core. That's where the satellite and the two people are now."

"But they're sealed off from us?"

"Yes."

"Then how do we get to them?"

"Have you ever used a glove box?" Burton asked.

Hall shook his head.

Burton explained that glove boxes were large clear plastic boxes used to handle sterile materials. The boxes had holes cut in the sides, and gloves attached with an airtight seal. To handle the contents, you slipped your hands into the gloves and reached into the box. But your fingers never touched the material, only the gloves.

"We've gone one step further," Burton said. "We have whole rooms that are nothing more than glorified glove boxes. Instead of a glove for your hand, there's a whole plastic suit, for your entire body. You'll see what I mean."

They walked down the curved corridor to a room marked CENTRAL CONTROL. Leavitt and Stone were there, working quietly. Central Control was a cramped room, stuffed with electronic equipment. One wall was glass, allowing the workers to look into the adjacent room.

Through the glass, Hall saw mechanical hands moving the capsule to a table and setting it down. Hall, who had never seen a capsule before, watched with interest. It was smaller than he had imagined, no more than a yard long; one end was seared and blackened from the heat of reentry.

The mechanical hands, under Stone's direction, opened the little scoop-shaped trough in the side of the capsule to expose the interior.

"There," Stone said, taking his hands from the controls. The controls looked like a pair of brass knuckles; the operator slipped his own hands into them and moved his hands as he wanted the mechanical hands to move.

"Our next step," he said, "is to determine whether there is still anything in the capsule which is biologically active. Suggestions?"

"A rat," Leavitt said. "Use a black Norway."

The black Norway rat was not black at all; the name simply designated a strain of laboratory animal, perhaps the most famous strain in all science. Once, of course, it had been both black and Norwegian; but years of breeding and countless generations had made it white, small, and docile. The biological explosion had created a demand for genetically uniform animals. In the last thirty years more than a thousand strains of "pure" animals had been evolved artificially. In the case of the black Norwegian, it was now possible for a scientist anywhere in the world to conduct experiments using this animal and be assured that other scientists elsewhere could repeat or enlarge upon his work using virtually identical organisms.

"Follow with a rhesus," Burton said. "We will want to get onto primates sooner or later."

The others nodded. Wildfire was prepared to conduct experiments with monkeys and apes, as well as smaller, cheaper animals. A monkey was exceedingly difficult to work with: the little primates were hostile, quick, intelligent. Among scientists, the New World monkeys, with their prehensile tails, were considered particularly trying. Many a scientist had engaged three or four lab assistants to hold down a monkey while he administered an injection—only to have the prehensile tail whip up, grasp the syringe, and fling it across the room.

The theory behind primate experimentation was that these animals were closer biologically to man. In the 1950's, several laboratories even attempted experiments on gorillas, going to great trouble and expense to work with these seemingly most human of animals. However, by 1960 it had been demonstrated that of the apes, the chimpanzee was biochemically more like man than the gorilla. (On the basis of similarity to man, the choice of laboratory animals is often surprising. For example, the hamster is preferred for immunological and cancer studies, since his responses are so similar to man's, while for studies of the heart and circulation, the pig is considered most like man.)

Stone put his hands back on the controls, moving them gently. Through the glass, they saw the black metal fingers move to the far wall of the adjoining room, where several caged lab animals were kept, separated from the room by hinged airtight doors. The wall reminded Hall oddly of an automat.

The mechanical hands opened one door and removed a rat in its cage, brought it into the room, and set it down next to the capsule.

The rat looked around the room, sniffed the air, and made

some stretching movements with its neck. A moment later it flopped over onto its side, kicked once, and was still.

It had happened with astonishing speed. Hall could hardly believe it had happened at all.

"My God," Stone said. "What a time course."

"That will make it difficult," Leavitt said.

Burton said, "We can try tracers . . ."

"Yes. We'll have to use tracers on it," Stone said. "How fast are our scans?"

"Milliseconds, if necessary."

"It will be necessary."

"Try the rhesus," Burton said. "You'll want a post on it, anyway."

Stone directed the mechanical hands back to the wall, opening another door and withdrawing a cage containing a large brown adult rhesus monkey. The monkey screeched as it was lifted and banged against the bars of its cage.

Then it died, after flinging one hand to its chest with a look of startled surprise.

Stone shook his head. "Well, at least we know it's still biologically active. Whatever killed everyone in Piedmont is still there, and still as potent as ever." He sighed. "If potent is the word."

Leavitt said, "We'd better start a scan of the capsule."

"I'll take these dead animals," Burton said, "and run the initial vector studies. Then I'll autopsy them."

Stone worked the mechanical hands once more. He picked up the cages that held the rat and monkey and set them on a rubber conveyor belt at the rear of the room. Then he pressed a button on a control console marked AUTOPSY. The conveyor belt began to move.

Burton left the room, walking down the corridor to the autopsy room, knowing that the conveyor belt, made to carry materials from one lab to another, would have automatically delivered the cages.

Stone said to Hall, "You're the practicing physician among us. I'm afraid you've got a rather tough job right now."

"Pediatrician and geriatrist?"

"Exactly. See what you can do about them. They're both in our miscellaneous room, the room we built precisely for unusual circumstances like this. There's a computer linkup there that should help you. The technician will show you how it works."

14.

Miscellaneous

HALL OPENED THE DOOR marked MIS-
CELLANEOUS, thinking to himself that his job was indeed miscellaneous—keeping alive an old man and a tiny infant. Both
of them vital to the project, and both of them, no doubt,
difficult to manage.

He found himself in another small room similar to the control room he had just left. This one also had a glass window,
looking inward to a central room. In the room were two beds,
and on the beds, Peter Jackson and the infant. But the incredible thing was the suits: standing upright in the room
were four clear plastic inflated suits in the shape of men. From
each suit, a tunnel ran back to the wall.

Obviously, one would have to crawl down the tunnel and
then stand up inside the suit. Then one could work with the
patients inside the room.

The girl who was to be his assistant was working in the
room, bent over the computer console. She introduced herself
as Karen Anson, and explained the working of the computer.

"This is just one substation of the Wildfire computer on
the first level," she said. "There are thirty substations through-

out the laboratory, all plugging into the computer. Thirty different people can work at once."

Hall nodded. Time-sharing was a concept he understood. He knew that as many as two hundred people had been able to use the same computer at once; the principle was that computers operated very swiftly—in fractions of a second—while people operated slowly, in seconds or minutes. One person using a computer was inefficient, because it took several minutes to punch in instructions, while the computer sat around idle, waiting. Once instructions were fed in, the computer answered almost instantaneously. This meant that a computer was rarely "working," and by permitting a number of people to ask questions of the computer simultaneously, you could keep the machine more continuously in operation.

"If the computer is really backed up," the technician said, "there may be a delay of one or two seconds before you get your answer. But usually it's immediate. What we are using here is the MEDCOM program. Do you know it?"

Hall shook his head.

"It's a medical-data analyzer," she said. "You feed in information and it will diagnose the patient and tell you what to do next for therapy, or to confirm the diagnosis."

"Sounds very convenient."

"It's fast," she said. "All our lab studies are done by automated machines. So we can have complex diagnoses in a matter of minutes."

Hall looked through the glass at the two patients. "What's been done on them so far?"

"Nothing. At Level I, they were started on intravenous infusions. Plasma for Peter Jackson, dextrose and water for the baby. They both seem well hydrated now, and in no distress. Jackson is still unconscious. He has no pupillary signs but is unresponsive and looks anemic."

Hall nodded. "The labs here can do everything?"

"Everything. Even assays for adrenal hormones and things

like partial thromboplastin times. Every known medical test is possible."

"All right. We'd better get started."

She turned on the computer. "This is how you order laboratory tests," she said. "Use this light pen here, and check off the tests you want. Just touch the pen to the screen."

She handed him a small penlight, and pushed the START button.

The screen glowed.

```
MEDCOM PROGRAM
LAB/ANALYS
CK/JGG/1223098


BLOOD
                                PROTEIN
      COUNTS  RBC
              RETIC             ALB
              PLATES            GLOB
              WBC               FIBRIN
              DIFF              TOTAL
      HEMATOCRIT                FRACTION
      HEMOGLOBIN
      INDICES  MCV        DIAGNOSTICS
               MCHC
      PROTIME                   CHOLEST
      PTT                       CREAT
      SED RATE                  GLUCOSE
                                PBI
CHEMISTRY                       BEI
                                I
      BRO                       IBC
      CA                        NPN
      CL                        BUN
      MG                        BILIRU, DIFF
      PO4                       CEPH/FLOC
      K                         THYMOL/TURB
      NA                        BSP
      CO2
```

ENZYMES	PULMONARY

ENZYMES

    AMYLASE
    CHOLINESTERASE
    LIPASE
    PHOSPHATASE, ACID
             ALKALINE
    LDH
    SGOT
    SGPT

STEROIDS
    ALDO
    L7-OH
    17-KS
    ACTH

VITS
    A
    ALL B
    C
    E
    K

PULMONARY

    TVC
    TV
    IC
    IRV
    ERV
    MBC

URINE

    SP GR
    PH
    PROT
    GLUC
    KETONE
    ALL ELECTROLYTES
    ALL STEROIDS
    ALL INORGANICS
    CATECHOLS
    PORPHYRINS
    UROBIL
    5-HIAA

Hall stared at the list. He touched the tests he wanted with the penlight; they disappeared from the screen. He ordered fifteen or twenty, then stepped back.

The screen went blank for a moment, and then the following appeared:

```
TESTS ORDERED WILL REQUIRE FOR EACH
SUBJECT

20 CC WHOLE BLOOD
10 CC OXALATED BLOOD
12 CC CITRATED BLOOD
15 CC URINE
```

The technician said, "I'll draw the bloods if you want to do physicals. Have you been in one of these rooms before?"

Hall shook his head.

"It's quite simple, really. We crawl through the tunnels into the suits. The tunnel is then sealed off behind us."

"Oh? Why?"

"In case something happens to one of us. In case the covering of the suit is broken—the integrity of the surface is ruptured, as the protocol says. In that case, bacteria could spread back through the tunnel to the outside."

"So we're sealed off."

"Yes. We get air from a separate system—you can see the thin lines coming in over there. But essentially you're isolated from everything, when you're in that suit. I don't think you need worry, though. The only way you might possibly break your suit is to cut it with a scalpel, and the gloves are triple-thickness to prevent just such an occurrence."

She showed him how to crawl through, and then, imitating her, he stood up inside the plastic suit. He felt like some kind of giant reptile, moving cumbersomely about, dragging his tunnel like a thick tail behind him.

After a moment, there was a hiss: his suit was being sealed off. Then another hiss, and the air turned cold as the special line began to feed air in to him.

The technician gave him his examining instruments. While she drew blood from the child, taking it from a scalp vein, Hall turned his attention to Peter Jackson.

An old man, and pale: anemia. Also thin: first thought, cancer. Second thought, tuberculosis, alcoholism, some other chronic process. And unconscious: he ran through the differential in his mind, from epilepsy to hypoglycemic shock to stroke.

Hall later stated that he felt foolish when the computer provided him with a differential, complete with probabilities of diagnosis. He was not at that time aware of the skill of the computer, the quality of its program.

He checked Jackson's blood pressure. It was low, 85/50. Pulse fast at 110. Temperature 97.8. Respirations 30 and deep.

He went over the body systematically, beginning with the head and working down. When he produced pain—by pressing on the nerve through the supraorbital notch, just below the eyebrow—the man grimaced and moved his arms to push Hall away.

Perhaps he was not unconscious after all. Perhaps just stuporous. Hall shook him.

"Mr. Jackson. Mr. Jackson."

The man made no response. And then, slowly, he seemed to revive. Hall shouted his name in his ear and shook him hard.

Peter Jackson opened his eyes, just for a moment, and said, "Go . . . away . . ."

Hall continued to shake him, but Jackson relaxed, going limp, his body slipping back to its unresponsive state. Hall gave up, returning to his physical examination. The lungs were clear and the heart seemed normal. There was some tenseness of the abdomen, and Jackson retched once, bringing up some bloody drooling material. Quickly, Hall did a basolyte test for blood: it was positive. He did a rectal exam and tested the stool. It was also positive for blood.

He turned to the technician, who had drawn all the bloods and was feeding the tubes into the computer analysis apparatus in one corner.

"We've got a GI bleeder here," he said. "How soon will the results be back?"

She pointed to a TV screen mounted near the ceiling. "The lab reports are flashed back as soon as they come in. They are displayed there, and on the console in the other room. The easy ones come back first. We should have hematocrit in two minutes."

Hall waited. The screen glowed, the letters printing out:

JACKSON, PETER
LABORATORY ANALYSES

TEST	NORMAL	VALUE
HEMATOCRIT	38 – 54	21

"Half normal," Hall said. He slapped an oxygen mask on Jackson's face, fixed the straps, and said, "We'll need at least four units. Plus two of plasma."

"I'll order them."

"To start as soon as possible."

She went to phone the blood bank on Level II and asked them to hurry on the requisition. Meantime, Hall turned his attention to the child.

It had been a long time since he had examined an infant, and he had forgotten how difficult it could be. Every time he tried to look at the eyes, the child shut them tightly. Every time he looked down the throat, the child closed his mouth. Every time he tried to listen to the heart, the child shrieked, obscuring all heart sounds.

Yet he persisted, remembering what Stone had said. These two people, dissimilar though they were, nonetheless represented the only survivors of Piedmont. Somehow they had managed to beat the disease. That was a link between the two, between the shriveled old man vomiting blood and the pink young child, howling and screaming.

At first glance, they were as different as possible; they were at opposite ends of the spectrum, sharing nothing in common.

And yet there must be something in common.

It took Hall half an hour to finish his examination of the child. At the end of that time he was forced to conclude that the infant was, to his exam, perfectly normal. Totally normal. Nothing the least bit unusual about him.

Except that, somehow, he had survived.

15.

Main Control

STONE SAT WITH LEAVITT in the main control room, looking into the inner room with the capsule. Though cramped, main control was complex and expensive: it had cost $2,000,000, the most costly single room in the Wildfire installation. But it was vital to the functioning of the entire laboratory.

Main control served as the first step in scientific examination of the capsule. Its chief function was detection—the room was geared to detect and isolate microorganisms. According to the Life Analysis Protocol, there were three main steps in the Wildfire program: detection, characterization, and control. First the organism had to be found. Then it had to be studied and understood. Only then could ways be sought to control it.

Main control was set up to find the organism.

Leavitt and Stone sat side by side in front of the banks of controls and dials. Stone operated the mechanical hands, while Leavitt manipulated the microscopic apparatus. Naturally it was impossible to enter the room with the capsule and examine it directly. Robot-controlled microscopes, with viewing screens in the control room, would accomplish this for them.

An early question had been whether to utilize television or some kind of direct visual linkup. Television was cheaper and more easily set up; TV image-intensifiers were already in use for electron microscopes, X-ray machines, and other devices. However, the Wildfire group finally decided that a TV screen was too imprecise for their needs; even a double-scan camera, which transmitted twice as many lines as the usual TV and gave better image resolution, would be insufficient. In the end, the group chose a fiber optics system in which a light image was transmitted directly through a snakelike bundle of glass fibers and then displayed on the viewers. This gave a clear, sharp image.

Stone positioned the capsule and pressed the appropriate controls. A black box moved down from the ceiling and began to scan the capsule surface. The two men watched the viewer screens.

"Start with five power," Stone said. Leavitt set the controls. They watched as the viewer automatically moved around the capsule, focusing on the surface of the metal. They watched one complete scan, then shifted up to twenty-power magnification. A twenty-power scan took much longer, since the field of view was smaller. They still saw nothing on the surface: no punctures, no indentations, nothing that looked like a small growth of any kind.

"Let's go to one hundred," Stone said. Leavitt adjusted the controls and sat back. They were beginning what they knew would be a long and tedious search. Probably they would find nothing. Soon they would examine the interior of the capsule; they might find something there. Or they might not. In either case, they would take samples for analysis, plating out the scrapings and swabs onto growth media.

Leavitt glanced from the viewing screens to look into the room. The viewer, suspended from the ceiling by a complex arrangement of rods and wires, was automatically moving in slow circles around the capsule. He looked back to the screens.

There were three screens in main control, and all showed exactly the same field of view. In theory, they could use three viewers projecting onto three screens, and cover the capsule in one third the time. But they did not want to do that—at least, not now. Both men knew that their interest and attention would fatigue as the day wore on. No matter how hard they tried, they could not remain alert all the time. But if two men watched the same image, there was less chance of missing something.

The surface area of the cone-shaped capsule, thirty-seven inches long and a foot in diameter at the base, was just over 650 square inches. Three scans, at five, twenty, and one hundred power, took them slightly more than two hours. At the end of the third scan, Stone said, "I suppose we ought to proceed with the 440 scan as well."

"But?"

"I am tempted to go directly to a scan of the interior. If we find nothing, we can come back outside and do a 440."

"I agree."

"All right," Stone said. "Start with five. On the inside."

Leavitt worked the controls. This time, it could not be done automatically; the viewer was programmed to follow the contours of any regularly shaped object, such as a cube, a sphere, or a cone. But it could not probe the interior of the capsule without direction. Leavitt set the lenses at five diameters and switched the remote viewer to manual control. Then he directed it down into the scoop opening of the capsule.

Stone, watching the screen, said, "More light."

Leavitt made adjustments. Five additional remote lights came down from the ceiling and clicked on, shining into the scoop.

"Better?"

"Fine."

Watching his own screen, Leavitt began to move the re-mote viewer. It took several minutes before he could do it smoothly; it was difficult to coordinate, rather like trying to write while you watched in a mirror. But soon he was scanning smoothly.

The five-power scan took twenty minutes. They found nothing except a small indentation the size of a pencil point. At Stone's suggestion, when they began the twenty-power scan they started with the indentation.

Immediately, they saw it: a tiny black fleck of jagged ma-terial no larger than a grain of sand. There seemed to be bits of green mixed in with the black.

Neither man reacted, though Leavitt later recalled that he was "trembling with excitement. I kept thinking, if this is it, if it's really something new, some brand new form of life . . ."

However, all he said was, "Interesting."

"We'd better complete the scan at twenty power," Stone said. He was working to keep his voice calm, but it was clear that he was excited too.

Leavitt wanted to examine the fleck at higher power im-mediately, but he understood what Stone was saying. They could not afford to jump to conclusions—any conclusions. Their only hope was to be grindingly, interminably thorough. They had to proceed methodically, to assure themselves at every point that they had overlooked nothing.

Otherwise, they could pursue a course of investigation for hours or days, only to find it ended nowhere, that they had made a mistake, misjudged the evidence, and wasted time.

So Leavitt did a complete scan of the interior at twenty power. He paused, once or twice, when they thought they saw other patches of green, and marked down the coordinates so they could find the areas later, under higher magnification. Half an hour passed before Stone announced he was satisfied with the twenty-power scan.

They took a break for caffeine, swallowing two pills with

water. The team had agreed earlier that amphetamines should not be used except in times of serious emergency; they were stocked in the Level V pharmacy, but for routine purposes caffeine was preferred.

The aftertaste of the caffeine pill was sour in his mouth as Leavitt clicked in the hundred-power lenses, and began the third scan. As before, they started with the indentation, and the small black fleck they had noted earlier.

It was disappointing: at higher magnification it appeared no different from their earlier views, only larger. They could see, however, that it was an irregular piece of material, dull, looking like rock. And they could see there were definitely flecks of green mined on the jagged surface of the material.

"What do you make of it?" Stone said.

"If that's the object the capsule collided with," Leavitt said, "it was either moving with great speed, or else it is very heavy. Because it's not big enough—"

"To knock the satellite out of orbit otherwise. I agree. And yet it did not make a very deep indentation."

"Suggesting?"

Stone shrugged. "Suggesting that it was either not responsible for the orbital change, or that it has some elastic properties we don't yet know about."

"What do you think of the green?"

Stone grinned. "You won't trap me yet. I am curious, nothing more."

Leavitt chuckled and continued the scan. Both men now felt elated and inwardly certain of their discovery. They checked the other areas where they had noted green, and confirmed the presence of the patches at higher magnification.

But the other patches looked different from the green on the rock. For one thing, they were larger, and seemed somehow more luminous. For another, the borders of the patches seemed quite regular, and rounded.

"Like small drops of green paint, spattered on the inside of the capsule," Stone said.

"I hope that's not what it is."

"We could probe," Stone said.

"Let's wait for 440."

Stone agreed. By now they had been scanning the capsule for nearly four hours, but neither man felt tired. They watched closely as the viewing screens blurred for a moment, the lenses shifting. When the screens came back into focus, they were looking at the indentation, and the black fleck with the green areas. At this magnification, the surface irregularities of the rock were striking—it was like a miniature planet, with jagged peaks and sharp valleys. It occurred to Leavitt that this was exactly what they were looking at: a minute, complete planet, with its life forms intact. But he shook his head, dismissing the thought from his mind. Impossible.

Stone said, "If that's a meteor, it's damned funny-looking."

"What bothers you?"

"That left border, over there." Stone pointed to the screen. "The surface of the stone—if it is stone—is rough everywhere except on that left border, where it is smooth and rather straight."

"Like an artificial surface?"

Stone sighed. "If I keep looking at it," he said, "I might start to think so. Let's see those other patches of green."

Leavitt set the coordinates and focused the viewer. A new image appeared on the screens. This time, it was a close-up of one of the green patches. Under high magnification the borders could be seen clearly. They were not smooth, but slightly notched: they looked almost like a gear from the inside of a watch.

"I'll be damned," Leavitt said.

"It's not paint. That notching is too regular."

As they watched, it happened: the green spot turned purple

for a fraction of a second, less than the blink of an eye. Then it turned green once more.

"Did you see that?"

"I saw it. You didn't change the lighting?"

"No. Didn't touch it."

A moment later, it happened again: green, a flash of purple, green again.

"Amazing."

"This may be——"

And then, as they watched, the spot turned purple and remained purple. The notches disappeared; the spot had enlarged slightly, filling in the V-shaped gaps. It was now a complete circle. It became green once more.

"It's growing," Stone said.

They worked swiftly. The movie cameras were brought down, recording from five angles at ninety-six frames per second. Another time-lapse camera clicked off frames at half-second intervals. Leavitt also brought down two more remote cameras, and set them at different angles from the original camera.

In main control, all three screens displayed different views of the green spot.

"Can we get more power? More magnification?" Stone said.

"No. You remember we decided 440 was the top."

Stone swore. To obtain higher magnification, they would have to go to a separate room, or else use the electron microscopes. In either case, it would take time.

Leavitt said, "Shall we start culture and isolation?"

"Yes. Might as well."

Leavitt turned the viewers back down to twenty power. They could now see that there were four areas of interest—three isolated green patches, and the rock with its indentation. On the control console, he pressed a button marked CULTURE, and a tray at the side of the room slid out, revealing stacks of circular, plastic-covered petri dishes. Inside each dish was a thin layer of growth medium.

The Wildfire project employed almost every known growth medium. The media were jellied compounds containing various nutrients on which bacteria would feed and multiply. Along with the usual laboratory standbys—horse and sheep blood agar, chocolate agar, simplex, Sabourad's medium—there were thirty diagnostic media, containing various sugars and minerals. Then there were forty-three specialized culture media, including those for growth of tubercule bacilli and unusual fungi, as well as the highly experimental media, designated by numbers: ME-997, ME-423, ME-A12, and so on.

With the tray of media was a batch of sterile swabs. Using the mechanical hands, Stone picked up the swabs singly and touched them to the capsule surface, then to the media. Leavitt punched data into the computer, so that they would know later where each swab had been taken. In this manner, they swabbed the outer surface of the entire capsule, and went to the interior. Very carefully, using high viewer magnification, Stone took scrapings from the green spots and transferred them to the different media.

Finally, he used fine forceps to pick up the rock and move it intact to a clean glass dish.

The whole process took better than two hours. At the end of that time, Leavitt punched through the MAXCULT computer program. This program automatically instructed the machine in the handling of the hundreds of petri dishes they had collected. Some would be stored at room temperature and pressure, with normal earth atmosphere. Others would be subjected to heat and cold; high pressure and vacuum; low oxygen and high oxygen; light and dark. Assigning the plates to the various culture boxes was a job that would take a man days to work out. The computer could do it in seconds.

When the program was running, Stone placed the stacks of petri dishes on the conveyor belt. They watched as the dishes moved off to the culture boxes.

There was nothing further they could do, except wait twenty-four to forty-eight hours, to see what grew out.

"Meantime," Stone said, "we can begin analysis of this piece of rock—if it actually is rock. How are you with an EM?"

"Rusty," Leavitt said. He had not used an electron microscope for nearly a year.

"Then I'll prepare the specimen. We'll also want mass spectometry done. That's all computerized. But before we do that, we ought to go to higher power. What's the highest light magnification we can get in Morphology?"

"A thousand diameters."

"Then let's do that first. Punch the rock through to Morphology."

Leavitt looked down at the console and pressed MORPHOL-OGY. Stone's mechanical hands placed the glass dish with the rock onto the conveyor belt.

They looked at the wall clock behind them. It showed 1100 hours; they had been working for eleven straight hours.

"So far," Stone said, "so good."

Leavitt grinned, and crossed his fingers.

16.

Autopsy

BURTON WAS WORKING in the autopsy room. He was nervous and tense, still bothered by his memories of Piedmont. Weeks later, in reviewing his work and his thoughts on Level V, he regretted his inability to concentrate.

Because in his initial series of experiments, Burton made several mistakes.

According to the protocol, he was required to carry out autopsies on dead animals, but he was also in charge of preliminary vector experiments. In all fairness, Burton was not the man to do this work; Leavitt would have been better suited to it. But it was felt that Leavitt was more useful working on preliminary isolation and identification.

So the vector experiments fell to Burton.

They were reasonably simple and straightforward, designed to answer the question of how the disease was transmitted. Burton began with a series of cages, lined up in a row. Each had a separate air supply; the air supplies could be interconnected in a variety of ways.

Burton placed the corpse of the dead Norway rat, which was contained in an airtight cage, alongside another cage containing a living rat. He punched buttons; air was allowed to pass freely from one cage to the other.

The living rat flopped over and died.

Interesting, he thought. Airborne transmission. He hooked up a second cage with a live rat, but inserted a millipore filter between the living and dead rat cages. This filter had perforations 100 angstroms in diameter—the size of a small virus.

He opened the passage between the two cages. The rat remained alive.

He watched for several moments, until he was satisfied. Whatever it was that transmitted the disease, it was larger than a virus. He changed the filter, replacing it with a larger one, and then another still larger. He continued in this way until the rat died.

The filter had allowed the agent to pass. He checked it: two microns in diameter, roughly the size of a small cell. He thought to himself that he had just learned something very valuable indeed: the size of the infectious agent.

This was important, for in a single simple experiment he had ruled out the possibility that a protein or a chemical molecule of some kind was doing the damage. At Piedmont, he and Stone had been concerned about a gas, perhaps a gas released as waste from the living organism.

Yet, clearly, no gas was responsible. The disease was transmitted by something the size of a cell that was very much bigger than a molecule, or gas droplet.

The next step was equally simple—to determine whether dead animals were potentially infectious.

He took one of the dead rats and pumped the air out of its cage. He waited until the air was fully evacuated. In the pressure fall, the rat ruptured, bursting open. Burton ignored this.

When he was sure all air was removed, he replaced the air with fresh, clean, filtered air. Then he connected the cage to the cage of a living animal.

Nothing happened.

Interesting, he thought. Using a remotely controlled scalpel, he sliced open the dead animal further, to make sure any organisms contained inside the carcass would be released into the atmosphere.

Nothing happened. The live rat scampered about its cage happily.

The results were quite clear: dead animals were not infectious. That was why, he thought, the buzzards could chew at the Piedmont victims and not die. Corpses could not transmit the disease; only the bugs themselves, carried in the air, could do so.

Bugs in the air were deadly.

Bugs in the corpse were harmless.

In a sense, this was predictable. It had to do with theories of accommodation and mutual adaptation between bacteria and man. Burton had long been interested in this problem, and had lectured on it at the Baylor medical school.

Most people, when they thought of bacteria, thought of diseases. Yet the fact was that only 3 per cent of bacteria produced human disease; the rest were either harmless or beneficial. In the human gut, for instance, there were a variety of bacteria that were helpful to the digestive process. Man needed them, and relied upon them.

In fact, man lived in a sea of bacteria. They were everywhere—on his skin, in his ears and mouth, down his lungs, in his stomach. Everything he owned, anything he touched, every breath he breathed, was drenched in bacteria. Bacteria were ubiquitous. Most of the time you weren't aware of it.

And there was a reason. Both man and bacteria had gotten used to each other, had developed a kind of mutual immunity. Each adapted to the other.

And this, in turn, for a very good reason. It was a principle of biology that evolution was directed toward increased reproductive potential. A man easily killed by bacteria was poorly adapted; he didn't live long enough to reproduce.

A bacteria that killed its host was also poorly adapted. Because any parasite that kills its host is a failure. It must die when the host dies. The successful parasites were those that could live off the host without killing him.

And the most successful hosts were those that could tolerate the parasite, or even turn it to advantage, to make it work for the host.

"The best adapted bacteria," Burton used to say, "are the ones that cause minor diseases, or none at all. You may carry the same single cell of *Strep. viridians* on your body for sixty or seventy years. During that time, you are growing and reproducing happily; so is the *Strep.* You can carry *Staph. aureus* around, and pay only the price of some acne and pimples. You can carry tuberculosis for many decades; you can carry syphilis for a lifetime. These last are not minor diseases, but they are much less severe than they once were, because both man and organism have adapted."

It was known, for instance, that syphilis had been a virulent disease four hundred years before, producing huge festering sores all over the body, often killing in weeks. But over the centuries, man and the spirochete had learned to tolerate each other.

Such considerations were not so abstract and academic as they seemed at first. In the early planning of Wildfire, Stone had observed that 40 per cent of all human disease was caused by microorganisms. Burton had countered by noting that only 3 per cent of all microorganisms caused disease. Obviously, while much human misery was attributable to bacteria, the chances of any particular bacteria being dangerous to man were very small. This was because the process of adaptation —of fitting man to bacteria—was complex.

"Most bacteria," Burton observed, "simply can't live within a man long enough to harm him. Conditions are, one way or another, unfavorable. The body is too hot or too cold, too acid or too alkaline, there is too much oxygen or not enough. Man's body is as hostile as Antarctica to most bacteria."

This meant that the chances of an organism from outer space being suited to harm man were very slim. Everyone recognized this, but felt that Wildfire had to be constructed in any event. Burton certainly agreed, but felt in an odd way that his prophecy had come true.

Clearly, the bug they had found could kill men. But it was not really adapted to men, because it killed and died within the organism. It could not be transmitted from corpse to corpse. It existed for a second or two in its host, and then died with it.

Satisfying intellectually, he thought.

But practically speaking they still had to isolate it, understand it, and find a cure.

Burton already knew something about transmission, and something about the mechanism of death: clotting of the blood. The question remained—How did the organisms get into the body?

Because transmission appeared to be airborne, contact with skin and lungs seemed likely. Possibly the organisms burrowed right through the skin surface. Or they might be inhaled. Or both.

How to determine it?

He considered putting protective suitings around an experimental animal to cover all but the mouth. That was possible, but it would take a long time. He sat and worried about the problem for an hour.

Then he hit upon a more likely approach.

He knew that the organism killed by clotting blood. Very likely it would initiate clotting at the point of entrance into the body. If skin, clotting would start near the surface. If lungs, it would begin in the chest, radiating outward.

This was something he could test. By using radioactively tagged blood proteins, and then following his animals with scintillometer scans, he could determine where in the body the blood first clotted.

He prepared a suitable animal, choosing a rhesus monkey because its anatomy was more human than a rat's. He infused the radioactive tagging substance, a magnesium isotope, into the monkey and calibrated the scanner. After allowing equilibration, he tied the monkey down and positioned the scanner overhead.

He was now ready to begin.

The scanner would print out its results on a series of human block outlines. He set the computer printing program and then exposed the rhesus to air containing the lethal microorganism.

Immediately, the printout began to clatter out from the computer:

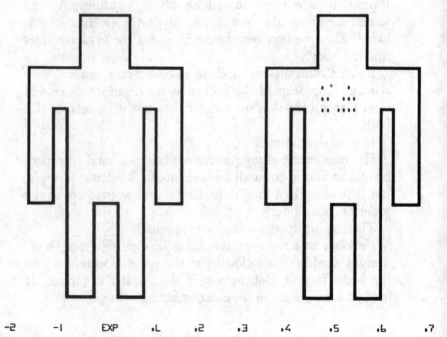

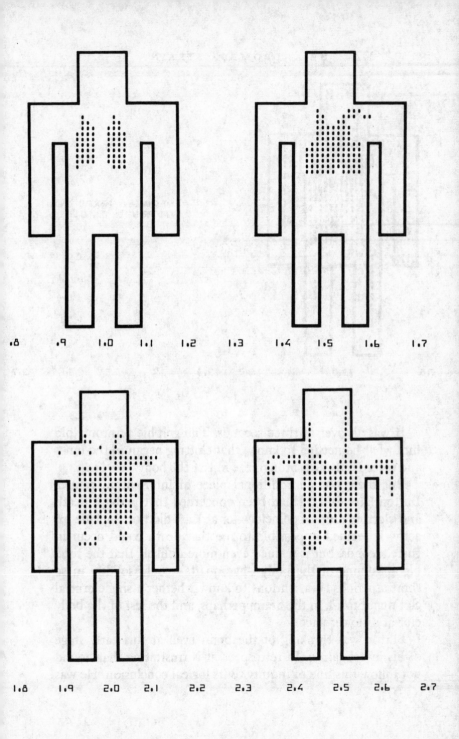

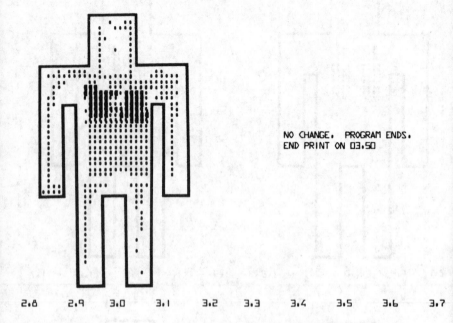

NO CHANGE. PROGRAM ENDS.
END PRINT ON 03.50

2.8   2.9   3.0   3.1   3.2   3.3   3.4   3.5   3.6   3.7

It was all over in three seconds. The graphic printout told him what he needed to know, that clotting began in the lungs and spread outward through the rest of the body.

But there was an additional piece of information gained. Burton later said, "I had been concerned that perhaps death and clotting did not coincide—or at least did not coincide exactly. It seemed impossible to me that death could occur in three seconds, but it seemed even more unlikely that the total blood volume of the body—five quarts—could solidify in so short a period. I was curious to know whether a single crucial clot might form, in the brain, perhaps, and the rest of the body clot at a slower pace."

Burton was thinking of the brain even at this early stage of his investigation. In retrospect, it is frustrating that he did not follow this line of inquiry to its logical conclusion. He was prevented from doing this by the evidence of the scans, which told him that clotting began in the lungs and progressed up the carotid arteries to the brain one or two seconds later.

So Burton lost immediate interest in the brain. And his mistake was compounded by his next experiment.

It was a simple test, not part of the regular Wildfire Protocol. Burton knew that death coincided with blood clotting. If clotting could be prevented, could death be avoided?

He took several rats and injected them with heparin, an anticoagulating drug—preventing blood-clot formation. Heparin was a rapid-acting drug widely used in medicine; its actions were thoroughly understood. Burton injected the drug intravenously in varying amounts, ranging from a low-normal dose to a massively excessive dose.

Then he exposed the rats to air containing the lethal organism.

The first rat, with a low dose, died in five seconds. The others followed within a minute. A single rat with a massive dose lived nearly three minutes, but he also succumbed in the end.

Burton was depressed by the results. Although death was delayed, it was not prevented. The method of symptomatic treatment did not work.

He put the dead rats to one side, and then made his crucial mistake.

Burton did not autopsy the anticoagulated rats.

Instead, he turned his attention to the original autopsy specimens, the first black Norway rat and the first rhesus monkey to be exposed to the capsule. He performed a complete autopsy on these animals, but discarded the anticoagulated animals.

It would be forty-eight hours before he realized his error.

The autopsies he performed were careful and good; he did them slowly, reminding himself that he must overlook nothing. He removed the internal organs from the rat and monkey and examined each, removing samples for both the light and electron microscopes.

To gross inspection, the animals had died of total, intravascular coagulation. The arteries, the heart, lungs, kidneys, liver and spleen—all the blood-containing organs—were rockhard, solid. This was what he had expected.

He carried his tissue slices across the room to prepare frozen sections for microscopic examination. As each section was completed by his technician, he slipped it under the microscope, examined it, and photographed it.

The tissues were normal. Except for the clotted blood, there was nothing unusual about them at all. He knew that these same pieces of tissue would now be sent to the microscopy lab, where another technician would prepare stained sections, using hematoxylin-eosin, periodic acid-Schiff, and Zenker-formalin stains. Sections of nerve would be stained with Nissl and Cajal gold preparations. This process would take an additional twelve to fifteen hours. He could hope, of course, that the stained sections would reveal something more, but he had no reason to believe they would.

Similarly, he was unenthusiastic about the prospects for electron microscopy. The electron microscope was a valuable tool, but occasionally it made things more difficult, not easier. The electron microscope could provide great magnification and clear detail—but only if you knew where to look. It was excellent for examining a single cell, or part of a cell. But first you had to know which cell to examine. And there were billions of cells in a human body.

At the end of ten hours of work, he sat back to consider what he had learned. He drew up a short list:

1. The lethal agent is approximately 1 micron in size. Therefore it is not a gas or molecule, or even a large protein

or virus. It is the size of a cell, and may actually be a cell of some sort.

2.   The lethal agent is transmitted by air. Dead organisms are not infectious.

3.   The lethal agent is inspired by the victim, entering the lungs. There it presumably crosses over into the bloodstream and starts coagulation.

4.   The lethal agent causes death through coagulation. This occurs within seconds, and coincides with total coagulation of the entire body vascular system.

5.   Anticoagulant drugs do not prevent this process.

6.   No other pathologic abnormalities are known to occur in the dying animal.

Burton looked at his list and shook his head. Anticoagulants might not work, but the fact was that *something* stopped the process. There was a way that it could be done. He knew that.

Because two people had survived.

17.

Recovery

AT 1147 HOURS, Mark Hall was bent over the computer, staring at the console that showed the laboratory results from Peter Jackson and the infant. The computer was giving results as they were finished by the automated laboratory equipment; by now, nearly all results were in.

The infant, Hall observed, was normal. The computer did not mince words:

```
SUBJECT CODED   -INFANT- SHOWS ALL LABORATORY VALUES
                  WITHIN NORMAL LIMITS
```

However, Peter Jackson was another problem entirely. His results were abnormal in several respects.

```
SUBJECT CODED   JACKSON, PETER
LABORATORY VALUES NOT WITHIN NORMAL LIMITS FOLLOW
```

TEST	NORMAL	VALUE
HEMATOCRIT	38 - 54	21 INITIAL
		25 REPEAT
		29 REPEAT
		33 REPEAT
		37 REPEAT
BUN	10 - 20	50
COUNTS RETIC	1	6

BLOOD SMEAR SHOWS MANY IMMATURE ERYTHROCYTE FORMS

TEST	NORMAL	VALUE
PRO TIME	12	12
BLOOD PH	7.40	7.31
SGOT	40	75
SED RATE	9	29
AMYLASE	70 - 200	450

Some of the results were easy to understand, others were not. The hematocrit, for example, was rising because Jackson was receiving transfusions of whole blood and packed red cells. The BUN, or blood urea nitrogen, was a test of kidney function and was mildly elevated, probably because of decreased blood flow.

Other analyses were consistent with blood loss. The reticulocyte count was up from 1 to 6 per cent—Jackson had been anemic for some time. He showed immature red-cell forms, which meant that his body was struggling to replace lost blood, and so had to put young, immature red cells into circulation.

The prothrombin time indicated that while Jackson was bleeding from somewhere in his gastrointestinal tract, he had no primary bleeding problem: his blood clotted normally.

The sedimentation rate and SGOT were indices of tissue destruction. Somewhere in Jackson's body, tissues were dying off.

But the pH of the blood was a bit of a puzzle. At 7.31, it was too acid, though not strikingly so. Hall was at a loss to explain this. So was the computer.

```
SUBJECT CODED JACKSON, PETER
DIAGNOSTIC PROBABILITIES
 1. ACUTE AND CHRONIC BLOOD LOSS
    ETIOLOGY GASTROINTESTINAL    .884
    NO OTHER STATISTICALLY SIGNIFICANT
    SOURCES.
 2. ACIDOSIS
    ETIOLOGY UNEXPLAINED
    FURTHER DATA REQUIRED
    SUGGEST HISTORY
```

Hall read the printout and shrugged. The computer might suggest he talk to the patient, but that was easier said than done. Jackson was comatose, and if he had ingested anything to make his blood acid, they would not find out until he revived.

On the other hand, perhaps he could test blood gases. He turned to the computer and punched in a request for blood gases.

The computer responded stubbornly.

PATIENT HISTORY PREFERABLE TO LABORATORY ANALYSES

Hall typed in: "Patient comatose."

The computer seemed to consider this, and then flashed back:

PATIENT MONITORS NOT COMPATIBLE WITH COMA

EEG SHOWS ALPHA WAVES DIAGNOSTIC OF SLEEP

"I'll be damned," Hall said. He looked through the window and saw that Jackson was, indeed, stirring sleepily. He crawled down through the tunnel to his plastic suit and leaned over the patient.

"Mr. Jackson, wake up . . ."

Slowly, he opened his eyes and stared at Hall. He blinked, not believing.

"Don't be frightened," Hall said quietly. "You're sick, and we have been taking care of you. Do you feel better?"

Jackson swallowed, and nodded. He seemed afraid to speak. But the pallor of his skin was gone; his cheeks had a slight pinkish tinge; his fingernails were no longer gray.

"How do you feel now?"

"Okay . . . Who are you?"

"I am Dr. Hall. I have been taking care of you. You were bleeding very badly. We had to give you a transfusion."

He nodded, accepting this quite calmly. Somehow, his manner rung a bell for Hall, who said, "Has this happened to you before?"

"Yes," he said. "Twice."

"How did it happen before?"

"I don't know where I am," he said, looking around the room. "Is this a hospital? Why are you wearing that thing?"

"No, this isn't a hospital. It is a special laboratory in Nevada."

"Nevada?" He closed his eyes and shook his head. "But I'm in Arizona . . ."

"Not now. We brought you here, so we could help you."

"How come that suit?"

"We brought you from Piedmont. There was a disease in Piedmont. You are now in an isolation chamber."

"You mean I'm contagious?"

"Well, we don't know for sure. But we must—"

"Listen," he said, suddenly trying to get up, "this place gives me the creeps. I'm getting out of here. I don't like it here."

He struggled in the bed, trying to move against the straps. Hall pushed him back gently.

"Just relax, Mr. Jackson. Everything will be all right, but you must relax. You've been a sick man."

Slowly, Jackson lay back. Then: "I want a cigarette."

"I'm afraid you can't have one."

"What the hell, I want one."

"I'm sorry, smoking is not allowed—"

"Look here, young fella, when you've lived as long as I have you'll know what you can do and what you can't do. They told me before. None of that Mexican food, no liquor, no butts. I tried it for a spell. You know how that makes a body feel? Terrible, just terrible."

"Who told you?"

"The doctors."

"What doctors?"

"Those doctors in Phoenix. Big fancy hospital, all that shiny equipment and all those shiny white uniforms. Real fancy hospital. I wouldn't have gone there, except for my sister. She insisted. She lives in Phoenix, you know, with that husband of hers, George. Stupid ninny. I didn't want no fancy hospital, I just wanted to rest up, is all. But she insisted, so I went."

"When was this?"

"Last year. June it was, or July."

"Why did you go to the hospital?"

"Why does anybody go to the hospital? I was sick, dammit."

"What was your problem?"

"This damn stomach of mine, same as always."

"Bleeding?"

"Christ, bleeding. Ever time I hiccoughed I came up with blood. Never knew a body had so much blood in it."

"Bleeding in your stomach?"

"Yeah. Like I said, I had it before. All these needles stuck in you"—he nodded to the intravenous lines—"and all the blood going into you. Phoenix last year, and then Tucson the year before that. Now, Tucson was a right nice place. Right nice. Had me a pretty little nurse and all." Abruptly, he closed his mouth. "How old are you, son, anyhow? You don't seem old enough to be a doctor."

"I'm a surgeon," Hall said.

"Surgeon! Oh no you don't. They kept trying to get me to do it, and I kept saying, Not on your sweet life. No indeedy. Not taking it out of me."

"You've had an ulcer for two years?"

"A bit more. The pains started out of the clear blue. Thought I had a touch of indigestion, you know, until the bleeding started up."

A two-year history, Hall thought. Definitely ulcer, not cancer.

"And you went to the hospital?"

"Yep. Fixed me up fine. Warned me off spicy foods and hard stuff and cigarettes. And I tried, sonny, I sure did. But it wasn't no good. A man gets used to his pleasures."

"So in a year, you were back in the hospital."

"Yeah. Big old place in Phoenix, with that stupid ninny George and my sister visiting me every day. He's a book-learning fool, you know. Lawyer. Talks real big, but he hasn't got the sense God gave a grasshopper's behind."

"And they wanted to operate in Phoenix?"

"Sure they did. No offense, sonny, but any doctor'll operate on you, give him half a chance. It's the way they think. I just told them I'd gone this far with my old stomach, and I reckoned I'd finish the stretch with it."

"When did you leave the hospital?"

"Must have been early August sometime. First week, or thereabouts."

"And when did you start smoking and drinking and eating the wrong foods?"

"Now don't lecture me, sonny," Jackson said. "I've been living for sixty-nine years, eating all the wrong foods and doing all the wrong things. I like it that way, and if I can't keep it up, well then the hell with it."

"But you must have had pain," Hall said, frowning.

"Oh, sure, it kicked up some. Specially if I didn't eat. But I found a way to fix that."

"Yes?"

"Sure. They gave me this milk stuff at the hospital, and wanted me to keep on with it. Hundred times a day, in little sips. Milk stuff. Tasted like chalk. But I found a better thing."

"What was that?"

"Aspirin," Jackson said.

"Aspirin?"

"Sure. Works real nice."

"How much aspirin did you take?"

"Fair bit, toward the end. I was doing a bottle a day. You know them bottles it comes in?"

Hall nodded. No wonder the man was acid. Aspirin was acetylsalicylic acid, and if it was taken in sufficient quantities, it would acidify you. Aspirin was a gastric irritant, and it could exacerbate bleeding.

"Didn't anybody tell you aspirin would make the bleeding worse?" he asked.

"Sure," Jackson said. "They told me. But I didn't mind none. Because it stopped the pains, see. That, plus a little squeeze."

"Squeeze?"

"Red-eye. You know."

Hall shook his head. He didn't know.

"Sterno. Pink lady. You take it, see, and put it in cloth, and squeeze it out . . ."

Hall sighed. "You were drinking Sterno," he said.

"Well, only when I couldn't get nothing else. Aspirin and squeeze, see, really kills that pain."

"Sterno isn't only alcohol. It's methanol, too."

"Doesn't hurt you, does it?" Jackson asked, in a voice suddenly concerned.

"As a matter of fact, it does. It can make you go blind, and it can even kill you."

"Well, hell, it made me feel better, so I took it," Jackson said.

"Did this aspirin and squeeze have any effect on you? On your breathing?"

"Well, now you mention it, I was a tad short of breath. But what the hell, I don't need much breath at my age."

Jackson yawned and closed his eyes.

"You're awful full of questions, boy. I want to sleep now."

Hall looked at him, and decided the man was right. It would be best to proceed slowly, at least for a time. He crawled back down the tunnel and out to the main room. He turned to his assistant:

"Our friend Mr. Jackson has a two-year history of ulcer. We'd better keep the blood going in for another couple of units, then we can stop and see what's happening. Drop an NG tube and start icewater lavage."

A gong rang, echoing softly through the room.

"What's that?"

"The twelve-hour mark. It means we have to change our clothing. And it means you have a conference."

"I do? Where?"

"The CR off the dining room."

Hall nodded, and left.

In delta sector, the computers hummed and clicked softly, as Captain Arthur Morris punched through a new program on the console. Captain Morris was a programmer; he had been sent to delta sector by the command on Level I because no MCN messages had been received for nine hours. It was possible, of course, that there had been no priority transmissions; but it was also unlikely.

And if there had been unreceived MCN messages, then the computers were not functioning properly. Captain Morris watched as the computer ran its usual internal check program, which read out as all circuits functioning.

Unsatisfied, he punched in the CHECKLIM program, a more rigorous testing of the circuit banks. It required 0.03 seconds for the machine to come back with its answer: a row of five green lights blinked on the console. He walked over to the teleprinter and watched as it typed:

MACHINE FUNCTION ON ALL CIRCUITS
WITHIN RATIONAL INDICES

He looked and nodded, satisfied. He could not have known, as he stood before the teleprinter, that there was indeed a fault, but that it was purely mechanical, not electronic, and hence could not be tested on the check programs. The fault lay within the teleprinter box itself. There a sliver of paper from the edge of the roll had peeled away and, curling upward, had lodged between the bell and striker, preventing the bell from ringing. It was for this reason that no MCN transmissions had been recorded.

Neither machine nor man was able to catch the error.

18.

The Noon Conference

ACCORDING TO PROTOCOL, the team met every twelve hours for a brief conference, at which results were summarized and new directions planned. In order to save time the conferences were held in a small room off the cafeteria; they could eat and talk at the same time.

Hall was the last to arrive. He slipped into a chair behind his lunch—two glasses of liquid and three pills of different colors—just as Stone said, "We'll hear from Burton first."

Burton shuffled to his feet and in a slow, hesitant voice outlined his experiments and his results. He noted first that he had determined the size of the lethal agent to be one micron.

Stone and Leavitt looked at each other. The green flecks they had seen were much larger than that; clearly, infection could be spread by a mere fraction of the green fleck.

Burton next explained his experiments concerning airborne transmission, and coagulation beginning at the lungs. He finished with his attempts at anticoagulation therapy.

"What about the autopsies?" Stone said. "What did they show?"

"Nothing we don't already know. The blood is clotted

throughout. No other demonstrable abnormalities at the light-microscope level."

"And clotting is initiated at the lungs?"

"Yes. Presumably the organisms cross over to the blood-stream there—or they may release a toxic substance, which crosses over. We may have an answer when the stained sections are finished. In particular, we will be looking for damage to blood vessels, since this releases tissue thromboplastin, and stimulates clotting at the site of damage."

Stone nodded and turned to Hall, who told of the tests carried out on his two patients. He explained that the infant was normal to all tests and that Jackson had a bleeding ulcer, for which he was receiving transfusions.

"He's revived," Hall said. "I talked with him briefly."

Everyone sat up.

"Mr. Jackson is a cranky old goat of sixty-nine who has a two-year history of ulcer. He's bled out twice before: two years ago, and again last year. Each time he was warned to change his habits; each time he went back to his old ways, and began bleeding again. At the time of the Piedmont contact, he was treating his problems with his own regimen: a bottle of aspirin a day, and some Sterno on top of it. He says this left him a little short of breath."

"And made him acidotic as hell," Burton said.

"Exactly."

Methanol, when broken down by the body, was converted to formaldehyde and formic acid. In combination with aspirin, it meant Jackson was consuming great quantities of acid. The body had to maintain its acid-base balance within fairly narrow limits or death would occur. One way to keep the balance was to breathe rapidly, and blow off carbon dioxide, decreasing carbonic acid in the body.

Stone said, "Could this acid have protected him from the organism?"

Hall shrugged. "Impossible to say."

Leavitt said, "What about the infant? Was it anemic?"

"No," Hall said. "But on the other hand, we don't know for sure that it was protected by the same mechanism. It might have something entirely different."

"How about the acid-base balance of the child?"

"Normal," Hall said. "Perfectly normal. At least it is now."

There was a moment of silence. Finally Stone said, "Well, you have some good leads here. The problem remains to discover what, if anything, that child and that old man have in common. Perhaps, as you suggest, there is nothing in common. But for a start, we have to assume that they were protected in the same way, by the same mechanism."

Hall nodded.

Burton said to Stone, "And what have you found in the capsule?"

"We'd better show you," Stone said.

"Show us what?"

"Something we believe may represent the organism," Stone said.

The door said MORPHOLOGY. Inside, the room was partitioned into a place for the experimenters to stand, and a glass-walled isolation chamber further in. Gloves were provided so the men could reach into the chamber and move instruments about.

Stone pointed to the glass dish, and the small fleck of black inside it.

"We think this is our 'meteor,'" he said. "We have found something apparently alive on its surface. There were also other areas within the capsule that may represent life. We've brought the meteor in here to have a look at it under the light microscope."

Reaching through with the gloves, Stone set the glass dish into an opening in a large chrome box, then withdrew his hands.

"The box," he said, "is simply a light microscope fitted with the usual image intensifiers and resolution scanners. We can go up to a thousand diameters with it, projected on the screen here."

Leavitt adjusted dials while Hall and the others stared at the viewer screen.

"Ten power," Leavitt said.

On the screen, Hall saw that the rock was jagged, blackish, dull. Stone pointed out green flecks.

"One hundred power."

The green flecks were larger now, very clear.

"We think that's our organism. We have observed it growing; it turns purple, apparently at the point of mitotic division."

"Spectrum shift?"

"Of some kind."

"One thousand power," Leavitt said.

The screen was filled with a single green spot, nestled down in the jagged hollows of the rock. Hall noticed the surface of the green, which was smooth and glistening, almost oily.

"You think that's a single bacterial colony?"

"We can't be sure it's a colony in the conventional sense," Stone said. "Until we heard Burton's experiments, we didn't think it was a colony at all. We thought it might be a single organism. But obviously the single units have to be a micron or less in size; this is much too big. Therefore it is probably a larger structure—perhaps a colony, perhaps something else."

As they watched, the spot turned purple, and green again.

"It's dividing now," Stone said. "Excellent."

Leavitt switched on the cameras.

"Now watch closely."

The spot turned purple and held the color. It seemed to expand slightly, and for a moment, the surface broke into fragments, hexagonal in shape, like a tile floor.

"Did you see that?"

"It seemed to break up."

"Into six-sided figures."

"I wonder," Stone said, "whether those figures represent single units."

"Or whether they are regular geometric shapes all the time, or just during division?"

"We'll know more," Stone said, "after the EM." He turned to Burton. "Have you finished your autopsies?"

"Yes."

"Can you work the spectrometer?"

"I think so."

"Then do that. It's computerized, anyway. We'll want an analysis of samples of both the rock and the green organism."

"You'll get me a piece?"

"Yes." Stone said to Leavitt: "Can you handle the AA analyzer?"

"Yes."

"Same tests on that."

"And a fractionation?"

"I think so," Stone said. "But you'll have to do that by hand."

Leavitt nodded; Stone turned back to the isolation chamber and removed a glass dish from the light microscope. He set it to one side, beneath a small device that looked like a miniature scaffolding. This was the microsurgical unit.

Microsurgery was a relatively new skill in biology—the ability to perform delicate operations on a single cell. Using microsurgical techniques, it was possible to remove the nucleus from a cell, or part of the cytoplasm, as neatly and cleanly as a surgeon performed an amputation.

The device was constructed to scale down human hand movements into fine, precise miniature motions. A series of gears and servomechanisms carried out the reduction; the movement of a thumb was translated into a shift of a knife blade millionths of an inch.

Using a high magnification viewer, Stone began to chip away delicately at the black rock, until he had two tiny fragments. He set them aside in separate glass dishes and proceeded to scrape away two small fragments from the green area.

Immediately, the green turned purple, and expanded.

"It doesn't like you," Leavitt said, and laughed.

Stone frowned. "Interesting. Do you suppose that's a nonspecific growth response, or a trophic response to injury and irradiation?"

"I think," Leavitt said, "that it doesn't like to be poked at."

"We must investigate further," Stone said.

19.

Crash

FOR ARTHUR MANCHEK, there was a certain kind of horror in the telephone conversation. He received it at home, having just finished dinner and sat down in the living room to read the newspapers. He hadn't seen a newspaper in the last two days, he had been so busy with the Piedmont business.

When the phone rang, he assumed that it must be for his wife, but a moment later she came in and said, "It's for you. The base."

He had an uneasy feeling as he picked up the receiver. "Major Manchek speaking."

"Major, this is Colonel Burns at Unit Eight." Unit Eight was the processing and clearing unit of the base. Personnel checked in and out through Unit Eight, and calls were transmitted through it.

"Yes, Colonel?"

"Sir, we have you down for notification of certain contingencies." His voice was guarded; he was choosing his words carefully on the open line. "I'm informing you now of an RTM crash forty-two minutes ago in Big Head, Utah."

Manchek frowned. Why was he being informed of a routine training-mission crash? It was hardly his province.

"What was it?"

"Phantom, sir. En route San Francisco to Topeka."

"I see," Manchek said, though he did not see at all.

"Sir, Goddard wanted you to be informed in this instance so that you could join the post team."

"Goddard? Why Goddard?" For a moment, as he sat there in the living room, staring at the newspaper headline absently —NEW BERLIN CRISIS FEARED—he thought that the colonel meant Lewis Goddard, chief of the codes section of Vandenberg. Then he realized he meant Goddard Spaceflight Center, outside Washington. Among other things, Goddard acted as collating center for certain special projects that fell between the province of Houston and the governmental agencies in Washington.

"Sir," Colonel Burns said, "the Phantom drifted off its flight plan forty minutes out of San Francisco and passed through Area WF."

Manchek felt himself slowing down. A kind of sleepiness came over him. "Area WF?"

"That is correct, sir."

"When?"

"Twenty minutes before the crash."

"At what altitude?"

"Twenty-three thousand feet, sir."

"When does the post team leave?"

"Half an hour, sir, from the base."

"All right," Manchek said. "I'll be there."

He hung up and stared at the phone lazily. He felt tired; he wished he could go to bed. Area WF was the designation for the cordoned-off radius around Piedmont, Arizona.

They should have dropped the bomb, he thought. They should have dropped it two days ago.

At the time of the decision to delay Directive 7–12, Manchek had been uneasy. But officially he could not express an opinion, and he had waited in vain for the Wildfire team, now located in the underground laboratory, to complain to Washington. He knew Wildfire had been notified; he had seen the cable that went to all security units; it was quite explicit.

Yet for some reason Wildfire had not complained. Indeed, they had paid no attention to it whatever.

Very odd.

And now there was a crash. He lit his pipe and sucked on it, considering the possibilities. Overwhelming was the likelihood that some green trainee had daydreamed, gone off his flight plan, panicked, and lost control of the plane. It had happened before, hundreds of times. The post team, a group of specialists who went out to the site of the wreckage to investigate all crashes, usually returned a verdict of "Agnogenic Systems Failure." It was military doubletalk for crash of unknown cause; it did not distinguish between mechanical failure and pilot failure, but it was known that most systems failures were pilot failures. A man could not afford to daydream when he was running a complex machine at two thousand miles an hour. The proof lay in the statistics: though only 9 per cent of flights occurred after the pilot had taken a leave or weekend pass, these flights accounted for 27 per cent of casualties.

Manchek's pipe went out. He stood, dropping the newspaper, and went into the kitchen to tell his wife he was leaving.

"This is movie country," somebody said, looking at the sandstone cliffs, the brilliant reddish hues, against the deepening blue of the sky. And it was true, many movies had been filmed in this area of Utah. But Manchek could not think of movies now. As he sat in the back of the limousine moving away from the Utah airport, he considered what he had been told.

During the flight from Vandenberg to southern Utah, the post team had heard transcripts of the flight transmission between the Phantom and Topeka Central. For the most part it was dull, except for the final moments before the pilot crashed.

The pilot had said: "Something is wrong."

And then, a moment later, "My rubber air hose is dissolving. It must be the vibration. It's just disintegrating to dust."

Perhaps ten seconds after that, a weak, fading voice said, "Everything made of rubber in the cockpit is dissolving."

There were no further transmissions.

Manchek kept hearing that brief communication, in his mind, over and over. Each time, it sounded more bizarre and terrifying.

He looked out the window at the cliffs. The sun was setting now, and only the tops of the cliffs were lighted by fading reddish sunlight; the valleys lay in darkness. He looked ahead at the other limousine, raising a small dust cloud as it carried the rest of the team to the crash site.

"I used to love westerns," somebody said. "They were all shot out here. Beautiful country."

Manchek frowned. It was astonishing to him how people could spend so much time on irrelevancies. Or perhaps it was just denial, the unwillingness to face reality.

The reality was cold enough: the Phantom had strayed into Area WF, going quite deep for a matter of six minutes before the pilot realized the error and pulled north again. However, once in WF, the plane had begun to lose stability. And it had finally crashed.

He said, "Has Wildfire been informed?"

A member of the group, a psychiatrist with a crew cut—all post teams had at least one psychiatrist—said, "You mean the germ people?"

"Yes."

"They've been told," somebody else said. "It went out on the scrambler an hour ago."

Then, thought Manchek, there would certainly be a reaction from Wildfire. They could not afford to ignore this.

Unless they weren't reading their cables. It had never occurred to him before, but perhaps it was possible—they weren't reading the cables. They were so absorbed in their work, they just weren't bothering.

"There's the wreck," somebody said. "Up ahead."

Each time Manchek saw a wreck, he was astonished. Somehow, one never got used to the idea of the sprawl, the mess—the destructive force of a large metal object striking the earth at thousands of miles an hour. He always expected a neat, tight little clump of metal, but it was never that way.

The wreckage of the Phantom was scattered over two square miles of desert. Standing next to the charred remnants of the left wing, he could barely see the others, on the horizon, near the right wing. Everywhere he looked, there were bits of twisted metal, blackened, paint peeling. He saw one with a small portion of a sign still intact, the stenciled letters clear: DO NOT. The rest was gone.

It was impossible to make anything of the remnants. The fuselage, the cockpit, the canopy were all shattered into a million fragments, and the fires had disfigured everything.

As the sun faded, he found himself standing near the remains of the tail section, where the metal still radiated heat from the smoldering fire. Half-buried in the sand he saw a bit of bone; he picked it up and realized with horror that it was human. Long, and broken, and charred at one end, it had obviously come from an arm or a leg. But it was oddly clean —there was no flesh remaining, only smooth bone.

Darkness descended, and the post team took out their

flashlights, the half-dozen men moving among smoking metal, flashing their yellow beams of light about.

It was late in the evening when a biochemist whose name he did not know came up to talk with him.

"You know," the biochemist said, "it's funny. That transcript about the rubber in the cockpit dissolving."

"How do you mean?"

"Well, no rubber was used in this airplane. It was all a synthetic plastic compound. Newly developed by Ancro; they're quite proud of it. It's a polymer that has some of the same characteristics as human tissue. Very flexible, lots of applications."

Manchek said, "Do you think vibrations could have caused the disintegration?"

"No," the man said. "There are thousands of Phantoms flying around the world. They all have this plastic. None of them has ever had this trouble."

"Meaning?"

"Meaning that I don't know what the hell is going on," the biochemist said.

20.

Routine

SLOWLY, the Wildfire installation settled into a routine, a rhythm of work in the underground chambers of a laboratory where there was no night or day, morning or afternoon. The men slept when they were tired, awoke when they were refreshed, and carried on their work in a number of different areas.

Most of this work was to lead nowhere. They knew that, and accepted it in advance. As Stone was fond of saying, scientific research was much like prospecting: you went out and you hunted, armed with your maps and your instruments, but in the end your preparations did not matter, or even your intuition. You needed your luck, and whatever benefits accrued to the diligent, through sheer, grinding hard work.

Burton stood in the room that housed the spectrometer along with several other pieces of equipment for radioactivity assays, ratio-density photometry, thermocoupling analysis, and preparation for X-ray crystallography.

The spectrometer employed in Level V was the standard Whittington model K-5. Essentially it consisted of a vapor-

izer, a prism, and a recórding screen. The material to be tested
was set in the vaporizer and burned. The light from its burning then passed through the prism, where it was broken down
to a spectrum that was projected onto a recording screen.
Since different elements gave off different wavelengths of
light as they burned, it was possible to analyze the chemical
makeup of a substance by analyzing the spectrum of light
produced.

In theory it was simple, but in practice the reading of
spectrometrograms was complex and difficult. No one in the
Wildfire laboratory was trained to do it well. Thus results
were fed directly into a computer, which performed the analysis. Because of the sensitivity of the computer, rough percentage compositions could also be determined.

Burton placed the first chip, from the black rock, onto the
vaporizer and pressed the button. There was a single bright
burst of intensely hot light; he turned away, avoiding the
brightness, and then put the second chip onto the lamp. Already, he knew, the computer was analyzing the light from
the first chip.

He repeated the process with the green fleck, and then
checked the time. The computer was now scanning the self-
developing photographic plates, which were ready for viewing
in seconds. But the scan itself would take two hours—the
electric eye was very slow.

Once the scan was completed, the computer would analyze
results and print the data within five seconds.

The wall clock told him it was now 1500 hours—three in
the afternoon. He suddenly realized he was tired. He punched
in instructions to the computer to wake him when analysis was
finished. Then he went off to bed.

In another room, Leavitt was carefully feeding similar chips
into a different machine, an amino-acid analyzer. As he did

so, he smiled slightly to himself, for he could remember how it had been in the old days, before AA analysis was automatic.

In the early fifties, the analysis of amino acids in a protein might take weeks, or even months. Sometimes it took years. Now it took hours—or at the very most, a day—and it was fully automatic.

Amino acids were the building blocks of proteins. There were twenty-four known amino acids, each composed of a half-dozen molecules of carbon, hydrogen, oxygen, and nitrogen. Proteins were made by stringing these amino acids together in a line, like a freight train. The order of stringing determined the nature of the protein—whether it was insulin, hemoglobin, or growth hormone. All proteins were composed of the same freight cars, the same units. Some proteins had more of one kind of car than another, or in a different order. But that was the only difference. The same amino acids, the same freight cars, existed in human proteins and flea proteins.

That fact had taken approximately twenty years to discover.

But what controlled the order of amino acids in the protein? The answer turned out to be DNA, the genetic-coding substance, which acted like a switching manager in a freight-yard.

That particular fact had taken another twenty years to discover.

But then once the amino acids were strung together, they began to twist and coil upon themselves; the analogy became closer to a snake than a train. The manner of coiling was determined by the order of acids, and was quite specific: a protein had to be coiled in a certain way, and no other, or it failed to function.

Another ten years.

Rather odd, Leavitt thought. Hundreds of laboratories, thousands of workers throughout the world, all bent on discovering such essentially simple facts. It had all taken years and years, decades of patient effort.

And now there was this machine. The machine would not, of course, give the precise order of amino acids. But it would give a rough percentage composition: so much valine, so much arginine, so much cystine and proline and leucine. And that, in turn, would give a great deal of information.

Yet it was a shot in the dark, this machine. Because they had no reason to believe that either the rock or the green organism was composed even partially of proteins. True, every living thing on earth had at least some proteins—but that didn't mean life elsewhere had to have it.

For a moment, he tried to imagine life without proteins. It was almost impossible: on earth, proteins were part of the cell wall, and comprised all the enzymes known to man. And life without enzymes? Was that possible?

He recalled the remark of George Thompson, the British biochemist, who had called enzymes "the matchmakers of life." It was true; enzymes acted as catalysts for all chemical reactions, by providing a surface for two molecules to come together and react upon. There were hundreds of thousands, perhaps millions, of enzymes, each existing solely to aid a single chemical reaction. Without enzymes, there could be no chemical reactions.

Without chemical reactions, there could be no life.

Or could there?

It was a long-standing problem. Early in planning Wildfire, the question had been posed: How do you study a form of life totally unlike any you know? How would you even know it was alive?

This was not an academic matter. Biology, as George Wald had said, was a unique science because it could not define its subject matter. Nobody had a definition for life. Nobody knew what it was, really. The old definitions—an organism that showed ingestion, excretion, metabolism, reproduction, and so on—were worthless. One could always find exceptions.

The group had finally concluded that energy conversion was the hallmark of life. All living organisms in some way took in energy—as food, or sunlight—and converted it to another form of energy, and put it to use. (Viruses were the exception to this rule, but the group was prepared to define viruses as nonliving.)

For the next meeting, Leavitt was asked to prepare a rebuttal to the definition. He pondered it for a week, and returned with three objects: a swatch of black cloth, a watch, and a piece of granite. He set them down before the group and said, "Gentlemen, I give you three living things."

He then challenged the team to prove that they were not living. He placed the black cloth in the sunlight; it became warm. This, he announced, was an example of energy conversion—radiant energy to heat.

It was objected that this was merely passive energy absorption, not conversion. It was also objected that the conversion, if it could be called that, was not purposeful. It served no function.

"How do you know it is not purposeful?" Leavitt had demanded.

They then turned to the watch. Leavitt pointed to the radium dial, which glowed in the dark. Decay was taking place, and light was being produced.

The men argued that this was merely release of potential energy held in unstable electron levels. But there was growing confusion; Leavitt was making his point.

Finally, they came to the granite. "This is alive," Leavitt said. "It is living, breathing, walking, and talking. Only we cannot see it, because it is happening too slowly. Rock has a lifespan of three billion years. We have a lifespan of sixty or seventy years. We cannot see what is happening to this rock for the same reason that we cannot make out the tune on a record being played at the rate of one revolution every century. And the rock, for its part, is not even aware of our existence because we are alive for only a brief instant of its lifespan. To it, we are like flashes in the dark."

He held up his watch.

His point was clear enough, and they revised their thinking in one important respect. They conceded that it was possible that they might not be able to analyze certain life forms. It was possible that they might not be able to make the slightest headway, the least beginning, in such an analysis.

But Leavitt's concerns extended beyond this, to the general problem of action in uncertainty. He recalled reading Talbert Gregson's "Planning the Unplanned" with close attention, poring over the complex mathematical models the author had devised to analyze the problem. It was Gregson's conviction that:

> All decisions involving uncertainty fall within two distinct categories—those with contingencies, and those without. The latter are distinctly more difficult to deal with.
>
> Most decisions, and nearly all human interaction, can be incorporated into a contingencies model. For example, a President may start a war, a man may sell his business, or divorce his wife. Such an action will produce a reaction; the number of reactions is infinite but the number of *probable* reactions is manageably small. Before making a decision, an individual can predict various reactions, and he can assess his original, or primary-mode, decision more effectively.
>
> But there is also a category which cannot be analyzed by contingencies. This category involves events and situations which are *absolutely* unpredictable, not merely disasters of all sorts, but those also including rare moments of discovery and insight, such as those which produced the laser, or penicillin. Because these moments are unpredictable, they cannot be planned for in any logical manner. The mathematics are wholly unsatisfactory.

We may only take comfort in the fact that such situations, for ill or for good, are exceedingly rare.

Jeremy Stone, working with infinite patience, took a flake of the green material and dropped it into molten plastic. The plastic was the size and shape of a medicine capsule. He waited until the flake was firmly imbedded, and poured more plastic over it. He then transferred the plastic pill to the curing room.

Stone envied the others their mechanized routines. The preparation of samples for electron microscopy was still a delicate task requiring skilled human hands; the preparation of a good sample was as demanding a craft as that ever practiced by an artisan—and took almost as long to learn. Stone had worked for five years before he became proficient at it.

The plastic was cured in a special high-speed processing unit, but it would still take five hours to harden to proper consistency. The curing room would maintain a constant temperature of 61° C. with a relative humidity of 10 per cent.

Once the plastic was hardened, he would scrape it away, and then flake off a small bit of green with a microtome. This would go into the electron microscope. The flake would have to be of the right thickness and size, a small round shaving 1,500 angstroms in depth, no more.

Only then could he look at the green stuff, whatever it was, at sixty thousand diameters magnification.

That, he thought, would be interesting.

In general, Stone believed the work was going well. They were making fine progress, moving forward in several promising lines of inquiry. But most important, they had time. There was no rush, no panic, no need to fear.

The bomb had been dropped on Piedmont. That would destroy airborne organisms, and neutralize the source of infection. Wildfire was the only place that any further infection could spread from, and Wildfire was specifically designed to prevent that. Should isolation be broken in the lab, the areas that were contaminated would automatically seal off. Within a half-second, sliding airtight doors would close, producing a new configuration for the lab.

This was necessary because past experience in other laboratories working in so-called axenic, or germ-free, atmospheres indicated that contamination occurred in 15 per cent of cases. The reasons were usually structural—a seal burst, a glove tore, a seam split—but the contamination occurred, nonetheless.

At Wildfire, they were prepared for that eventuality. But if it did not happen, and the odds were it would not, then they could work safely here for an indefinite period. They could spend a month, even a year, working on the organism. There was no problem, no problem at all.

Hall walked through the corridor, looking at the atomic-detonator substations. He was trying to memorize their positions. There were five on the floor, positioned at intervals along the central corridor. Each was the same: small silver boxes no larger than a cigarette packet. Each had a lock for the key, a green light that was burning, and a dark-red light.

Burton had explained the mechanism earlier. "There are sensors in all the duct systems and in all the labs. They monitor the air in the rooms by a variety of chemical, electronic, and straight bioassay devices. The bioassay is just a mouse whose heartbeat is being monitored. If anything goes wrong with the sensors, the lab automatically seals off. If the whole floor is contaminated, it will seal off, and the atomic device will cut in. When that happens, the green light will go out, and the red light will begin to blink. That signals the start of the three-minute interval. Unless you lock in your key, the bomb will go off at the end of three minutes."

"And I have to do it myself?"

Burton nodded. "The key is steel. It is conductive. The

lock has a system which measures the capacitance of the person holding the key. It responds to general body size, particularly weight, and also the salt content of sweat. It's quite specific, actually, for you."

"So I'm really the only one?"

"You really are. And you only have one key. But there's a complicating problem. The blueprints weren't followed exactly; we only discovered the error after the lab was finished and the device installed. But there is an error: we are short three detonator substations. There are only five, instead of eight."

"Meaning?"

"Meaning that if the floor starts to contaminate, you must rush to locate yourself at a substation. Otherwise there is a chance you could be sealed off in a sector without a substation. And then, in the event of a malfunction of the bacteriologic sensors, a false positive malfunction, the laboratory could be destroyed needlessly."

"That seems a rather serious error in planning."

"It turns out," Burton said, "that three new substations were going to be added next month. But that won't help us now. Just keep the problem in mind, and everything'll be all right."

Leavitt awoke quickly, rolling out of bed and starting to dress. He was excited: he had just had an idea. A fascinating thing, wild, crazy, but fascinating as hell.

It had come from his dream.

He had been dreaming of a house, and then of a city—a huge, complex, interconnecting city around the house. A man lived in the house, with his family; the man lived and worked and commuted within the city, moving about, acting, reacting.

And then, in the dream, the city was suddenly eliminated, leaving only the house. How different things were then! A

single house, standing alone, without the things it needed—
water, plumbing, electricity, streets. And a family, cut off
from the supermarkets, schools, drugstores. And the husband,
whose work was in the city, interrelated to others in the city,
suddenly stranded.

The house became a different organism altogether. And
from that to the Wildfire organism was but a single step, a
single leap of the imagination . . .

He would have to discuss it with Stone. Stone would laugh,
as usual—Stone always laughed—but he would also pay attention. Leavitt knew that, in a sense, he operated as the idea
man for the team. The man who would always provide the
most improbable, mind-stretching theories.

Well, Stone would at least be interested.

He glanced at the clock. 2200 hours. Getting on toward
midnight. He hurried to dress.

He took out a new paper suit and slipped his feet in. The
paper was cool against his bare flesh.

And then suddenly it was warm. A strange sensation. He
finished dressing, stood, and zipped up the one-piece suit. As
he left, he looked once again at the clock.

2210.

Oh, Christ, he thought.

It had happened again. And this time, for ten minutes.
What had gone on? He couldn't remember. But it was ten
minutes gone, disappeared, while he had dressed—an action
that shouldn't have taken more than thirty seconds.

He sat down again on the bed, trying to remember, but he
could not.

Ten minutes gone.

It was terrifying. Because it was happening again, though he
had hoped it would not. It hadn't happened for months, but
now, with the excitement, the odd hours, the break in his
normal hospital schedule, it was starting once more.

For a moment, he considered telling the others, then shook

his head. He'd be all right. It wouldn't happen again. He was going to be just fine.

He stood. He had been on his way to see Stone, to talk to Stone about something. Something important and exciting.

He paused.

He couldn't remember.

The idea, the image, the excitement was gone. Vanished, erased from his mind.

He knew then that he should tell Stone, admit the whole thing. But he knew what Stone would say and do if he found out. And he knew what it would mean to his future, to the rest of his life, once the Wildfire Project was finished. Everything would change, if people knew. He couldn't ever be normal again—he would have to quit his job, do other things, make endless adjustments. He couldn't even drive a car.

No, he thought. He would not say anything. And he would be all right: as long as he didn't look at blinking lights.

Jeremy Stone was tired, but knew he was not ready for sleep. He paced up and down the corridors of the laboratory, thinking about the birds at Piedmont. He ran over everything they had done: how they had seen the birds, how they had gassed them with chlorazine, and how the birds had died. He went over it in his mind, again and again.

Because he was missing something. And that something was bothering him.

At the time, while he had been inside Piedmont itself, it had bothered him. Then he had forgotten, but his nagging doubts had been revived at the noon conference, while Hall was discussing the patients.

Something Hall had said, some fact he had mentioned, was related, in some off way, to the birds. But what was it? What was the exact thought, the precise words, that had triggered the association?

Stone shook his head. He simply couldn't dig it out. The clues, the connection, the keys were all there, but he couldn't bring them to the surface.

He pressed his hands to his head, squeezing against the bones, and he damned his brain for being so stubborn.

Like many intelligent men, Stone took a rather suspicious attitude toward his own brain, which he saw as a precise and skilled but temperamental machine. He was never surprised when the machine failed to perform, though he feared those moments, and hated them. In his blackest hours, Stone doubted the utility of all thought, and all intelligence. There were times when he envied the laboratory rats he worked with; their brains were so simple. Certainly they did not have the intelligence to destroy themselves; that was a peculiar invention of man.

He often argued that human intelligence was more trouble than it was worth. It was more destructive than creative, more confusing than revealing, more discouraging than satisfying, more spiteful than charitable.

There were times when he saw man, with his giant brain, as equivalent to the dinosaurs. Every schoolboy knew that dinosaurs had outgrown themselves, had become too large and ponderous to be viable. No one ever thought to consider whether the human brain, the most complex structure in the known universe, making fantastic demands on the human body in terms of nourishment and blood, was not analogous. Perhaps the human brain had become a kind of dinosaur for man and perhaps, in the end, would prove his downfall.

Already, the brain consumed one quarter of the body's blood supply. A fourth of all blood pumped from the heart went to the brain, an organ accounting for only a small percentage of body mass. If brains grew larger, and better, then perhaps they would consume more—perhaps so much that, like an infection, they would overrun their hosts and kill the bodies that transported them.

Or perhaps, in their infinite cleverness, they would find a way to destroy themselves and each other. There were times when, as he sat at State Department or Defense Department meetings, and looked around the table, he saw nothing more than a dozen gray, convoluted brains sitting on the table. No flesh and blood, no hands, no eyes, no fingers. No mouths, no sex organs—all these were superfluous.

Just brains. Sitting around, trying to decide how to outwit other brains, at other conference tables.

Idiotic.

He shook his head, thinking that he was becoming like Leavitt, conjuring up wild and improbable schemes.

Yet, there was a sort of logical consequence to Stone's ideas. If you really feared and hated your brain, you would attempt to destroy it. Destroy your own, and destroy others.

"I'm tired," he said aloud, and looked at the wall clock. It was 2340 hours—almost time for the midnight conference.

21.

The Midnight Conference

THEY MET AGAIN, in the same room, in the same way. Stone glanced at the others and saw they were tired; no one, including himself, was getting enough sleep.

"We're going at this too hard," he said. "We don't need to work around the clock, and we shouldn't do so. Tired men will make mistakes, mistakes in thinking and mistakes in action. We'll start to drop things, to screw things up, to work sloppily. And we'll make wrong assumptions, draw incorrect inferences. That mustn't happen."

The team agreed to get at least six hours sleep in each twenty-four-hour period. That seemed reasonable, since there was no problem on the surface; the infection at Piedmont had been halted by the atomic bomb.

Their belief might never have been altered had not Leavitt suggested that they file for a code name. Leavitt stated that they had an organism and that it required a code. The others agreed.

In a corner of the room stood the scrambler typewriter. It had been clattering all day long, typing out material sent in from the outside. It was a two-way machine; material transmitted had to be typed in lowercase letters, while received material was printed out in capitals.

No one had really bothered to look at the input since their arrival on Level V. They were all too busy; besides, most of the input had been routine military dispatches that were sent to Wildfire but did not concern it. This was because Wildfire was one of the Cooler Circuit substations, known facetiously as the Top Twenty. These substations were linked to the basement of the White House and were the twenty most important strategic locations in the country. Other substations included Vandenberg, Kennedy, NORAD, Patterson, Detrick, and Virginia Key.

Stone went to the typewriter and printed out his message. The message was directed by computer to Central Codes, a station that handled the coding of all projects subsumed under the system of Cooler.

The transmission was as follows:

open line to transmit
UNDERSTAND TRANSMIT STATE ORIGIN
stone project wildfire
STATE DESTINATION
central codes
UNDERSTAND CENTRAL CODES
message follows
SEND
have isolated extraterrestrial organism secondary to return
of scoop seven wish coding for organism
end message
TRANSMITTED

There followed a long pause. The scrambler teleprinter hummed and clicked, but printed nothing. Then the typewriter began to spit out a message on a long roll of paper.

MESSAGE FROM CENTRAL CODES FOLLOWS
UNDERSTAND ISOLATION OF NEW ORGANISM PLEASE
CHARACTERIZE
END MESSAGE

Stone frowned. "But we don't know enough." However, the teleprinter was impatient:

TRANSMIT REPLY TO CENTRAL CODES

After a moment, Stone typed back:

message to central codes follows
cannot characterize at this time but suggest
tentative classification as bacterial strain
end message

MESSAGE FROM CENTRAL CODES FOLLOWS

UNDERSTAND REQUEST FOR BACTERIAL CLASSIFICATION
OPENING NEW CATEGORY CLASSIFICATION ACCORDING TO
ICDA STANDARD REFERENCE
CODE FOR YOUR ORGANISM WILL BE ANDROMEDA
CODE WILL READ OUT ANDROMEDA STRAIN
FILED UNDER ICDA LISTINGS AS 053.9 [UNSPECIFIED ORGANISM]
FURTHER FILING AS E866 [AIRCRAFT ACCIDENT]
THIS FILING REPRESENTS CLOSEST FIT TO
ESTABLISHED CATEGORIES

Stone smiled. "It seems we don't fit the established categories."

He typed back:

understand coding as andromeda strain
accepted
end message
TRANSMITTED

"Well," Stone said, "that's that."

Burton had been looking over the sheaves of paper behind the teleprinter. The teleprinter wrote its messages out on a long roll of paper, which fell into a box. There were dozens of yards of paper that no one had looked at.

Silently, he read a single message, tore it from the rest of the strip, and handed it to Stone.

```
1134/443/KK/Y-U/9
INFORMATION STATUS
TRANSMIT TO ALL STATIONS
CLASSIFICATION TOP SECRET

REQUEST FOR DIRECTIVE 7-12 RECEIVED TODAY BY
EXEC AND NSC-COBRA
ORIGIN VANDENBERG/WILDFIRE
CORROBORATION NASA/AMC
AUTHORITY PRIMARY MANCHEK, ARTHUR, MAJOR USA
IN CLOSED SESSION THIS DIRECTIVE HAS NOT
BEEN ACTED UPON
FINAL DECISION HAS BEEN POSTPONED TWENTY
FOUR TO FORTY EIGHT HOURS
RECONSIDERATION AT THAT TIME
ALTERNATIVE TROOP DEPLOYMENT ACCORDING TO
DIRECTIVE 7-11 NOW IN EFFECT
NO NOTIFICATION
END MESSAGE

TRANSMIT ALL STATIONS
CLASSIFICATION TOP SECRET
END TRANSMISSION
```

The team stared at the message in disbelief. No one said anything for a long time. Finally, Stone ran his fingers along the upper corner of the sheet and said in a low voice, "This was a 443. That makes it an MCN transmission. It should have rung the bell down here."

"There's no bell on this teleprinter," Leavitt said. "Only on Level I, at sector five. But they're supposed to notify us whenever—"

"Get sector five on the intercom," Stone said.

Ten minutes later, the horrified Sergeant Morris had connected Stone to Robertson, the head of the President's Science Advisory Committee, who was in Houston.

Stone spoke for several minutes with Robertson, who expressed initial surprise that he hadn't heard from Wildfire earlier. There then followed a heated discussion of the President's decision not to call a Directive 7–12.

"The President doesn't trust scientists," Robertson said. "He doesn't feel comfortable with them."

"It's your job to make him comfortable," Stone said, "and you haven't been doing it."

"Jeremy—"

"There are only two sources of contamination," Stone said. "Piedmont, and this installation. We're adequately protected here, but Piedmont—"

"Jeremy, I agree the bomb should have been dropped."

"Then work on him. Stay on his back. Get him to call a 7–12 as soon as possible. It may already be too late."

Robertson said he would, and would call back. Before he hung up, he said, "By the way, any thoughts about the Phantom?"

"The what?"

"The Phantom that crashed in Utah."

There was a moment of confusion before the Wildfire group understood that they had missed still another important teleprinter message.

"Routine training mission. The jet strayed over the closed zone, though. That's the puzzle."

"Any other information?"

"The pilot said something about his air hose dissolving. Vibration, or something. His last communication was pretty bizarre."

"Like he was crazy?" Stone asked.

"Like that," Robertson said.

"Is there a team at the wreck site now?"

"Yes, we're waiting for information from them. It could come at any time."

"Pass it along," Stone said. And then he stopped. "If a 7–11 was ordered, instead of a 7–12," he said, "then you have troops in the area around Piedmont."

"National Guard, yes."

"That's pretty damned stupid," Stone said.

"Look, Jeremy, I agree—"

"When the first one dies," Stone said, "I want to know when, and how. And most especially, *where*. The wind there is from the east predominantly. If you start losing men west of Piedmont—"

"I'll call, Jeremy," Robertson said.

The conversation ended, and the team shuffled out of the conference room. Hall remained behind a moment, going through some of the rolls in the box, noting the messages. The majority were unintelligible to him, a weird set of non-sense messages and codes. After a time he gave up; he did so before he came upon the reprinted news item concerning the peculiar death of Officer Martin Willis, of the Arizona highway patrol.

day 4

SPREAD

22

The Analysis

WITH THE NEW PRESSURES of time, the results of spectrometry and amino-acid analysis, previously of peripheral interest, suddenly became matters of major concern. It was hoped that these analyses would tell, in a rough way, how foreign the Andromeda organism was to earth life forms.

It was thus with interest that Leavitt and Burton looked over the computer printout, a column of figures written on green paper:

```
MASS SPECTROMETRY DATA OUTPUT
PRINT
PERCENTAGE OUTPUT SAMPLE I  - BLACK OBJECT UNIDENTIFIED ORIGIN -
```

H	HE								
21.07	0								
LI	BE	B	C	N	O	F			
0	0	0	54.90	0	18.00	0			
NA	MG	AL	SI	P	S	CL			
0	0	0	00.20	-	01.01	0			
K	CA	SC	TI	V	CR	MN	FE	CO	NI
0	0	0	-	-	-	-	-	-	-
CU	ZN	GA	GE	AS	SE	BR			
-	-	0	0	0	00.34	0			

```
ALL HEAVIER METALS SHOW ZERO CONTENT


SAMPLE 2  - GREEN OBJECT UNIDENTIFIED ORIGIN -


H      HE
27.00  0
LI     BE     B      C      N      O      F
0      0      0      45.00  05.00  23.00  0


ALL HEAVIER METALS SHOW ZERO CONTENT


END PRINT


END PROGRAM


- STOP -
```

What all this meant was simple enough. The black rock contained hydrogen, carbon, and oxygen, with significant amounts of sulfur, silicon, and selenium, and with trace quantities of several other elements.

The green spot, on the other hand, contained hydrogen, carbon, nitrogen, and oxygen. Nothing else at all. The two men found it peculiar that the rock and the green spot should be so similar in chemical makeup. And it was peculiar that the green spot should contain nitrogen, while the rock contained none at all.

The conclusion was obvious: the "black rock" was not rock at all, but some kind of material similar to earthly organic life. It was something akin to plastic.

And the green spot, presumably alive, was composed of elements in roughly the same proportion as earth life. On earth, these same four elements—hydrogen, carbon, nitrogen, and oxygen—accounted for 99 per cent of all the elements in life organisms.

The men were encouraged by these results, which suggested similarity between the green spot and life on earth. Their hopes were, however, short-lived as they turned to the amino-acid analysis:

```
AMINO ACID ANALYSIS DATA OUTPUT
PRINT
SAMPLE 1  - BLACK OBJECT UNIDENTIFIED ORIGIN -
SAMPLE 2  - GREEN OBJECT UNIDENTIFIED ORIGIN -
```

	SAMPLE 1	SAMPLE 2
NEUTRAL AMINO ACIDS		
GLYCINE	00.00	00.00
ALANINE	00.00	00.00
VALINE	00.00	00.00
ISOLEUCINE	00.00	00.00
SERINE	00.00	00.00
THREONINE	00.00	00.00
LEUCINE	00.00	00.00
AROMATIC AMINO ACIDS		
PHENYLALANINE	00.00	00.00
TYROSINE	00.00	00.00
TRYPTOPHAN	00.00	00.00
SULFURIC AMINO ACIDS		
CYSTINE	00.00	00.00
CYSTEINE	00.00	00.00
METHIONINE	00.00	00.00

	SAMPLE 1	SAMPLE 2
SECONDARY AMINO ACIDS		
PROLINE	00.00	00.00
HYDROXYPROLINE	00.00	00.00
DICARBOXYLIC AMINO ACIDS		
ASPARTIC ACID	00.00	00.00
GLUTAMIC ACID	00.00	00.00
BASIC AMINO ACIDS		
HISTIDINE	00.00	00.00
ARGININE	00.00	00.00
LYSINE	00.00	00.00
HYDROXYLYSINE	00.00	00.00
TOTAL AMINO ACID CONTENT		
	00.00	00.00

END PRINT
END PROGRAM

- STOP -

"Christ," Leavitt said, staring at the printed sheet. "Will you look at that."

"No amino acids," Burton said. "No proteins."

"Life without proteins," Leavitt said. He shook his head; it seemed as if his worst fears were realized.

On earth, organisms had evolved by learning to carry out

biochemical reactions in a small space, with the help of protein enzymes. Biochemists were now learning to duplicate these reactions, but only by isolating a single reaction from all others.

Living cells were different. There, within a small area, reactions were carried out that provided energy, growth, and movement. There was no separation, and man could not duplicate this any more than a man could prepare a complete dinner from appetizers to dessert by mixing together the ingredients for everything into a single large dish, cooking it, and hoping to separate the apple pie from the cheese dip later on.

Cells could keep the hundreds of separate reactions straight, using enzymes. Each enzyme was like a single worker in a kitchen, doing just one thing. Thus a baker could not make a steak, any more than a steak griller could use his equipment to prepare appetizers.

But enzymes had a further use. They made possible chemical reactions that otherwise would not occur. A biochemist could duplicate the reactions by using great heat, or great pressure, or strong acids. But the human body, or the individual cell, could not tolerate such extremes of environment. Enzymes, the matchmakers of life, helped chemical reactions to go forward at body temperature and atmospheric pressure.

Enzymes were essential to life on earth. But if another form of life had learned to do without them, it must have evolved in a wholly different way.

Therefore, they were dealing with an entirely alien organism.

And this in turn meant that analysis and neutralization would take much, much longer.

In the room marked MORPHOLOGY, Jeremy Stone removed the small plastic capsule in which the green fleck had been imbedded. He set the now-hard capsule into a vise, fixing it firmly, and then took a dental drill to it, shaving away the plastic until he exposed bare green material.

This was a delicate process, requiring many minutes of concentrated work. At the end of that time, he had shaved the plastic in such a way that he had a pyramid of plastic, with the green fleck at the peak of the pyramid.

He unscrewed the vise and lifted the plastic out. He took it to the microtome, a knife with a revolving blade that cut very thin slices of plastic and imbedded green tissue. These slices were round; they fell from the plastic block into a dish of water. The thickness of the slice could be measured by looking at the light as it reflected off the slices—if the light was faint silver, the slice was too thick. If, on the other hand, it was a rainbow of colors, then it was the right thickness, just a few molecules in depth.

That was how thick they wanted a slice of tissue to be for the electron microscope.

When Stone had a suitable piece of tissue, he lifted it carefully with forceps and set it onto a small round copper grid. This in turn was inserted into a metal button. Finally, the button was set into the electron microscope, and the microscope sealed shut.

The electron microscope used by Wildfire was the BVJ model JJ-42. It was a high-intensity model with an image-resolution attachment. In principle, the electron microscope was simple enough: it worked exactly like a light microscope, but instead of focusing light rays, it focused an electron beam. Light is focused by lenses of curved glass. Electrons are focused by magnetic fields.

In many respects, the EM was not a great deal different from television, and in fact, the image was displayed on a television screen, a coated surface that glowed when electrons struck it. The great advantage of the electron microscope was that it could magnify objects far more than the light microscope. The reason for this had to do with quantum mechanics and the waveform theory of radiation. The best simple explanation had come from the electron microscopist Sidney Polton, also a racing enthusiast.

"Assume," Polton said, "that you have a road, with a sharp corner. Now assume that you have two automobiles, a sports car and a large truck. When the truck tries to go around the corner, it slips off the road; but the sports car manages it easily. Why? The sports car is lighter, and smaller, and faster; it is better suited to tight, sharp curves. On large, gentle curves, the automobiles will perform equally well, but on sharp curves, the sports car will do better.

"In the same way, an electron microscope will 'hold the road' better than a light microscope. All objects are made of corners, and edges. The electron wavelength is smaller than the quantum of light. It cuts the corners closer, follows the road better, and outlines it more precisely. With a light microscope—like a truck—you can follow only a large road. In microscopic terms this means only a large object, with large edges and gentle curves: cells, and nuclei. But an electron microscope can follow all the minor routes, the byroads, and can outline very small structures within the cell—micochondria, ribosomes, membranes, reticula."

In actual practice there were several drawbacks to the electron microscope, which counterbalanced its great powers of magnification. For one thing, because it used electrons instead of light, the inside of the microscope had to be a vacuum. This meant it was impossible to examine living creatures.

But the most serious drawback had to do with the sections of specimen. These were extremely thin, making it difficult to get a good three-dimensional concept of the object under study.

Again, Polton had a simple analogy. "Let us say you cut an

automobile in half down the middle. In that case, you could guess the complete, 'whole' structure. But if you cut a very thin slice from the automobile, and if you cut it on a strange angle, it could be more difficult. In your slice, you might have only a bit of bumper, and rubber tire, and glass. From such a slice, it would be hard to guess the shape and function of the full structure."

Stone was aware of all the drawbacks as he fitted the metal button into the EM, sealed it shut, and started the vacuum pump. He knew the drawbacks and he ignored them, because he had no choice. Limited as it was, the electron microscope was their only available high-power tool.

He turned down the room lights and clicked on the beam. He adjusted several dials to focus the beam. In a moment, the image came into focus, green and black on the screen.

It was incredible.

Jeremy Stone found himself staring at a single unit of the organism. It was a perfect, six-sided hexagon, and it interlocked with other hexagons on each side. The interior of the hexagon was divided into wedges, each meeting at the precise center of the structure. The overall appearance was accurate, with a kind of mathematical precision he did not associate with life on earth.

It looked like a crystal.

He smiled: Leavitt would be pleased. Leavitt liked spectacular, mind-stretching things. Leavitt had also frequently considered the possibility that life might be based upon crystals of some kind, that it might be ordered in some regular pattern.

He decided to call Leavitt in.

As soon as he arrived, Leavitt said, "Well, there's our answer."

"Answer to what?"

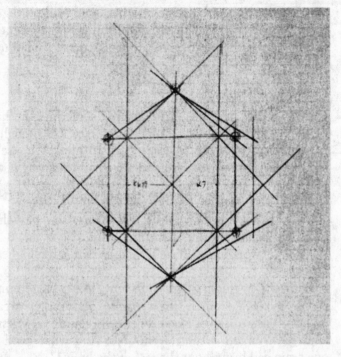

Early sketch by Jeremy Stone of hexagonal Andromeda configuration.

Photo courtesy Project Wildfire

"To how this organism functions. I've seen the results of spectrometry and amino-acid analysis."

"And?"

"The organism is made of hydrogen, carbon, oxygen, and nitrogen. But it has no amino acids at all. None. Which means that it has no proteins as we know them, and no enzymes. I was wondering how it could survive without protein-based organization. Now I know."

"The crystalline structure."

"Looks like it," Leavitt said, peering at the screen. "In three dimensions, it's probably a hexagonal slab, like a piece of tile. Eight-sided, with each face a hexagon. And on the inside, those wedge-shaped compartments leading to the center."

"They would serve to separate biochemical functions quite well."

"Yes," Leavitt said. He frowned.

"Something the matter?"

Leavitt was thinking, remembering something he had forgotten. A dream, about a house and a city. He thought for a moment and it began to come back to him. A house and a city. The way the house worked alone, and the way it worked in a city.

It all came back.

"You know," he said, "it's interesting, the way this one unit interlocks with the others around it."

"You're wondering if we're seeing part of a higher organism?"

"Exactly. Is this unit self-sufficient, like a bacterium, or is it just a block from a larger organ, or a larger organism? After all, if you saw a single liver cell, could you guess what kind of an organ it came from? No. And what good would one brain cell be without the rest of the brain?"

Stone stared at the screen for a long time. "A rather unusual pair of analogies. Because the liver can regenerate, can grow back, but the brain cannot."

Leavitt smiled. "The Messenger Theory."

"One wonders," Stone said.

The Messenger Theory had come from John R. Samuels, a communications engineer. Speaking before the Fifth Annual Conference on Astronautics and Communication, he had reviewed some theories about the way in which an alien culture might choose to contact other cultures. He argued that the most advanced concepts in communications in earth technology were inadequate, and that advanced cultures would find better methods.

"Let us say a culture wishes to scan the universe," he said.

"Let us say they wish to have a sort of 'coming-out party' on a galactic scale—to formally announce their existence. They wish to spew out information, clues to their existence, in every direction. What is the best way to do this? Radio? Hardly—radio is too slow, too expensive, and it decays too rapidly. Strong signals weaken within a few billion miles. TV is even worse. Light rays are fantastically expensive to generate. Even if one learned a way to detonate whole stars, to explode a sun as a kind of signal, it would be costly.

"Besides expense, all these methods suffer the traditional drawback to any radiation, namely decreasing strength with distance. A light bulb may be unbearably bright at ten feet; it may be powerful at a thousand feet; it may be visible at ten miles. But at a million miles, it is completely obscure, because radiant energy decreases according to the fourth power of the radius. A simple, unbeatable law of physics.

"So you do not use physics to carry your signal. You use biology. You create a communications system that does not diminish with distance, but rather remains as powerful a million miles away as it was at the source.

"In short, you devise an organism to carry your message. The organism would be self-replicating, cheap, and could be produced in fantastic numbers. For a few dollars, you could produce trillions of them, and send them off in all directions into space. They would be tough, hardy bugs, able to withstand the rigors of space, and they would grow and duplicate and divide. Within a few years, there would be countless numbers of these in the galaxy, speeding in all directions, waiting to contact life.

"And when they did? Each single organism would carry the potential to develop into a full organ, or a full organism. They would, upon contacting life, begin to grow into a complete communicating mechanism. It is like spewing out a billion brain cells, each capable of regrowing a complete brain under the proper circumstances. The newly grown brain would then speak to the new culture—informing it of the presence of the other, and announcing ways in which contact might be made."

Samuels's theory of the Messenger Bug was considered amusing by practical scientists, but it could not be discounted now.

"Do you suppose," Stone said, "that it is already developing into some kind of organ of communication?"

"Perhaps the cultures will tell us more," Leavitt said.

"Or X-ray crystallography," Stone said. "I'll order it now."

Level V had facilities for X-ray crystallography, though there had been much heated discussion during Wildfire planning as to whether such facilities were necessary. X-ray crystallography represented the most advanced, complex, and expensive method of structural analysis in modern biology. It was a little like electron microscopy, but one step further along the line. It was more sensitive, and could probe deeper—but only at great cost in terms of time, equipment, and personnel.

The biologist R. A. Janek has said that "increasing vision is increasingly expensive." He meant by this that any machine to enable men to see finer or fainter details increased in cost faster than it increased in resolving power. This hard fact of research was discovered first by the astronomers, who learned painfully that construction of a two-hundred-inch telescope mirror was far more difficult and expensive than construction of a one-hundred-inch mirror.

In biology this was equally true. A light microscope, for example, was a small device easily carried by a technician in one hand. It could outline a cell, and for this ability a scientist paid about $1,000.

An electron microscope could outline small structures within the cell. The EM was a large console and cost up to $100,000.

In contrast, X-ray crystallography could outline individual

molecules. It came as close to photographing atoms as science could manage. But the device was the size of a large automobile, filled an entire room, required specially trained operators, and demanded a computer for interpretation of results.

This was because X-ray crystallography did not produce a direct visual picture of the object being studied. It was not, in this sense, a microscope, and it operated differently from either the light or electron microscope.

It produced a diffraction pattern instead of an image. This appeared as a pattern of geometric dots, in itself rather mysterious, on a photographic plate. By using a computer, the pattern of dots could be analyzed and the structure deduced.

It was a relatively new science, retaining an old-fashioned name. Crystals were seldom used any more; the term "X-ray crystallography" dated from the days when crystals were chosen as test objects. Crystals had regular structures and thus the pattern of dots resulting from a beam of X rays shot at a crystal were easier to analyze. But in recent years the X rays had been shot at irregular objects of varying sorts. The X rays were bounced off at different angles. A computer could "read" the photographic plate and measure the angles, and from this work back to the shape of the object that had caused such a reflection.

The computer at Wildfire performed the endless and tedious calculations. All this, if done by manual human calculation, would take years, perhaps centuries. But the computer could do it in seconds.

"How are you feeling, Mr. Jackson?" Hall asked.

The old man blinked his eyes and looked at Hall, in his plastic suit.

"All right. Not the best, but all right."

He gave a wry grin.

"Up to talking a little?"

"About what?"

"Piedmont."

"What about it?"

"That night," Hall said. "The night it all happened."

"Well, I tell you. I've lived in Piedmont all my life. Traveled a bit—been to LA, and even up to Frisco. Went as far east as St. Louis, which was far enough for me. But Piedmont, that's where I've lived. And I have to tell you—"

"The night it all happened," Hall repeated.

He stopped, and turned his head away. "I don't want to think about it," he said.

"You have to think about it."

"No."

He continued to look away for a moment, and then turned back to Hall. "They all died, did they?"

"Not all. One other survived." He nodded to the crib next to Jackson.

Jackson peered over at the bundle of blankets. "Who's that?"

"A baby."

"Baby? Must be the Ritter child. Jamie Ritter. Real young, is it?"

"About two months."

"Yep. That's him. A real little heller. Just like the old man. Old Ritter likes to kick up a storm, and his kid's the same way. Squalling morning, noon, and night. Family couldn't keep the windas open, on account of the squalling."

"Is there anything else unusual about Jamie?"

"Nope. Healthy as a water buffalo, except he squalls. I remember he was squalling like the dickens that night."

Hall said, "What night?"

"The night Charley Thomas brought the damned thing in. We all seen it, of course. It came down like one of them shooting stars, all glowing, and landed just to the north.

Everybody was excited, and Charley Thomas went off to get it. Came back about twenty minutes later with the thing in the back of his Ford station wagon. Brand-new wagon. He's real proud of it."

"Then what happened?"

"Well, we all gathered around, looking at it. Reckoned it must be one of those space things. Annie figured it was from Mars, but you know how Annie is. Lets her mind carry her off, at times. The rest of us, we didn't feel it was no Martian thing, we just figured it was something sent up from Cape Canaveral. You know, that place in Florida where they shoot the rockets?"

"Yes. Go on."

"So, once we figured that out good and proper, we didn't know what to do. Nothing like that ever happened in Piedmont, you know. I mean, once we had that tourist with the gun, shot up the Comanche Chief motel, but that was back in '48 and besides, he was just a GI had a little too much to drink, and there were exterminating circumstances. His gal run out on him while he was in Germany or some damn place. Nobody gave him a bad time; we understood how it was. But nothing happened since, really. Quiet town. That's why we like it, I reckon."

"What did you do with the capsule?"

"Well, we didn't know what to do with it. Al, he said open 'er up, but we didn't figure that was right, especially since it might have some scientific stuff inside, so we thought awhile. And then Charley, who got it in the first place, Charley says, let's give it to Doc. That's Doc Benedict. He's the town doctor. Actually, he takes care of everybody around, even the Indians. But he's a good fella anyhow, and he's been to lots of schools. Got these degrees on the walls? Well, we figured Doc Benedict would know what to do with the thing. So we brought it to him."

"And then?"

"Old Doc Benedict, he's not so old actually, he looks 'er over real careful, like it was his patient, and then he allows as how it might be a thing from space, and it might be one of ours, or it might be one of theirs. And he says he'll take care of it, and maybe make a few phone calls, and let everybody know in a few hours. See, Doc always played poker Monday nights with Charley and Al and Herb Johnstone, over at Herb's place, and we figured that he'd spread the word around then. Besides, it was getting on suppertime and most of us were a bit hungry, so we all kind of left it with Doc."

"When was that?"

"Bout seven-thirty or so."

"What did Benedict do with the satellite?"

"Took it inside his house. None of us saw it again. It was about eight, eight-thirty that it all started up, you see. I was over at the gas station, having a chat with Al, who was working the pump that night. Chilly night, but I wanted a chat to take my mind off the pain. And to get some soda from the machine, to wash down the aspirin with. Also, I was thirsty, squeeze makes you right thirsty, you know."

"You'd been drinking Sterno that day?"

"Bout six o'clock I had some, yes."

"How did you feel?"

"Well, when I was with Al, I felt good. Little dizzy, and my stomach was paining me, but I felt good. And Al and me were sitting inside the office, you know, talking, and suddenly he shouts, 'Oh God, my head!' He ups and runs outside, and falls down. Right there in the street, not a word from him.

"Well, I didn't know what to make of it. I figured he had a heart attack or a shock, but he was pretty young for that, so I went after him. Only he was dead. Then . . . they all started coming out. I believe Mrs. Langdon, the Widow Langdon, was next. After that, I don't recall, there was so many of them. Just pouring outside, it seemed like. And they just grab their chests and fall, like they slipped. Only they wouldn't get up afterward. And never a word from any of them."

"What did you think?"

"I didn't know what to think, it was so damned peculiar. I was scared, I don't mind telling you, but I tried to stay calm. I couldn't, naturally. My old heart was thumping, and I was wheezin' and gaspin'. I was scared. I thought everybody was dead. Then I heard the baby crying, so I knew not *everybody* could be dead. And then I saw the General."

"The General?"

"Oh, we just called him that. He wasn't no general, just been in the war, and liked to be remembered. Older'n me, he is. Nice fella, Peter Arnold. Steady as a rock all his life. and he's standing by the porch, all got up in his military clothes. It's dark, but there's a moon, and he sees me in the street and he says, 'That you, Peter?' We both got the same name, see. And I says, 'Yes it is.' And he says, 'What the hell's happening? Japs coming in?' And I think that's a mighty peculiar thing for him to be saying. And he says, 'I think it must be the Japs, come to kill us all.' And I say, 'Peter, you gone loco?' And he says he don't feel too good and he goes inside. Course, he must have gone loco, 'cause he shot himself. But others went loco, too. It was the disease."

"How do you know?"

"People don't burn themselves, or drown themselves, if they got sense, do they? All them in that town were good, normal folks until that night. Then they just seemed to go crazy."

"What did you do?"

"I thought to myself, Peter, you're dreaming. You had too much to drink. So I went home and got into bed, and figured I'd be better in the morning. Only about ten o'clock, I hear a noise, and it's a car, so I go outside to see who it is. It's some kind of car, you know, one of those vans. Two fellers inside. I go up to them, and damn but they don't fall over dead. Scariest thing you ever saw. But it's funny."

"What's funny?"

"That was the only other car to come through all night. Normally, there's lots of cars."

"There was another car?"

"Yep. Willis, the highway patrol. He came through about fifteen, thirty seconds before it all started. Didn't stop, though; sometimes he doesn't. Depends if he's late on his schedule; he's got a regular patrol, you know, he has to stick to."

Jackson sighed and let his head fall back against the pillow. "Now," he said, "if you don't mind, I'm going to get me some sleep. I'm all talked out."

He closed his eyes. Hall crawled back down the tunnel, out of the unit, and sat in the room looking through the glass at Jackson, and the baby in the crib alongside. He stayed there, just looking, for a long time.

23.

Topeka

THE ROOM WAS HUGE, the size of a football field. It was furnished sparsely, just a few tables scattered about. Inside the room, voices echoed as the technicians called to each other, positioning the pieces of wreckage. The post team was reconstructing the wreck in this room, placing the clumps of twisted metal from the Phantom in the same positions as they had been found on the sand.

Only then would the intensive examination begin.

Major Manchek, tired, bleary-eyed, clutching his coffee cup, stood in a corner and watched. To him, there was something surrealistic about the scene: a dozen men in a long, white-washed room in Topeka, rebuilding a crash.

One of the biophysicists came up to him, holding a clear plastic bag. He waved the contents under Manchek's nose.

"Just got it back from the lab," he said.

"What is it?"

"You'll never guess." The man's eyes gleamed in excitement.

All right, Manchek thought irritably, I'll never guess. "What is it?"

"A depolymerized polymer," the biochemist said, smacking his lips with satisfaction. "Just back from the lab."

"What kind of polymer?"

A polymer was a repeating molecule, built up from thousands of the same units, like a stack of dominos. Most plastics, nylon, rayon, plant cellulose, and even glycogen in the human body were polymers.

"A polymer of the plastic used on the air hose of the Phantom jet. The face mask to the pilot. We thought as much."

Manchek frowned. He looked slowly at the crumbly black powder in the bag. "Plastic?"

"Yes. A polymer, depolymerized. It was broken down. Now that's no vibration effect. It's a biochemical effect, purely organic."

Slowly, Manchek began to understand. "You mean something tore the plastic apart?"

"Yes, you could say that," the biochemist replied. "It's a simplification, of course, but—"

"What tore it apart?"

The biochemist shrugged. "Chemical reaction of some sort. Acid could do it, or intense heat, or . . ."

"Or?"

"A microorganism, I suppose. If one existed that could eat plastic. If you know what I mean."

"I think," Manchek said, "that I know what you mean."

He left the room and went to the cable transmitter, located in another part of the building. He wrote out his message to the Wildfire group, and gave it to the technician to transmit. While he waited, he said, "Has there been any reply yet?"

"Reply, sir?" the technician asked.

"From Wildfire," Manchek said. It was incredible to him that no one had acted upon the news of the Phantom crash. It was so obviously linked . . .

"Wildfire, sir?" the technician asked.

Manchek rubbed his eyes. He was tired: he would have to remember to keep his big mouth shut.

"Forget it," he said.

After his conversation with Peter Jackson, Hall went to see Burton. Burton was in the autopsy room, going over his slides from the day before.

Hall said, "Find anything?"

Burton stepped away from the microscope and sighed. "No. Nothing."

"I keep wondering," Hall said, "about the insanity. Talking with Jackson reminded me of it. A large number of people in that town went insane—or at least became bizarre and suicidal—during the evening. Many of those people were old."

Burton frowned. "So?"

"Old people," Hall said, "are like Jackson. They have lots wrong with them. Their bodies are breaking down in a variety of ways. The lungs are bad. The hearts are bad. The livers are shot. The vessels are sclerotic."

"And this alters the disease process?"

"Perhaps. I keep wondering, What makes a person become rapidly insane?"

Burton shook his head.

"And there's something else," Hall said. "Jackson recalls hearing one victim say, just before he died, 'Oh God, my head.'"

Burton stared away into space. "Just before death?"

"Just before."

"You're thinking of hemorrhage?"

Hall nodded. "It makes sense," he said. "At least to check."

If the Andromeda Strain produced hemorrhage inside the brain for any reason, then it might produce rapid, unusual mental aberrations.

"But we already know the organism acts by clotting—"

"Yes," Hall said, "in most people. Not all. Some survive, and some go mad."

Burton nodded. He suddenly became excited. Suppose that the organism acted by causing damage to blood vessels. This damage would initiate clotting. Anytime the wall of a blood vessel was torn, or cut, or burned, then the clotting sequence would begin. First platelets would clump around the injury, protecting it, preventing blood loss. Then red cells would accumulate. Then a fibrin mesh would bind all the elements together. And finally, the clot would become hard and firm.

That was the normal sequence.

But if the damage was extensive, if it began at the lungs and worked its way . . .

"I'm wondering," Hall said, "if our organism attacks vessel walls. If so, it would initiate clotting. But if clotting were prevented in certain persons, then the organism might eat away and cause hemorrhage in those persons."

"And insanity," Burton said, hunting through his slides. He found three of the brain, and checked them.

No question.

The pathology was striking. Within the internal layer of cerebral vessels were small deposits of green. Burton had no doubt that, under higher magnification, they would turn out to be hexagonal in shape.

Quickly, he checked the other slides, for vessels in lung, liver, and spleen. In several instances he found green spots in the vessel walls, but never in the profusion he found for cerebral vessels.

Obviously the Andromeda Strain showed a predilection for cerebral vasculature. It was impossible to say why, but it was known that the cerebral vessels are peculiar in several respects. For instance, under circumstances in which normal body vessels dilate or contract—such as extreme cold, or exercise—the brain vasculature does not change, but maintains a steady, constant blood supply to the brain.

In exercise, the blood supply to muscle might increase five to twenty times. But the brain always has a steady flow: whether its owner is taking an exam or a nap, chopping wood or watching TV. The brain receives the same amount of blood every minute, hour, day.

The scientists did not know why this should be, or how, precisely, the cerebral vessels regulate themselves. But the phenomenon is known to exist, and cerebral vessels are regarded as a special case among the body's arteries and veins. Clearly, something is different about them.

And now there was an example of an organism that destroyed them preferentially.

But as Burton thought about it, the action of Andromeda did not seem so unusual. For example, syphilis causes an inflammation of the aorta, a very specific, peculiar reaction. Schistosomiasis, a parasitic infection, shows a preference for bladder, intestine, or colonic vessels—depending on the species. So such specificity was not impossible.

"But there's another problem," he said. "In most people, the organism begins clotting at the lungs. We know that. Presumably vessel destruction begins there as well. What is different about—"

He stopped.

He remembered the rats he had anticoagulated. The ones who had died anyway, but had had no autopsies.

"My God," he said.

He drew out one of the rats from cold storage and cut it open. It bled. Quickly he incised the head, exposing the brain. There he found a large hemorrhage over the gray surface of the brain.

"You've got it," Hall said.

"If the animal is normal, it dies from coagulation, beginning at the lungs. But if coagulation is prevented, then the organism erodes through the vessels of the brain, and hemorrhage occurs."

"And insanity."

"Yes." Burton was now very excited. "And coagulation could be prevented by any blood disorder. Or too little vitamin K. Malabsorption syndrome. Poor liver function. Impaired protein synthesis. Any of a dozen things."

"All more likely to be found in an old person," Hall said.

"Did Jackson have any of those things?"

Hall took a long time to answer, then finally said, "No. He has liver disease, but not significantly."

Burton sighed. "Then we're back where we started."

"Not quite. Because Jackson and the baby both survived. They didn't hemorrhage—as far as we know—they survived untouched. Completely untouched."

"Meaning?"

"Meaning that they somehow prevented the primary process, which is invasion of the organism into the vessel walls of the body. The Andromeda organism didn't get to the lungs, or the brain. It didn't get anywhere."

"But why?"

"We'll know that," Hall said, "when we know why a sixty-nine-year-old Sterno drinker with an ulcer is like a two-month-old baby."

"They seem pretty much opposites," Burton said.

"They do, don't they?" Hall said. It would be hours before he realized Burton had given him the answer to the puzzle —but an answer that was worthless.

24.

Evaluation

SIR WINSTON CHURCHILL ONCE SAID that "true genius resides in the capacity for evaluation of uncertain, hazardous, and conflicting information." Yet it is a peculiarity of the Wildfire team that, despite the individual brilliance of team members, the group grossly misjudged their information at several points.

One is reminded of Montaigne's acerbic comment: "Men under stress are fools, and fool themselves." Certainly the Wildfire team was under severe stress, but they were also prepared to make mistakes. They had even predicted that this would occur.

What they did not anticipate was the magnitude, the staggering dimensions of their error. They did not expect that their ultimate error would be a compound of a dozen small clues that were missed, a handful of crucial facts that were dismissed.

The team had a blind spot, which Stone later expressed this way: "We were problem-oriented. Everything we did and thought was directed toward finding a solution, a cure to Andromeda. And, of course, we were fixed on the events that had occurred at Piedmont. We felt that if we did not find a solution, no solution would be forthcoming, and the whole world would ultimately wind up like Piedmont. We were very slow to think otherwise."

The error began to take on major proportions with the cultures.

Stone and Leavitt had taken thousands of cultures from the original capsule. These had been incubated in a wide variety of atmospheric, temperature, and pressure conditions. The results of this could only be analyzed by computer.

Using the GROWTH/TRANSMATRIX program, the computer did not print out results from all possible growth combinations. Instead, it printed out only significant positive and negative results. It did this after first weighing each petri dish, and examining any growth with its photoelectric eye.

When Stone and Leavitt went to examine the results, they found several striking trends. Their first conclusion was that growth media did not matter at all—the organism grew equally well on sugar, blood, chocolate, plain agar, or sheer glass.

However, the gases in which the plates were incubated were crucial, as was the light.

Ultraviolet light stimulated growth under all circumstances. Total darkness, and to a lesser extent infrared light, inhibited growth.

Oxygen inhibited growth in all circumstances, but carbon dioxide stimulated growth. Nitrogen had no effect.

Thus, best growth was achieved in 100-per cent carbon dioxide, lighted by ultraviolet radiation. Poorest growth occurred in pure oxygen, incubated in total darkness.

"What do you make of it?" Stone said.

"It looks like a pure conversion system," Leavitt said.

"I wonder," Stone said.

He punched through the coordinates of a closed-growth system. Closed-growth systems studied bacterial metabolism by measuring intake of gases and nutrients, and output of waste products. They were completely sealed and self-con-

```
]00000000000000000000000000000000000000000000000000000000000000000000000000000000000000
]000000000000000000000000000000.....................000000000000000000000000000000000000
]0000000000000000000000000.................00000000000000000000000000000000000000000
]00000000000000000000000.............11221...........0000000000000000000000000000000000
]0000000000000000000000..............112332111.........000000000000000000000000000000000
]000000000000000000.................11223321.........00000000000000000000000000000000
]0000000000000000..............11221...........000000000000000000000000000000000
]000000000000000............................11............000000000000000000000000000000
]00000000000000...........................................00000000000000000000000000000
]0000000000000.............................................00000000000000000000000000000
]000000000000.............................................00000000000000000000000000000
]000000000000................11..............................00000000000000000000000000
]0000000000000.....................112221.....................0000000000000000000000000
]00000000000000..........11234432221.....................00000000000000000000000000
]00000000000000........122345677654322 1...................00000000000000000000000000
]000000000000000........1223456788776543211................00000000000000000000000000
]00000000000000.......12334567899876543221...............0000000000000000000000000000
]0000000000000000.......11234455678899876543211...............000000000000000000000000
]00000000000000........12345567889876543211..............00000000000000000000000
]000000000000000.......11235677676542221...............00000000000000000000000000
]0000000000000000.......11234564321..............0000000000000000000000000000
]000000000000000000.......123221................00000000000000000000000000000
]000000000000000000000.....1221................00000000000000000000000000000000
]0000000000000000000000..11..................000000000000000000000000000000000
]00000000000000000000000000.............00000000000000000000000000000000000000
]00000000000000000000000000000000000000000000000000000000000000000000000000000000000
```

CULTURE DESIG - 779,223,187,
ANDROMEDA
MEDIA DESIG - 779
ATMOSPHERE DESIG - 223
LUMIN DESIG - L87 UV/HI
FINAL SCANNER PRINT

An example of a scanner printout from the photoelectric eye that examined all growth media. Within the circular petri dish the computer has noted the presence of two separate colonies. The colonies are "read" in two-millimeter-square segments, and graded by density on a scale from one to nine.

tained. A plant in such a system, for example, would consume carbon dioxide and give off water and oxygen.

But when they looked at the Andromeda Strain, they found something remarkable. The organism had no excretions. If incubated with carbon dioxide and ultraviolet light, it grew steadily until all carbon dioxide had been consumed. Then growth stopped. There was no excretion of any kind of gas or waste product at all.

No waste.

"Clearly efficient," Stone said.

"You'd expect that," Leavitt said.

This was an organism highly suited to its environment. It consumed everything, wasted nothing. It was perfect for the barren existence of space.

He thought about this for a moment, and then it hit him. It hit Leavitt at the same time.

"Good Christ."

Leavitt was already reaching for the phone. "Get Robertson," he said. "Get him immediately."

"Incredible," Stone said softly. "No waste. It doesn't require growth media. It can grow in the presence of carbon, oxygen, and sunlight. Period."

"I hope we're not too late," Leavitt said, watching the computer console screen impatiently.

Stone nodded. "If this organism is really converting matter to energy, and energy to matter—directly—then it's functioning like a little reactor."

"And an atomic detonation . . ."

"Incredible," Stone said. "Just incredible."

The screen came to life; they saw Robertson, looking tired, smoking a cigarette.

"Jeremy, you've got to give me time. I haven't been able to get through to—"

"Listen," Stone said, "I want you to make sure Directive

7–12 is not carried out. It is imperative: no atomic device must be detonated around the organisms. That's the last thing in the world, literally, that we want to do."

He explained briefly what he had found.

Robertson whistled. "We'd just provide a fantastically rich growth medium."

"That's right," Stone said.

The problem of a rich growth medium was a peculiarly distressing one to the Wildfire team. It was known, for example, that checks and balances exist in the normal environment. These manage to dampen the exuberant growth of bacteria.

The mathematics of uncontrolled growth are frightening. A single cell of the bacterium *E. coli* would, under ideal circumstances, divide every twenty minutes. That is not particularly disturbing until you think about it, but the fact is that bacteria multiply geometrically: one becomes two, two become four, four become eight, and so on. In this way, it can be shown that in a single day, one cell of *E. coli* could produce a supercolony equal in size and weight to the entire planet earth.

This never happens, for a perfectly simple reason: growth cannot continue indefinitely under "ideal circumstances." Food runs out. Oxygen runs out. Local conditions within the colony change, and check the growth of organisms.

On the other hand, if you had an organism that was capable of directly converting matter to energy, and if you provided it with a huge rich source of energy, like an atomic blast . . .

"I'll pass along your recommendation to the President," Robertson said. "He'll be pleased to know he made the right decision on the 7–12."

"You can congratulate him on his scientific insight," Stone said, "for me."

Robertson was scratching his head. "I've got some more data on the Phantom crash. It was over the area west of Piedmont at twenty-three thousand feet. The post team has found evidence of the disintegration the pilot spoke of, but the material that was destroyed was a plastic of some kind. It was depolymerized."

"What does the post team make of that?"

"They don't know what the hell to make of it," Robertson admitted. "And there's something else. They found a few pieces of bone that have been identified as human. A bit of humerus and tibia. Notable because they are clean—almost polished."

"Flesh burned away?"

"Doesn't look that way," Robertson said.

Stone frowned at Leavitt.

"What *does* it look like?"

"It looks like clean, polished bone," Robertson said. "They say it's weird as hell. And there's something else. We checked into the National Guard around Piedmont. The 112th is stationed in a hundred-mile radius, and it turns out they've been running patrols into the area for a distance of fifty miles. They've had as many as one hundred men west of Piedmont. No deaths."

"None? You're quite sure?"

"Absolutely."

"Were there men on the ground in the area the Phantom flew over?"

"Yes. Twelve men. They reported the plane to the base, in fact."

Leavitt said, "Sounds like the plane crash is a fluke."

Stone nodded. To Robertson: "I'm inclined to agree with Peter. In the absence of fatalities on the ground . . ."

"Maybe it's only in the upper air."

"Maybe. But we know at least this much: we know how Andromeda kills. It does so by coagulation. Not disintegration, or bone-cleaning, or any other damned thing. By coagulation."

"All right," Robertson said, "let's forget the plane for the time being."

It was on that note that the meeting ended.

Stone said, "I think we'd better check our cultured organisms for biologic potency."

"Run some of them against a rat?"

Stone nodded. "Make sure it's still virulent. Still the same."

Leavitt agreed. They had to be careful the organism didn't mutate, didn't change to something radically different in its effects.

As they were about to start, the Level V monitor clicked on and said, "Dr. Leavitt. Dr. Leavitt."

Leavitt answered. On the computer screen was a pleasant young man in a white lab coat.

"Yes?"

"Dr. Leavitt, we have gotten our electroencephalograms back from the computer center. I'm sure it's all a mistake, but . . ."

His voice trailed off.

"Yes?" Leavitt said. "Is something wrong?"

"Well, sir, yours were read as grade four, atypical, probably benign. But we would like to run another set."

Stone said, "It must be a mistake."

"Yes," Leavitt said. "It must be."

"Undoubtedly, sir," the man said. "But we would like another set of waves to be certain."

"I'm rather busy now," Leavitt said.

Stone broke in, talking directly to the technician. "Dr. Leavitt will get a repeat EEG when he has the chance."

"Very good, sir," the technician said.

When the screen was blank, Stone said, "There are times when this damned routine gets on anybody's nerves."

Leavitt said, "Yes."

They were about to begin biologic testing of the various culture media when the computer flashed that preliminary reports from X-ray crystallography were prepared. Stone and Leavitt left the room to check the results, delaying the biologic tests of media. This was a most unfortunate decision, for had they examined the media, they would have seen that their thinking had already gone astray, and that they were on the wrong track.

25.

Willis

X-RAY CRYSTALLOGRAPHY ANALYSIS showed that the Andromeda organism was not composed of component parts, as a normal cell was composed of nucleus, mitochondria, and ribosomes. Andromeda had no subunits, no smaller particules. Instead, a single substance seemed to form the walls and interior. This substance produced a characteristic precession photograph, or scatter pattern of X-rays.

Looking at the results, Stone said, "A series of six-sided rings."

"And nothing else," Leavitt said. "How the hell does it operate?"

The two men were at a loss to explain how so simple an organism could utilize energy for growth.

"A rather common ring structure," Leavitt said. "A phenolic group, nothing more. It should be reasonably inert."

"Yet it can convert energy to matter."

Leavitt scratched his head. He thought back to the city analogy, and the brain-cell analogy. The molecule was simple in its building blocks. It possessed no remarkable powers, taken as single units. Yet collectively, it had great powers.

"Perhaps there is a critical level," he suggested. "A structural complexity that makes possible what is not possible in a similar but simple structure."

"The old chimp-brain argument," Stone said.

Leavitt nodded. As nearly as anyone could determine, the chimp brain was as complex as the human brain. There were minor differences in structure, but the major difference was size—the human brain was larger, with more cells, more interconnections.

And that, in some subtle way, made the human brain different. (Thomas Waldren, the neurophysiologist, once jokingly noted that the major difference between the chimp and human

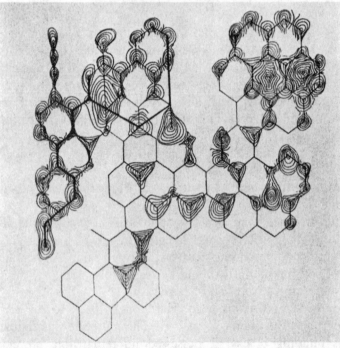

Electron-density mapping of Andromeda structure as derived from micrographic studies. It was this mapping which disclosed activity variations within an otherwise uniform structure.

Photo courtesy Project Wildfire

brain was that "we can use the chimp as an experimental animal, and not the reverse.")

Stone and Leavitt puzzled over the problem for several minutes until they came to the Fourier electron-density scans. Here, the probability of finding electrons was mapped for the structure on a chart that resembled a topological map.

They noticed something odd. The structure was present but the Fourier mapping was inconstant.

"It almost looks," Stone said, "as if part of the structure is switched off in some way."

"It's not uniform after all," Leavitt said.

Stone sighed, looking at the map. "I wish to hell," he said, "that we'd brought a physical chemist along on the team."

Unspoken was the added comment, "instead of Hall."

Tired, Hall rubbed his eyes and sipped the coffee, wishing he could have sugar. He was alone in the cafeteria, which was silent except for the muted ticking of the teleprinter in the corner.

After a time he got up and went over to the teleprinter, examining the rolls of paper that had come from it. Most of the information was meaningless to him.

But then he saw one item which had come from the DEATH-MATCH program. DEATHMATCH was a news-scanning computer program that recorded all significant deaths according to whatever criterion the computer was fed. In this case, the computer was alerted to pick up all deaths in the Arizona-Nevada-California area, and to print them back.

The item he read might have gone unnoticed, were it not for Hall's conversation with Jackson. At the time, it had seemed like a pointless conversation to Hall, productive of little and consuming a great deal of time.

But now, he wondered.

```
PRINT PROGRAM
DEATHWATCH
DEATHMATCH/998
SCALE 7,Y,0.  X,4,0
PRINT AS
ITEM FROM ASSOCIATED PRESS VERBATIM  778-778
```

BRUSH RIDGE, ARIZ. — — —,: An Arizona highway patrol officer was allegedly involved in the death today of five persons in a highway diner. Miss Sally Conover, waitress at the Dine-eze diner on Route 15, ten miles south of Flagstaff, was the sole survivor of the incident.

Miss Conover told investigators that at 2:40 a.m., Officer Martin Willis entered the diner and ordered coffee and donut. Officer Willis had frequently visited the diner in the past. After eating, he stated that he had a severe headache and that "his ulcer was acting up." Miss Conover gave him two aspirin and a tablespoon of bicarbonate of soda. According to her statement, Officer Willis then looked suspiciously at the other people in the diner and whispered, "They're after me."

Before the waitress could reply, Willis took out his revolver and shot the other customers in the diner, moving methodically from one to the next, shooting each in the forehead. Then, he allegedly turned to Miss Conover and, smiling, said "I love you, Shirley Temple," placed the barrel in his mouth, and fired the last bullet.

Miss Conover was released by police here after questioning. The names of the deceased customers are not known at this time.

```
END ITEM VERBATIM
END PRINT
END PROGRAM

TERMINATE
```

Hall remembered that Officer Willis had gone through Piedmont earlier in the evening—just a few minutes before the disease broke out. He had gone through without stopping.

And had gone mad later on.

Connection?

He wondered. There might be. Certainly, he could see many similarities: Willis had an ulcer, had taken aspirin, and had, eventually, committed suicide.

That didn't prove anything, of course. It might be a wholly unrelated series of events. But it was certainly worth checking.

He punched a button on the computer console. The TV screen lighted and a girl at a switchboard, with a headset pressing down her hair, smiled at him.

"I want the chief medical officer for the Arizona highway patrol. The western sector, if there is one."

"Yes sir," she said briskly.

A few moments later, the screen came back on. It was the operator. "We have a Dr. Smithson who is the medical officer for the Arizona highway patrol west of Flagstaff. He has no television monitor but you can speak to him on audio."

"Fine," Hall said.

There was a crackling, and a mechanical hum. Hall watched the screen, but the girl had shut down her own audio and was busy answering another call from elsewhere in the Wildfire station. While he watched her, he heard a deep, drawling voice ask tentatively, "Anyone there?"

"Hello, Doctor," Hall said. "This is Dr. Mark Hall, in . . . Phoenix. I'm calling for some information about one of your patrolmen, Officer Willis."

"The girl said it was some government thing," Smithson drawled. "That right?"

"That is correct. We require—"

"Dr. Hall," Smithson said, still drawling, "perhaps you'd identify yourself and your agency."

It occurred to Hall that there was probably a legal problem involved in Officer Willis's death. Smithson might be worried about that.

Hall said, "I am not at liberty to tell you exactly what it is—"

"Well, look here, Doctor. I don't give out information over the phone, and especially I don't when the feller at the other end won't tell me what it's all about."

Hall took a deep breath. "Dr. Smithson, I must ask you—"

"Ask all you want. I'm sorry, I simply won't—"

At that moment, a bell sounded on the line, and a flat mechanical voice said:

"Attention please. This is a recording. Computer monitors have analyzed cable properties of this communication and have determined that the communication is being recorded by the outside party. All parties should be informed that the penalty for outside recording of a classified government communication is a minimum of five years' prison sentence. If the recording is continued this connection will automatically be broken. This is a recording. Thank you."

There was a long silence. Hall could imagine the surprise Smithson was feeling; he felt it himself.

"What the hell kind of a place are you calling from, anyhow?" Smithson said, finally.

"Turn it off," Hall said.

There was a pause, a click, then: "All right. It's off."

"I am calling from a classified government installation," Hall said.

"Well, look here, mister—"

"Let me be perfectly plain," Hall said. "This is a matter of considerable importance and it concerns Officer Willis. No doubt there's a court inquiry pending on him, and no doubt you'll be involved. We may be able to demonstrate that Officer Willis was not responsible for his actions, that he was suffering from a purely medical problem. But we can't do that unless you tell us what you know about his medical status. And if you don't tell us, Dr. Smithson, and tell us damned fast, we can have you locked away for twelve years for obstructing an official government inquiry. I don't care whether you believe that or not. I'm telling you, and you'd better believe it."

There was a very long pause, and finally the drawl: "No need to get excited, Doctor. Naturally, now that I understand the situation—"

"Did Willis have an ulcer?"

"Ulcer? No. That was just what he said, or was reported to have said. He never had an ulcer that I know of."

"Did he have any medical problem?"

"Diabetes," Smithson said.

"Diabetes?"

"Yeah. And he was pretty casual about it. We diagnosed him five, six years ago, at the age of thirty. Had a pretty severe case. We put him on insulin, fifty units a day, but he was casual, like I said. Showed up in the hospital once or twice in coma, because he wouldn't take his insulin. Said he hated the needles. We almost put him off the force, because we were afraid to let him drive a car—thought he'd go into acidosis at the wheel and conk out. We scared him plenty and he promised to go straight. That was three years ago, and as far as I know, he took his insulin regularly from then on."

"You're sure of that?"

"Well, I think so. But the waitress at that restaurant, Sally Conover, told one of our investigators that she figured Willis had been drinking, because she could smell liquor on his breath. And I know for a fact that Willis never touched a drop in his life. He was one of these real religious fellows. Never smoked and never drank. Always led a clean life. That was why his diabetes bothered him so: he felt he didn't deserve it."

Hall relaxed in his chair. He was getting near now, coming closer. The answer was within reach; the final answer, the key to it all.

"One last question," Hall said. "Did Willis go through Piedmont on the night of his death?"

"Yes. He radioed in. He was a little behind schedule, but he passed through. Why? Is it something about the government tests being held there?"

"No," Hall said, but he was sure Smithson didn't believe him.

"Well, listen, we're stuck here with a bad case, and if you have any information which would—"

"We will be in touch," Hall promised him, and clicked off.

The girl at the switchboard came back on.

"Is your call completed, Dr. Hall?"

"Yes. But I need information."

"What kind of information?"

"I want to know if I have the authority to arrest someone."

"I will check, sir. What is the charge?"

"No charge. Just to hold someone."

There was a moment while she looked over at her computer console.

"Dr. Hall, you may authorize an official Army interview with anyone involved in project business. This interview may last up to forty-eight hours."

"All right," Hall said. "Arrange it."

"Yes sir. Who is the person?"

"Dr. Smithson," Hall said.

The girl nodded and the screen went blank. Hall felt sorry for Smithson, but not very sorry; the man would have a few hours of sweating, but nothing more serious than that. And it was essential to halt rumors about Piedmont.

He sat back in his chair and thought about what he had learned. He was excited, and felt on the verge of an important discovery.

Three people:

A diabetic in acidosis, from failure to take insulin.

An old man who drank Sterno and took aspirin, also in acidosis.

A young infant.

One had survived for hours, the other two had survived longer, apparently permanently. One had gone mad, the other two had not. Somehow, they were all interrelated.

In a very simple way.

Acidosis. Rapid breathing. Carbon-dioxide content. Oxygen saturation. Dizziness. Fatigue. Somehow they were all logically coordinated. And they held the key to beating Andromeda.

At that moment, the emergency bell sounded, ringing in a high-pitched, urgent way as the bright-yellow light began to flash.

He jumped up and left the room.

26.

The Seal

IN THE CORRIDOR, he saw the flashing sign that indicated the source of the trouble: AUTOPSY. Hall could guess the problem—somehow the seals had been broken, and contamination had occurred. That would sound the alarm.

As he ran down the corridor, a quiet, soothing voice on the loudspeakers said, "Seal has been broken in Autopsy. Seal has been broken in Autopsy. This is an emergency."

His lab technician came out of the lab and saw him. "What is it?"

"Burton, I think. Infection spread."

"Is he all right?"

"Doubt it," Hall said, running. She ran with him.

Leavitt came out of the MORPHOLOGY room and joined them, sprinting down the corridor, around the gentle curves. Hall thought to himself that Leavitt was moving quite well, for an older man, when suddenly Leavitt stopped.

He stood riveted to the ground. And stared straight forward at the flashing sign, and the light above it, blinking on and off.

Hall looked back. "Come on," he said.

Then the technician: "Dr. Hall, he's in trouble."

Leavitt was not moving. He stood, eyes open, but otherwise he might have been asleep. His arms hung loosely at his sides.

"Dr. Hall."

Hall stopped, and went back.

"Peter, boy, come on, we need your—"

He said nothing more, for Leavitt was not listening. He was staring straight forward at the blinking light. When Hall passed his hand in front of his face, he did not react. And then Hall remembered the other blinking lights, the lights Leavitt had turned away from, had joked off with stories.

"The son of a bitch," Hall said. "Now, of all times."

"What is it?" the technician said.

A small dribble of spittle was coming from the corner of Leavitt's mouth. Hall quickly stepped behind him and said to the technician, "Get in front of him and cover his eyes. Don't let him look at the blinking light."

"Why?"

"Because it's blinking three times a second," Hall said.

"You mean—"

"He'll go any minute now."

Leavitt went.

With frightening speed, his knees gave way and he collapsed to the floor. He lay on his back and his whole body began to vibrate. It began with his hands and feet, then involved his entire arms and legs, and finally his whole body. He clenched his teeth and gave a gasping, loud cry. His head hammered against the floor; Hall slipped his foot beneath the back of Leavitt's head and let him bang against his toes. It was better than having him hit the hard floor.

"Don't try to open his mouth," Hall said. "You can't do it. He's clenched tight."

As they watched, a yellow stain began to spread at Leavitt's waist.

"He may go into status," Hall said. "Go to the pharmacy

and get me a hundred milligrams of phenobarb. Now. In a syringe. We'll get him onto Dilantin later, if we have to."

Leavitt was crying, through his clenched teeth, like an animal. His body rapped like a tense rod against the floor.

A few moments later, the technician came back with the syringe. Hall waited until Leavitt relaxed, until his body stopped its seizures, and then he injected the barbiturate.

"Stay with him," he said to the girl. "If he has another seizure, just do what I did—put your foot under his head. I think he'll be all right. Don't try to move him."

And Hall ran down to the autopsy lab.

For several seconds, he tried to open the door to the lab, and then he realized it had been sealed off. The lab was contaminated. He went on to main control, and found Stone looking at Burton through the closed-circuit TV monitors.

Burton was terrified. His face was white and he was breathing in rapid, shallow gasps, and he could not speak. He looked exactly like what he was: a man waiting for death to strike him.

Stone was trying to reassure him. "Just take it easy, boy. Take it easy. You'll be okay. Just take it easy."

"I'm scared," Burton said. "Oh Christ, I'm scared . . ."

"Just take it easy," Stone said in a soft voice. "We know that Andromeda doesn't do well in oxygen. We're pumping pure oxygen through your lab now. For the moment, that should hold you."

Stone turned to Hall. "You took your time getting here. Where's Leavitt?"

"He fitted," Hall said.

"What?"

"Your lights flash at three per second, and he had a seizure."

"*What?*"

"Petit mal. It went on to a grand-mal attack: tonic clonic

seizure, urinary incontinence, the whole bit. I got him onto phenobarb and came as soon as I could."

"Leavitt has epilepsy?"

"That's right."

Stone said, "He must not have known. He must not have realized."

And then Stone remembered the request for a repeat electroencephalogram.

"Oh," Hall said, "he knew, all right. He was avoiding flashing lights, which will bring on an attack. I'm sure he knew. I'm sure he has attacks where he suddenly doesn't know what happened to him, where he just loses a few minutes from his life and can't remember what went on."

"Is he all right?"

"We'll keep him sedated."

Stone said, "We've got pure oxygen running into Burton. That should help him, until we know something more." Stone flicked off the microphone button connecting voice transmission to Burton. "Actually, it will take several minutes to hook in, but I've told him we've already started. He's sealed off in there, so the infection is stopped at that point. The rest of the base is okay, at least."

Hall said, "How did it happen? The contamination."

"Seal must have broken," Stone said. In a lower voice, he added, "We knew it would, sooner or later. All isolation units break down after a certain time."

Hall said, "You think it was just a random event?"

"Yes," Stone said. "Just an accident. So many seals, so much rubber, of such-and-such a thickness. They'd all break, given time. Burton happened to be there when one went."

Hall didn't see it so simply. He looked in at Burton, who was breathing rapidly, his chest heaving in terror.

Hall said, "How long has it been?"

Stone looked up at the stop-clocks. The stop-clocks were special timing clocks that automatically cut in during emergencies. The stop-clocks were now timing the period since the seal broke.

"Four minutes."

Hall said, "Burton's still alive."

"Yes, thank God." And then Stone frowned. He realized the point.

"*Why,*" Hall said, "*is he still alive?*"

"The oxygen . . ."

"You said yourself the oxygen isn't running yet. What's protecting Burton?"

At that moment, Burton said over the intercom, "Listen. I want you to try something for me."

Stone flicked on the microphone. "What?"

"Kalocin," Burton said.

"No." Stone's reaction was immediate.

"Dammit, it's my life."

"No," Stone said.

Hall said, "Maybe we should try—"

"Absolutely not. We don't dare. Not even once."

Kalocin was perhaps the best-kept American secret of the last decade. Kalocin was a drug developed by Jensen Pharmaceuticals in the spring of 1965, an experimental chemical designated UJ-44759W, or K-9 in the short abbreviation. It had been found as a result of routine screening tests employed by Jensen for all new compounds.

Like most pharmaceutical companies, Jensen tested all new drugs with a scatter approach, running the compounds through a standard battery of tests designed to pick up any significant biologic activity. These tests were run on laboratory animals —rats, dogs, and monkeys. There were twenty-four tests in all.

Jensen found something rather peculiar about K-9. It inhibited growth. An infant animal given the drug never attained full adult size.

This discovery prompted further tests, which produced even more intriguing results. The drug, Jensen learned, inhibited metaplasia, the shift of normal body cells to a new and bizarre form, a precursor to cancer. Jensen became excited, and put the drug through intensive programs of study.

By September 1965, there could be no doubt: Kalocin stopped cancer. Through an unknown mechanism, it inhibited the reproduction of the virus responsible for myelogenous leukemia. Animals taking the drug did not develop the disease, and animals already demonstrating the disease showed a marked regression as a result of the drug.

The excitement at Jensen could not be contained. It was soon recognized that the drug was a broad-spectrum antiviral agent. It killed the virus of polio, rabies, leukemia, and the common wart. And, oddly enough, Kalocin also killed bacteria.

And fungi.

And parasites.

Somehow, the drug acted to destroy all organisms built on a unicellular structure, or less. It had no effect on organ systems—groups of cells organized into larger units. The drug was perfectly selective in this respect.

In fact, Kalocin was the universal antibiotic. It killed everything, even the minor germs that caused the common cold. Naturally, there were side effects—the normal bacteria in the intestines were destroyed, so that all users of the drug experienced massive diarrhea—but that seemed a small price to pay for a cancer cure.

In December 1965, knowledge of the drug was privately circulated among government agencies and important health officials. And then for the first time, opposition to the drug arose. Many men, including Jeremy Stone, argued that the drug should be suppressed.

But the arguments for suppression seemed theoretical, and Jensen, sensing billions of dollars at hand, fought hard for a clinical test. Eventually the government, the HEW, the FDA, and others agreed with Jensen and sanctioned further clinical testing over the protests of Stone and others.

In February 1966, a pilot clinical trial was undertaken. It involved twenty patients with incurable cancer, and twenty normal volunteers from the Alabama state penitentiary. All forty subjects took the drug daily for one month. Results were as expected: normal subjects experienced unpleasant side effects, but nothing serious. Cancer patients showed striking remission of symptoms consistent with cure.

On March 1, 1966, the forty men were taken off the drug. Within six hours, they were all dead.

It was what Stone had predicted from the start. He had pointed out that mankind had, over centuries of exposure, developed a carefully regulated immunity to most organisms. On his skin, in the air, in his lungs, gut, and even bloodstream were hundreds of different viruses and bacteria. They were potentially deadly, but man had adapted to them over the years, and only a few could still cause disease.

All this represented a carefully balanced state of affairs. If you introduced a new drug that killed *all* bacteria, you upset the balance and undid the evolutionary work of centuries. And you opened the way to superinfection, the problem of new organisms, bearing new diseases.

Stone was right: the forty volunteers each had died of obscure and horrible diseases no one had ever seen before. One man experienced swelling of his body, from head to foot, a hot, bloated swelling until he suffocated from pulmonary edema. Another man fell prey to an organism that ate away his stomach in a matter of hours. A third was hit by a virus that dissolved his brain to a jelly.

And so it went.

Jensen reluctantly took the drug out of further study. The government, sensing that Stone had somehow understood what was happening, agreed to his earlier proposals, and viciously suppressed all knowledge and experimentation with the drug Kalocin.

And that was where the matter had rested for two years.

Now Burton wanted to be given the drug.

"No," Stone said. "Not a chance. It might cure you for a while, but you'd never survive later, when you were taken off."

"That's easy for you to say, from where you are."

"It's not easy for me to say. Believe me, it's not." He put his hand over the microphone again. To Hall: "We know that oxygen inhibits growth of the Andromeda Strain. That's what we'll give Burton. It will be good for him—make him a little giddy, a little relaxed, and slow his breathing down. Poor fellow is scared to death."

Hall nodded. Somehow, Stone's phrase stuck in his mind: scared to death. He thought about it, and then began to see that Stone had hit upon something important. That phrase was a clue. It was the answer.

He started to walk away.

"Where are you going?"

"I've got some thinking to do."

"About what?"

"About being scared to death."

27.

Scared to Death

HALL WALKED BACK TO HIS LAB and
stared through the glass at the old man and the infant. He
looked at the two of them and tried to think, but his brain
was running in frantic circles. He found it difficult to think
logically, and his earlier sensation of being on the verge of a
discovery was lost.

For several minutes, he stared at the old man while brief
images passed before him: Burton dying, his hand clutched to
his chest. Los Angeles in panic, bodies everywhere, cars going
haywire, out of control . . .

It was then that he realized that he, too, was scared. Scared
to death. The words came back to him.

Scared to death.

Somehow, that was the answer.

Slowly, forcing his brain to be methodical, he went over it
again.

A cop with diabetes. A cop who didn't take his insulin and
had a habit of going into ketoacidosis.

An old man who drank Sterno, which gave him methanol-
ism, and acidosis.

A baby, who did . . . what? What gave him acidosis?

Hall shook his head. Always, he came back to the baby, who was normal, not acidotic. He sighed.

Take it from the beginning, he told himself. Be logical. If a man has metabolic acidosis—any kind of acidosis—what does he do?

He has too much acid in his body. He can die from too much acid, just as if he had injected hydrochloric acid into his veins.

Too much acid meant death.

But the body could compensate. By breathing rapidly. Because in that manner, the lungs blew off carbon dioxide, and the body's supply of carbonic acid, which was what carbon dioxide formed in the blood, decreased.

A way to get rid of acid.

Rapid breathing.

And Andromeda? What happened to the organism, when you were acidotic and breathing fast?

Perhaps fast breathing kept the organism from getting into your lungs long enough to penetrate to blood vessels. Maybe that was the answer. But as soon as he thought of it, he shook his head. No: something else. Some simple, direct fact. Something they had always known, but somehow never recognized.

The organism attacked through the lungs.

It entered the bloodstream.

It localized in the walls of arteries and veins, particularly of the brain.

It produced damage.

This led to coagulation. Which was dispersed throughout the body, or else led to bleeding, insanity, and death.

But in order to produce such rapid, severe damage, it would take many organisms. Millions upon millions, collecting in the arteries and veins. Probably you did not breathe in so many.

So they must multiply in the bloodstream.

At a great rate. A fantastic rate.

And if you were acidotic? Did that halt multiplication? Perhaps.

Again, he shook his head. Because a person with acidosis like Willis or Jackson was one thing. But what about the baby?

The baby was normal. If it breathed rapidly, it would become alkalotic—basic, too little acid—not acidotic. The baby would go to the opposite extreme.

Hall looked through the glass, and as he did, the baby awoke. Almost immediately it began to scream, its face turning purple, the little eyes wrinkling, the mouth, toothless and smooth-gummed, shrieking.

Scared to death.

And then the birds, with the fast metabolic rate, the fast heart rates, the fast breathing rates. The birds, who did everything fast. They, too, survived.

Breathing fast?

Was it as simple as that?

He shook his head. It couldn't be.

He sat down and rubbed his eyes. He had a headache, and he felt tired. He kept thinking of Burton, who might die at any minute. Burton, sitting there in the sealed room.

Hall felt the tension was unbearable. He suddenly felt an overwhelming urge to escape it, to get away from everything.

The TV screen clicked on. His technician appeared and said, "Dr. Hall, we have Dr. Leavitt in the infirmary."

And Hall found himself saying, "I'll be right there."

He knew he was acting strangely. There was no reason to see Leavitt. Leavitt was all right, perfectly fine, in no danger. In going to see him, Hall knew that he was trying to forget the other, more immediate problems. As he entered the infirmary, he felt guilty.

His technician said, "He's sleeping."

"Post-ictal," Hall said. Persons after a seizure usually slept. "Shall we start Dilantin?"

"No. Wait and see. Perhaps we can hold him on phenobarb."

He began a slow and meticulous examination of Leavitt. His technician watched him and said, "You're tired."

"Yes," said Hall. "It's past my bedtime."

On a normal day, he would now be driving home on the expressway. So would Leavitt: going home to his family in Pacific Palisades. The Santa Monica Expressway.

He saw it vividly for a moment, the long lines of cars creeping slowly forward.

And the signs by the side of the road. Speed limit 65 maximum, 40 minimum. They always seemed like a cruel joke at rush hour.

Maximum and minimum.

Cars that drove slowly were a menace. You had to keep traffic moving at a fairly constant rate, little difference between the fastest and the slowest, and you had to . . .

He stopped.

"I've been an idiot," he said.

And he turned to the computer.

In later weeks, Hall referred to it as his "highway diagnosis." The principle of it was so simple, so clear and obvious, he was surprised none of them had thought of it before.

He was excited as he punched in instructions for the GROWTH program into the computer; he had to punch in the directions three times; his fingers kept making mistakes.

At last the program was set. On the display screen, he saw what he wanted: growth of Andromeda as a function of pH, of acidity-alkalinity.

The results were quite clear:

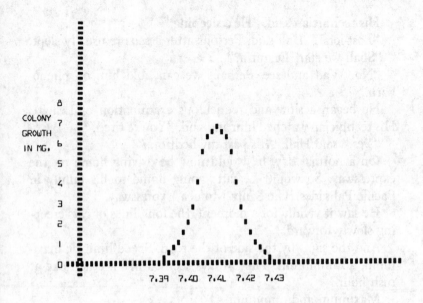

ACIDITY OF MEDIUM AS LOG H - ION CONCENTRATION

CORRECTED FOR SKEW
MEANS, MODES, S.D. FOUND
IN CORREL/PRINT
MM -76
CALL COORDINATES
0,Y,88,Z,09,

REVIEW CHECK

END PRINT

The Andromeda Strain grew within a narrow range. If the medium for growth was too acid, the organism would not multiply. If it was too basic, it would not multiply. Only within the range of pH 7.39 to 7.42 would it grow well.

He stared at the graph for a moment, then ran for the door. On his way out he grinned at his assistant and said, "It's all over. Our troubles are finished."

He could not have been more wrong.

28.

The Test

IN THE MAIN CONTROL ROOM, Stone was watching the television screen that showed Burton in the sealed lab.

"The oxygen's going in," Stone said.

"Stop it," Hall said.

"What?"

"Stop it now. Put him on room air."

Hall was looking at Burton. On the screen, it was clear that the oxygen was beginning to affect him. He was no longer breathing so rapidly; his chest moved slowly.

He picked up the microphone.

"Burton," he said, "this is Hall. I've got the answer. The Andromeda Strain grows within a narrow range of pH. Do you understand? A very narrow range. If you're either acidotic or alkalotic, you'll be all right. I want you to go into respiratory alkalosis. I want you to breathe as fast as you can."

Burton said, "But this is pure oxygen. I'll hyperventilate and pass out. I'm a little dizzy now."

"No. We're switching back to air. Now start breathing as fast as you can."

Hall turned back to Stone. "Give him a higher carbon-dioxide atmosphere."

"But the organism flourishes in carbon dioxide!"

"I know, but not at an unfavorable pH of the blood. You see, that's the problem: air doesn't matter, but blood does. We have to establish an unfavorable acid balance for Burton's blood."

Stone suddenly understood. "The child," he said. "It screamed."

"Yes."

"And the old fellow with the aspirin hyperventilated."

"Yes. And drank Sterno besides."

"And both of them shot their acid-base balance to hell," Stone said.

"Yes," Hall said. "My trouble was, I was hung up on the acidosis. I didn't understand how the baby could become acidotic. The answer, of course, was that it didn't. It became basic—too little acid. But that was all right—you could go either way, too much acid or too little—as long as you got out of the growth range of Andromeda."

He turned back to Burton. "All right now," he said. "Keep breathing rapidly. Don't stop. Keep your lungs going and blow off your carbon dioxide. How do you feel?"

"Okay," Burton panted. "Scared . . . but . . . okay."

"Good."

"Listen," Stone said, "we can't keep Burton that way forever. Sooner or later—"

"Yes," Hall said. "We'll alkalinize his blood."

To Burton: "Look around the lab. Do you see anything we could use to raise your blood pH?"

Burton looked. "No, not really."

"Bicarbonate of soda? Ascorbic acid? Vinegar?"

Burton searched frantically among the bottles and reagents on the lab shelf, and finally shook his head. "Nothing here that will work."

Hall hardly heard him. He had been counting Burton's respirations; they were up to thirty-five a minute, deep and full. That would hold him for a time, but sooner or later he would become exhausted—breathing was hard work—or pass out.

He looked around the lab from his vantage point. And it was while doing this that he noticed the rat. A black Norway, sitting calmly in its cage in a corner of the room, watching Burton.

He stopped.

"That rat . . ."

It was breathing slowly and easily. Stone saw the rat and said, "What the hell . . ."

And then, as they watched, the lights began to flash again, and the computer console blinked on:

EARLY DEGENERATIVE CHANGE IN GASKET V-112-6886

"Christ," Stone said.

"Where does that gasket lead?"

"It's one of the core gaskets; it connects all the labs. The main seal is—"

The computer came back on.

DEGENERATIVE CHANGE IN GASKETS A-009-5478

V-430-0030

N-966-6656

They looked at the screen in astonishment. "Something is wrong," Stone said. "Very wrong."

In rapid succession the computer flashed the number of nine more gaskets that were breaking down.

"I don't understand . . ."

And then Hall said, "The child. Of course!"

"The child?"

"And that damned airplane. It all fits."

"What are you talking about?" Stone said.

"The child was normal," Hall said. "It could cry, and disrupt its acid-base balance. Well and good. That would prevent the Andromeda Strain from getting into its bloodstream, and multiplying, and killing it."

"Yes, yes," Stone said. "You've told me all that."

"*But what happens when the child stops crying?*"

Stone stared at him. He said nothing.

"I mean," Hall said, "that sooner or later, that kid had to stop crying. It couldn't cry forever. Sooner or later it would stop, and its acid-base balance would return to normal. Then it would be vulnerable to Andromeda."

"True."

"But it didn't die."

"Perhaps some rapid form of immunity—"

"No. Impossible. There are only two explanations. When the child stopped crying, either the organism was no longer there—had been blown away, cleared from the air—or else the organism—"

"Changed," Stone said. "Mutated."

"Yes. Mutated to a noninfectious form. And perhaps it is still mutating. Now it is no longer directly harmful to man, but it eats rubber gaskets."

"The airplane."

Hall nodded. "National guardsmen could be on the ground, and not be harmed. But the pilot had his aircraft destroyed because the plastic was dissolved before his eyes."

"So Burton is now exposed to a harmless organism. That's why the rat is alive."

"That's why Burton is alive," Hall said. "The rapid breathing isn't necessary. He's only alive because Andromeda changed."

"It may change again," Stone said. "and if most mutations

occur at times of multiplication, when the organism is growing most rapidly—"

The sirens went off, and the computer flashed a message in red.

GASKET INTEGRITY ZERO.   LEVEL V CONTAMINATED AND SEALED.

Stone turned to Hall. "Quick," he said, "get out of here. There's no substation in this lab. You have to go to the next sector."

For a moment, Hall did not understand. He continued to sit in his seat, and then, when the realization hit him, he scrambled for the door and hurried outside to the corridor. As he did so he heard a hissing sound, and a thump as a massive steel plate slid out from a wall and closed off the corridor.

Stone saw it and swore. "That does it," he said. "We're trapped here. And if that bomb goes off, it'll spread the organism all over the surface. There will be a thousand mutations, each killing in a different way. We'll never be rid of it."

Over the loudspeaker, a flat mechanical voice was saying, "The level is closed. The level is closed. This is an emergency. The level is closed."

There was a moment of silence, and then a scratching sound as a new recording came on, and Miss Gladys Stevens of Omaha, Nebraska, said quietly, "There are now three minutes to atomic self-destruct."

29.

Three Minutes

A NEW RISING AND FALLING siren came on, and all the clocks snapped their hands back to 1200 hours, and the second hands began to sweep out the time. The stop-clocks all glowed red, with a green line on the dial to indicate when detonation would occur.

And the mechanical voice repeated calmly, "There are now three minutes to self-destruct."

"Automatic," Stone said quietly. "The system cuts in when the level is contaminated. We can't let it happen."

Hall was holding the key in his hand. "There's no way to get to a substation?"

"Not on this level. Each sector is sealed from every other."

"But there *are* substations, on the other levels?"

"Yes . . ."

"How do I get up?"

"You can't. All the conventional routes are sealed."

"What about the central core?" The central core communicated with all levels.

Stone shrugged. "The safeguards . . ."

Hall remembered talking to Burton earlier about the central-core safeguards. In theory, once inside the central core you could go straight to the top. But in practice, there were ligamine sensors located around the core to prevent this. Originally intended to prevent escape of lab animals that might break free into the core, the sensors released ligamine, a curare derivative that was water-soluble, in the form of a gas. There were also automatic guns that fired ligamine darts.

The mechanical voice said, "There are now two minutes forty-five seconds to self-destruct."

Hall was already moving back into the lab and staring through the glass into the inner work area; beyond that was the central core.

Hall said, "What are my chances?"

"They don't exist," Stone explained.

Hall bent over and crawled through a tunnel into a plastic suit. He waited until it had sealed behind him, and then he picked up a knife and cut away the tunnel, like a tail. He breathed in the air of the lab, which was cool and fresh, and laced with Andromeda organisms.

Nothing happened.

Back in the lab, Stone watched him through the glass. Hall saw his lips move, but heard nothing; then a moment later the speakers cut in and he heard Stone say, "—best that we could devise."

"What was?"

"The defense system."

"Thanks very much," Hall said, moving toward the rubber gasket. It was circular and rather small, leading into the central core.

"There's only one chance," Stone said. "The doses are low. They're calculated for a ten-kilogram animal, like a large monkey, and you weigh seventy kilograms or so. You can stand a fairly heavy dose before—"

"Before I stop breathing," Hall said. The victims of curare suffocate to death, their chest muscles and diaphragms paralyzed. Hall was certain it was an unpleasant way to die.

"Wish me luck," he said.

"There are now two minutes thirty seconds to self-destruct," Gladys Stevens said.

Hall slammed the gasket with his fist, and it crumbled in a dusty cloud. He moved out into the central core.

It was silent. He was away from the sirens and flashing lights of the level, and into a cold, metallic, echoing space. The central core was perhaps thirty feet wide, painted a utilitarian gray; the core itself, a cylindrical shaft of cables and machinery, lay before him. On the walls he could see the rungs of a ladder leading upward to Level IV.

"I have you on the TV monitor," Stone's voice said. "Start up the ladder. The gas will begin any moment."

A new recorded voice broke in. "The central core has been contaminated," it said. "Authorized maintenance personnel are advised to clear the area immediately."

"Go!" Stone said.

Hall climbed. As he went up the circular wall, he looked back and saw pale clouds of white smoke blanketing the floor.

"That's the gas," Stone said. "Keep going."

Hall climbed quickly, hand over hand, moving up the rungs. He was breathing hard, partly from the exertion, partly from emotion.

"The sensors have you," Stone said. His voice was dull.

Stone was sitting in the Level V laboratory, watching on the consoles as the computer electric eyes picked up Hall and outlined his body moving up the wall. To Stone he seemed painfully vulnerable. Stone glanced over at a third screen, which showed the ligamine ejectors pivoting on their wall brackets, the slim barrels coming around to take aim.

"Go!"

On the screen, Hall's body was outlined in red on a vivid green background. As Stone watched, a crosshair was superimposed over the body, centering on the neck. The computer was programmed to choose a region of high blood flow; for most animals, the neck was better than the back.

Hall, climbing up the core wall, was aware only of the distance and his fatigue. He felt strangely and totally exhausted, as if he had been climbing for hours. Then he realized that the gas was beginning to affect him.

"The sensors have picked you up," Stone said. "But you have only ten more yards."

Hall glanced back and saw one of the sensor units. It was aimed directly at him. As he watched, it fired, a small puff of bluish smoke spurting from the barrel. There was a whistling sound, and then something struck the wall next to him, and fell to the ground.

"Missed that time. Keep going."

Another dart slammed into the wall near his neck. He tried to hurry, tried to move faster. Above, he could see the door with the plain white markings LEVEL IV. Stone was right; less than ten yards to go.

A third dart, and then a fourth. He still was untouched. For an ironic moment he felt irration: the damned computers weren't worth anything, they couldn't even hit a simple target . . .

The next dart caught him in the shoulder, stinging as it entered his flesh, and then there was a second wave of burning pain as the liquid was injected. Hall swore.

Stone watched it all on the monitor. The screen blandly recorded STRIKE and then proceeded to rerun a tape of the sequence, showing the dart moving through the air, and hitting Hall's shoulder. It showed it three times in succession.

The voice said, "There are now two minutes to self-destruct."

"It's a low dose," Stone said to Hall. "Keep going."

Hall continued to climb. He felt sluggish, like a four-hundred-pound man, but he continued to climb. He reached the next door just as a dart slammed into the wall near his cheekbone.

"Nasty."

"Go! Go!"

The door had a seal and handle. He tugged at the handle while still another dart struck the wall.

"That's it, that's it, you're going to make it," Stone said.

"There are now ninety seconds to self-destruct," the voice said.

The handle spun. With a hiss of air the door came open. He moved into an inner chamber just as a dart struck his leg with a brief, searing wave of heat. And suddenly, instantly, he was a thousand pounds heavier. He moved in slow motion as he reached for the door and pulled it shut behind him.

"You're in an airlock," Stone said. "Turn the next door handle."

Hall moved toward the inner door. It was several miles away, an infinite trip, a distance beyond hope. His feet were encased in lead; his legs were granite. He felt sleepy and achingly tired as he took one step, and then another, and another.

"There are now sixty seconds to self-destruct."

Time was passing swiftly. He could not understand it; everything was so fast, and he was so slow.

The handle. He closed his fingers around it, as if in a dream. He turned the handle.

"Fight the drug. You can do it," Stone said.

What happened next was difficult to recall. He saw the handle turn, and the door open; he was dimly aware of a girl, a technician, standing in the hallway as he staggered through. She watched him with frightened eyes as he took a single clumsy step forward.

"Help me," he said.

She hesitated; her eyes got wider, and then she ran down the corridor away from him.

He watched her stupidly, and fell to the ground. The substation was only a few feet away, a glittering, polished metal plate on the wall.

"Forty-five seconds to self-destruct," the voice said, and then he was angry because the voice was female, and seductive, and recorded, because someone had planned it this way, had written out a series of inexorable statements, like a script, which was now being followed by the computers, together with all the polished, perfect machinery of the laboratory. It was as if this was his fate, planned from the beginning.

And he was angry.

Later, Hall could not remember how he managed to crawl the final distance; nor could he remember how he was able to get to his knees and reach up with the key. He did remember twisting it in the lock, and watching as the green light came on again.

"Self-destruct has been canceled," the voice announced, as if it were quite normal.

Hall slid to the floor, heavy, exhausted, and watched as blackness closed in around him.

day 5

RESOLUTION

30.

The Last Day

A VOICE FROM VERY FAR AWAY said, "He's fighting it."

"Is he?"

"Yes. Look."

And then, a moment later, Hall coughed as something was pulled from his throat, and he coughed again, gasped for air, and opened his eyes.

A concerned female face looked down at him. "You okay? It wears off quickly."

Hall tried to answer her but could not. He lay very still on his back, and felt himself breathe. It was a little stiff at first, but soon became much easier, his ribs going in and out without effort. He turned his head and said, "How long?"

"About forty seconds," the girl said, "as nearly as we can figure. Forty seconds without breathing. You were a little blue when we found you, but we got you intubated right away, and onto a respirator."

"When was that?"

"Twelve, fifteen minutes ago. Ligamine is short-acting, but even so, we were worried about you. . . . How are you feeling?"

"Okay."

He looked around the room. He was in the infirmary on Level IV. On the far wall was a television monitor, which showed Stone's face.

"Hello," Hall said.

Stone grinned. "Congratulations."

"I take it the bomb didn't?"

"The bomb didn't," Stone said.

"That's good," Hall said, and closed his eyes. He slept for more than an hour, and when he awoke the television screen was blank. A nurse told him that Dr. Stone was talking to Vandenberg.

"What's happening?"

"According to predictions, the organism is over Los Angeles now."

"And?"

The nurse shrugged. "Nothing. It seems to have no effect at all."

"None whatsoever," Stone said, much later. "It has apparently mutated to a benign form. We're still waiting for a bizarre report of death or disease, but it's been six hours now, and it gets less likely with every minute. We suspect that ultimately it will migrate back out of the atmosphere, since there's too much oxygen down here. But of course if the bomb had gone off in Wildfire . . ."

Hall said, "How much time was left?"

"When you turned the key? About thirty-four seconds."

Hall smiled. "Plenty of time. Hardly even exciting."

"Perhaps from where you were," Stone said. "But down on Level V, it was very exciting indeed. I neglected to tell you that in order to improve the subterranean detonation characteristics of the atomic device, all air is evacuated from Level V, beginning thirty seconds before explosion."

"Oh," Hall said.

"But things are now under control," Stone said. "We have the organism, and can continue to study it. We've already begun to characterize a variety of mutant forms. It's a rather astonishing organism in its versatility." He smiled. "I think we can be fairly confident that the organism will move into the upper atmosphere without causing further difficulty on the surface, so there's no problem there. And as for us down here, we understand what's happening now, in terms of the mutations. That's the important thing. That we understand."

"Understand," Hall repeated.

"Yes," Stone said. "We have to understand."

EPILOGUE

OFFICIALLY, THE LOSS OF ANDROS V, the manned spacecraft that burned up as it reentered the atmosphere, was explained on the basis of mechanical failure. The tungsten-and-plastic-laminate heat shield was said to have eroded away under the thermal stress of returning to the atmosphere, and an investigation was ordered by NASA into production methods for the heat shield.

In Congress, and in the press, there was clamor for safer spacecraft. As a result of governmental and public pressure, NASA elected to postpone future manned flights for an indefinite period. This decision was announced by Jack Marriott, "the voice of Andros," in a press conference at the Manned Spaceflight Center in Houston. A partial transcript of the conference follows:

Q: Jack, when does this postponement go into effect?
A: Immediately. Right as I talk to you, we are shutting down.
Q: How long do you anticipate this delay will last?
A: I'm afraid that's impossible to say.
Q: Could it be a matter of months?
A: It could.
Q: Jack, could it be as long as a year?

A: It's just impossible for me to say. We must wait for the findings of the investigative committee.

Q: Does this postponement have anything to do with the Russian decision to curtail their space program after the crash of Zond 19?

A: You'd have to ask the Russians about that.

Q: I see that Jeremy Stone is on the list of the investigative committee. How did you happen to include a bacteriologist?

A: Professor Stone has served on many scientific advisory councils in the past. We value his opinion on a broad range of subjects.

Q: What will this delay do to the Mars-landing target date?

A: It will certainly set the scheduling back.

Q: Jack, how far?

A: I'll tell you frankly, it's something that all of us here would like to know. We regard the failure of Andros V as a scientific error, a breakdown in systems technology, and not as a specifically human error. The scientists are going over the problem now, and we'll have to wait for their findings. The decision is really out of our hands.

Q: Jack, would you repeat that?

A: The decision is out of our hands.

REFERENCES

Listed below is a selected bibliography of unclassified documents, reports, and references that formed the background to the book.

DAY ONE

1. Merrick, J. J. "Frequencies of Biologic Contact According to Speciation Probabilities," *Proceedings of the Cold Springs Harbor Symposia* 10:443–57.
2. Toller, G. G. *Essence and Evolution.* New Haven: Yale Univ. Press, 1953.
3. Stone, J., et al. "Multiplicative Counts in Solid Plating," *J. Biol. Res.* 17:323–7.
4. Stone, J., et al. "Liquid-Pure Suspension and Monolayer Media: A Review," *Proc. Soc. Biol. Phys.* 9:101–14.
5. Stone, J., et al. "Linear Viral Transformation Mechanisms," *Science* 107:2201–4.
6. Stone, J. "Sterilization of Spacecraft," *Science* 112:1198–2001.
7. Morley, A., et al. "Preliminary Criteria for a Lunar Receiving Laboratory," *NASA Field Reports*, #7703A, 123 pp.
8. Worthington, A., et al. "The Axenic Environment and Life Support Systems Delivery," *Jet Propulsion Lab Tech. Mem.* 9:404–11.
9. Ziegler, V. A., et al. "Near Space Life: A Predictive Model for Retrieval Densities," *Astronaut. Aeronaut. Rev.* 19:449–507.
10. Testimony of Jeremy Stone before the Senate Armed Services Subcommittee, Space and Preparedness Subcommittee (see Appendix).
11. Manchek, A. "Audiometric Screening by Digital Computer," *Ann. Tech.* 7:1033–9.
12. Wilson, L. O., et al. "Unicentric Directional Routing," *J. Space Comm.* 43:34–41.

13. *Project Procedures Manual: Scoop.* U.S. Gov't Printing Office, publication #PJS–4431.

14. Comroe, L. "Critical Resonant Frequencies in Higher Vertebrate Animals," *Rev. Biol. Chem.* 109:43–59.

15. Pockran, A. *Culture, Crisis and Change.* Chicago: Univ. of Chicago Press, 1964.

16. Manchek, A. "Module Design for High-Impact Landing Ratios," *NASA Field Reports* #3–3476.

17. Lexwell, J. F., et al. "Survey Techniques by Multiple Spectrology," *USAF Technical Pubs.*, #55A–789.

18. Jaggers, N. A., et al. "The Direct Interpretation of Infrared Intelligence Data," *Tech. Rev. Soc.* 88:111–19.

19. Vanderlink, R. E. "Binominate Analysis of Personality Characteristics: A Predictive Model," *Pubs. NIMH* 3:199.

20. Vanderlink, R. E. "Multicentric Problems in Personnel Prediction," *Proc. Symp. NIMH* 13:404–512.

21. Sanderson, L. L. "Continuous Screen Efficiency in Personnel Review," *Pubs. NIMH* 5:98.

DAY TWO

1. Metterlinck, J. "Capacities of a Closed Cable-Link Communications System with Limited Entry Points," *J. Space Comm.* 14:777–801.

2. Leavitt, P. "Metabolic Changes in *Ascaris* with Environmental Stress," *J. Microbiol. Parasitol.* 97:501–44.

3. Herrick, L. A. "Induction of Petit-Mal Epilepsy with Flashing Lights," *Ann. Neurol.* 8:402–19.

4. Burton, C., et al. "*Endotoxic properties of Staphylococcus aureus,*" *NEJM* 14:11–39.

5. Kenniston, N. N., et al. "Geographics by Computer: A Critical Review," *J. Geog. Geol.* 98:1–34.

6. Blakley, A. K. "Computerbase Output Mapping as a Predictive Technique," *Ann. Comp. Tech.* 18:8–40.

7. Vorhees, H. G. "The Time Course of Enzymatic Blocking Agents," *J. Phys. Chem.* 66:303–18.

8. Garrod, D. O. "Effects of Chlorazine on Aviary Metabolism: A Rate-Dependent Decoupler," *Rev. Biol. Sci.* 9:13–39.

9. Bagdell, R. L. "Prevailing Winds in the Southwest United States," *Gov. Weather Rev.* 81:291–9.

10. Jaegers, A. A. *Suicide and Its Consequences.* Ann Arbor: Michigan Univ. Press, 1967.

11. Revell, T. W. "Optical Scanning in Machine-Score Programs," *Comp. Tech.* 12:34–51.

12. Kendrew, P. W. "Voice Analysis by Phonemic Inversion," *Ann. Biol. Comp. Tech.* 19:35–61.

13. Ulrich, V., et al. "The Success of Battery Vaccinations in Previously Immunized Healthy Subjects," *Medicine* 180:901–6.

14. Rodney, K. G. "Electronic Body Analyzers with Multifocal Input," *NASA Field Reports* #2–223–1150.

15. Stone, J., et al. "Gradient Decontamination Procedures to Life Tolerances," *Bull. Soc. Biol. Microbiol.* 16:84–90.

16. Howard, E. A. "Realtime Functions in Autoclock Transcription," *NASA Field Reports* #4–564–0002.

17. Edmundsen, T. E. "Long Wave Asepsis Gradients," *Proc. Biol. Soc.* 13:343–51.

DAY THREE

1. Karp, J. "Sporulation and Calcium Dipicolonate Concentrations in Cell Walls," *Microbiol.* 55:180.

2. *Weekly Reports of the United States Air Force Satellite Tracking Stations,* NASA Res. Pubs, ——.

3. Wilson, G. E. "Glove-box Asepsis and Axenic Environments," *J. Biol. Res.* 34:88–96.

4. Yancey, K. L., et. al. "Serum Electrophoresis of Plasma Globulins in Man and the Great Apes," *Nature* 89:1101–9.

5. Garrison, H. W. "Laboratory Analysis by Computer: A Maximin Program," *Med. Adv.* 17:9–41.

6. Urey, W. W. "Image Intensification from Remote Modules," *Jet Propulsion Lab Tech. Mem.* 33:376–86.

7. Isaacs, I. V. "Physics of Non-Elastic Interactions," *Phys. Rev.* 80:97–104.

8. Quincy, E. W. "Virulence as a Function of Gradient Adaptation to Host," *J. Microbiol.* 99:109–17.

9. Danvers, R. C. "Clotting Mechanisms in Disease States," *Ann. Int. Med.* 90:404–81.

10. Henderson, J. W., et al. "Salicylism and Metabolic Acidosis," *Med. Adv.* 23:77–91.

DAY FOUR

1. Livingston, J. A. "Automated Analysis of Amino Acid Substrates," *J. Microbiol.* 100:44–57.

2. Laandgard, Q. *X-Ray Crystallography.* New York: Columbia Univ. Press, 1960.

3. Polton, S., et al. "Electron Waveforms and Microscopic Resolution Ratios," *Ann. Anatomy* 5:90–118.

4. Twombley, E. R., et al. "Tissue Thromboplastin in Timed Release from Graded Intimal Destruction," *Path. Res.* 19:1–53.

5. Ingersoll, H. G. "Basal Metabolism and Thyroid Indices in Bird Metabolic Stress Contexts," *J. Zool.* 50:223–304.

6. Young, T. C., et al. "Diabetic Ketoacidosis Induced by Timed Insulin Withdrawal," *Rev. Med. Proc.* 96:87–96.

7. Ramsden, C. C. "Speculations on a Universal Antibiotic," *Nature* 112:44–8.

8. Yandell, K. M. "Ligamine Metabolism in Normal Subjects," *JAJA* 44:109–10.

DAY FIVE

1. Hepley, W. E., et al. "Studies in Mutagenic Transformation of Bacteria from Non-virulent to Virulent Forms," *J. Biol. Chem.* 78:90–9.

2. Drayson, V. L. "Does Man Have a Future?" *Tech Rev.* 119:1–13.

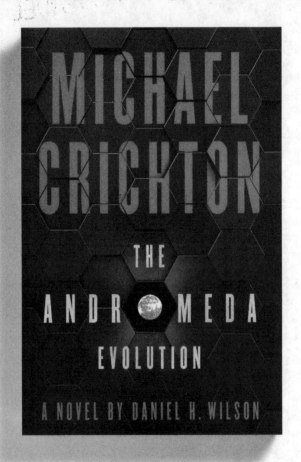